WAYNE STINNETT

RISING FURY

A JESSE MCDERMITT NOVEL

Caribbean Adventure Series
Volume 12

2017

Published by DOWN ISLAND PRESS, 2017
Lady's Island, SC
Copyright © 2017 by Wayne Stinnett

Library of Congress cataloging-in-publication Data
Stinnett, Wayne
Rising Storm/Wayne Stinnett
p. cm. - (A Jesse McDermitt novel)
ISBN-13: 978-0-9981285-7-3 (Down Island Press)
ISBN-10: 0-9981285-7-0
Cover photograph by Pieter Jordaan
Graphics by Wicked Good Book Covers
Edited by Larks & Katydids
Final Proofreading by Donna Rich
Interior Design by WDR Book Designs

FOREWORD

This past fall, my wife and I watched the Breaking Bad series, again. The scenes in the RV got me thinking. How hard would it be to hide a meth lab in the hold of a shrimp trawler? Apparently, not that hard. I hope you enjoy it.

As always, my wife gave me a lot of insight when I first came up with this idea. Together, we figured out logistical problems, like how to keep anyone from smelling the fumes from the lab, or how to keep a Coast Guard inspection from finding the hidden lab. As always, I thank Greta for pushing me onward.

I have a private Facebook group, just for my beta readers. There are sailing ship captains in this group, along with doctors, former and current military, explorers, pilots, and folks from very diverse backgrounds among the twenty or so people who help me polish my work, pre-editing.

Many thanks to Dana Vihlen, David Parsons, Katy McKnight, Alan Fader, Deg Priest, Karl Schulte, John Trainer, Dan Horn, Mike Ramsey, Ron Ramey, Drew Mutch, Debbie Kocol, Dan Horn, Charles Hofbauer, Marc Lowe, Glenn Hibbert, Linda Winner, and Tom Crisp. Your recommendations are worth far more than the pittance I offer. Thank you for all your help.

I extend my deep appreciation to my friend and talented musician and songwriter, Eric Stone, for his appearance in this book. Eric once owned Dockside in Marathon, but now tours with his wife Kim and their three birds, Chief, Harley, and Marley. He takes his trop-rock sound all over the country, singing his own tunes and a few favorite covers. The timeline in my stories was a bit before when he owned Dockside, so I've been looking forward to catching this series up closer to current time. The events that befell Dockside and led to Eric and Kim buying the place are appropriate for the time this book is set, late 2008.

At the end of this book, you'll find the lyrics to a song he recently recorded (at my bold request), "The Rusty Anchor Bar & Grill." It's sure to be a perennial favorite very soon. As of this writing, I've yet to hear the song, and the studio date is four days away. But I've read the lyrics and really like the story. I'm eagerly looking forward to this merger between trop-rock and trop-fiction. To download Eric's music, including The Rusty Anchor Bar & Grill, visit his website at www.islanderic.com and tell him I sent you.

There are a bunch of friends I need to thank, as well—other writers who have given me a lot of sage council over the last couple of years. We sit in a corner reserved just for us, and talk shop and gossip. A casual listener might think we were planning a government coup or mass genocide, or something similar. It's just us, being us, in the author's corner.

Lastly, thank you to the hundreds of professional authors of Novelist, Inc. for honoring me with the task of leading the organization in 2019. I enjoy the NINC conferences immensely and will do all I can in 2018 to assist incoming president Julie Ortolon, and to learn the role from her as the incoming president-elect.

For my readers who might be concerned that my role at NINC could interfere with my writing, don't worry. I plan to continue releasing something new, in either the Jesse or Charity series every four to six months, just as I always have. Enduring Charity will be released in the spring, and Rising Force in the fall, with four more releases scheduled for 2019.

DEDICATION

Dedicated to the memory of Ginger, the most ferocious chi-weenie the world has ever known. For more than two years, this nine-pound, black-and-tan miniature long-haired dachshund and Chihuahua mix, would sit beside me as I worked. I often read dialogue to her. Had anyone told me I'd ever own, much less love, such a tiny, whining lapdog, I'd have said they were nuts. She was a senior when we adopted her; we made sure her final years were good ones and she knew she was loved when she passed away sitting on my lap last spring. I'll see you at the Rainbow Bridge, Short-Round.

"You can say any foolish thing to a dog, and the dog will give you a look that says, 'Wow, you're right! I never would've thought of that!'"

— Dave Barry

If you'd like to receive my newsletter, please sign up on my website:

WWW.WAYNESTINNETT.COM

Every two weeks, I'll bring you insights into my private life and writing habits, with updates on what I'm working on, special deals I hear about, and new books by other authors that I'm reading.

THE CHARITY STYLES
CARIBBEAN THRILLER SERIES
Merciless Charity
Ruthless Charity
Reckless Charity
Enduring Charity (Spring, 2018)

THE JESSE MCDERMITT
CARIBBEAN ADVENTURE SERIES

Fallen Out
Fallen Palm
Fallen Hunter
Fallen Pride
Fallen Mangrove
Fallen King
Fallen Honor
Fallen Tide
Fallen Angel
Fallen Hero
Rising Storm
Rising Fury
Rising Force (Fall, 2018)

The Gaspar's Revenge Ship's Store is now open. There you can purchase all kinds of swag related to my books.
WWW.GASPARS-REVENGE.COM

RISING
FURY

MAPS

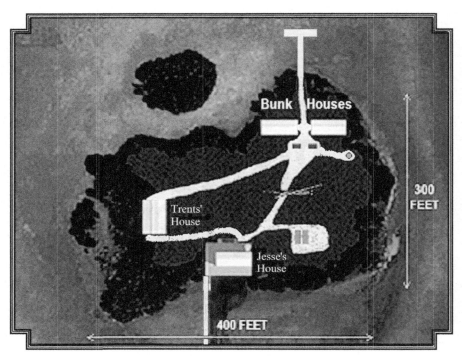

Jesse's Island

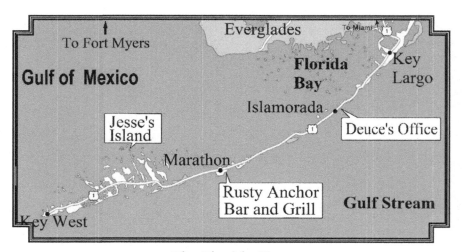

The Florida Keys

CHAPTER ONE

The thump and rattle of the anchor chain was the only sound in the still morning air. It created a low, rumbling clatter as the rode slowly came up from the anchor locker in the bow, lumbered across the roller on the pulpit, and splashed into the water as the current gradually carried the boat toward the southwest.

To the east, the sun was just beginning to turn the sky from inky black to a dark gray, as one by one, the stars in that direction winked out. The forecast called for cloudless skies, with little to no wind, and as it quickly grew lighter, it became apparent the weather guy was right.

The sea was about as smooth as a polished granite countertop, with the graying eastern sky reflecting off its surface. Where the sea and sky actually met seemed uncertain. The water was so calm they melded as one, creating a sense of floating in space.

Captain Al Fader knew it was going to be a hot day, and he wasn't looking forward to it. Warming weather was good for shrimping, but for the last week, it had been ten degrees hotter than normal for the middle of December, and the air conditioner onboard *Night Moves* wasn't working at its best. Not anticipating a hot December, Al had put off repairing it until the season ended in a few more months. Most of the men were eating their meals out on the work deck. The galley was just too uncomfortable. Hot temperatures made for hot tempers.

Other boats were going through pretty much the same daily drill as the crew of *Night Moves*. The early morning hours were all about cleaning the deck and sides of the boat and cleaning, maintaining, and repairing the nets and equipment. Only after the work was done would the hungry crew wolf down a hot meal and sleep through the heat of the day. Or try to.

Shrimping wasn't like other jobs; there wasn't any going home after a hard night's work. Most of the time, home for a shrimper was on board the boat. The shrimp boats left the docks early on Monday and didn't return until the holds were full. It didn't matter if that took four days or six. When the run was exceptionally good, the holds might be full in three days and the crew would gladly put back out on Thursday afternoon to catch more. A second run was all bonus money, even if it meant staying out until Saturday and only half-filling the holds on the week's second run. For some, that meant an extra car or house payment. For others, a higher time at the many bars on Duval Street.

Captain Fader leaned out the starboard door of the pilothouse and looked back before reversing the engine. Far astern, another boat was anchoring, but it was almost half a mile off. Shifting to reverse, Al backed the boat up slowly while letting out more rode.

"That's enough," Al called out to his first mate, standing ready at the anchor windlass.

JoAnn engaged the brake on the windlass, and Al continued to back down, taking up some of the slack in the rode and setting the heavy anchor deep in the sandy bottom. Once satisfied, Al shifted to neutral and monitored the gauges for a moment before shutting down the engine.

"Good night's work, Skipper," JoAnn said, entering the small wheelhouse. "A little over five hundred pounds."

JoAnn Thaxton was a Carolina girl. She'd arrived in Key West two years earlier, nearly broke, carrying all she owned in a single large duffel. A lot of people arrived in Key West that way. Many of them left with nothing at all, just weeks or months later. When JoAnn arrived, she had something in her duffel bag that set her apart from the thousands of other people who came seeking tropical paradise at the end of the highway—she had papers that indicated she was a Coast-Guard-licensed Near Coastal Mate.

Al hired her on a temporary basis and she quickly proved she wasn't afraid of hard work. Two weeks later, he made it permanent. At the end of that first season, his old first mate quit and moved north, and Al asked JoAnn if she'd be willing to take the job. The crew had no trouble working under her; she was as knowledgeable, capable, and competent as any man in the fleet and was well-respected for that and her work ethic.

"That boat back there," Al said, jerking a thumb astern. "It came up on the radar a couple of hours ago, out of the north."

JoAnn stepped out of the pilothouse with a pair of binoculars and looked back toward the other boat. "Shrimper, but it's none I've ever seen. It came from the north?"

"Yeah," Al said, stepping out into the gathering light. He took the binos and trained them on the other boats in the fleet scattered across New Ground to the east and north of *Night Moves*. He counted five. "Not one of ours that strayed off. Everyone's here."

Turning, Al looked aft at the strange boat in the distance. He raised the binoculars and studied it a moment. It was too far away to make out any details, but in the gray light of dawn, he could see the outriggers and nets clearly.

"How far is the mainland?" JoAnn asked.

"'Bout a hundred miles to Naples," Al replied, still watching the boat. "Another twenty to Fort Myers and Port Charlotte. That'd be the nearest cities a shrimper might be out of. Well, except Havana."

"Think that's where they came from?"

"No way to tell. Stern's away and she don't have name boards on the bow." Al lowered the binos and measured the distance to the boat with his eyes: half a mile. He turned and looked at the other boats, all within a quarter mile. "Happens just about every winter. A rogue boat from one of the fisheries up on the mainland comes down for the pink run."

Hearing a series of clicks from the VHF radio in the pilothouse, Al stepped back inside and hung up the binos. He and the other skippers from the Key West fleet used several non-commercial radio frequencies to talk to each other in private, but if you announced which channel to go to, anyone could listen in. They'd devised a code to let one another know which channel to go to without announcing it to the world.

Turning to channel seventy-two, he heard Bob Talbot, the skipper of *Miss Charlie* speaking. "Came in from the north a couple of hours ago."

Al keyed the mic. "Anyone have an idea who it is?"

"Hey, Al," Charlie Hofbauer, the skipper on *Morning Mist* said. "Nobody knows. We were just talking about whether we oughta take my tender to go and find out."

Al leaned out of the pilothouse. "JoAnn, have someone launch the dinghy." Then he keyed the mic again. "Stop by here, Charlie. We're putting a boat in now."

A few minutes later, Al heard the buzzing of a small engine and looked forward. Charlie's fourteen-foot tender was skimming across the water toward *Night Moves*. Charlie was at the helm, with his first mate, Ernie King, standing to one side of the console and Bob on the other.

Al went aft to the work deck, where JoAnn waited at the transom.

"What's going on, Skipper?" Lee Cordero asked. Lee was a new deck hand, young and as green as a key lime—but the kid had muscles on muscles and didn't mind the heat.

"Dunno," Al replied to the broad-shouldered young man. "How about you come along?"

"Sure thing," Lee said, rising quickly to his feet and moving to the trash can to scrape the rest of his supper away.

"Take it with you, Lee," JoAnn said. "Never waste food. A time'll come when you'll have to skip a meal."

The two men climbed down into the little inflatable boat and Al started the small outboard. JoAnn loosed the line from the transom cleat and tossed it to Lee, who caught it and quickly coiled the painter at his feet. He sat down and began shoveling food in his mouth as Al steered away from *Night Moves* to wait for the other boat.

Charlie slowed his tender, bringing it down off plane and then stopping as he came alongside Al's dinghy.

"These guys are like herpes," Charlie said, as the two boats rocked on the disturbed water. "They just keep coming back."

"I don't think they wetted a net yet," Al said. "I first spotted them on radar several hours ago. They'd been on a southwest heading at five knots, in deep water the whole time, so they haven't taken any pinks."

"How do you wanna handle it?" Bob asked.

Being the oldest of the fleet's captains, Al was the unofficial spokesman for the hearty group of men and women who pulled their livelihood out of the water every night.

"Same as we always do," Al said. "We politely but firmly tell them they wasted their time and fuel getting down here."

The other two skippers nodded in firm agreement. Al sat down astraddle the small aft bench seat. He shifted the little outboard to forward and twisted the throttle on the tiller arm. Steering the little dinghy around the larger tender, he accelerated in a straight line toward the unwelcome shrimp boat. The bow of Charlie's tender rose as he throttled up too.

It only took a few minutes for the two small boats to reach the trawler and they slowed as they neared it. There were two men on the boat's port-side deck, watching their approach.

"What do you want?" one of the men yelled, when the two small boats slowed to idle speed.

"Where are you from?" Al shouted back, as the small dinghy drew nearer the larger vessel. Al could see that it was a big boat, probably more than sixty feet. There was something about it that wasn't right, but he couldn't put his finger on what it was.

"I asked first," the man on the deck sneered. "And that's close enough. What do you want?"

"What we want," Charlie said, shifting to neutral and rising from the helm, "is for you to go back up to wherever you came from and leave our fishery be."

"We ain't here for your shrimp," the man on the deck said with disdain. "And we'll leave when we're damned good and ready."

Al shifted to forward and twisted the throttle. He circled the big shrimp boat quickly, noting the name *Eliminator* on the transom, with its home port of Cape Coral stenciled below that.

The second man on the deck of the shrimp boat raced around to the starboard side, then aft, keeping an eye on what Al was doing. After circling the boat, Al stopped alongside Charlie's tender and glared up at the man on the deck.

"I suggest you just go on back up to the Caloosahatchee where you came from," Al shouted. "Wet those nets around here and there's gonna be hell to pay."

"Like I said, mister, we ain't here to catch no shrimp and we'll be moving along as soon as it gets dark."

"See that you do," Charlie shouted, turning the wheel and shifting to forward.

Both boats moved away from the trawler toward their own fleet. Nearing *Night Moves*, they slowed and then stopped.

"If they ain't here to shrimp," Ernie said, "what the hell are they doing here? It's a friggin' shrimp boat, and more than a hundred miles from its home port."

"Something about that crew strike you as odd?" Bob asked Al.

"Yeah, but I couldn't put my finger on it till you just mentioned it. You're right; it was the guys on the rail. They weren't like other fishermen I've met. Downwind, that damned boat stunk to high Heaven."

"All our boats stink," Charlie said, "but I agree. There was something that just didn't sit right about those guys. Who do we know up in the Fort Myers area?"

CHAPTER TWO

"**D**ammit!" Rusty Thurman cursed, crashing the phone down in its cradle and shoving it roughly under the bar.

"What's the matter?" Jimmy asked, sitting on the other side.

"Sorry," Rusty said somewhat sheepishly as he realized Angie Trent was sitting at the bar with Jimmy. Rusty had a colorful vocabulary to say the least, but not usually in mixed company. "That was Jodi. He ran aground and ain't gonna be back in time to play tonight, and maybe not tomorrow."

"How does the dude get stuck for a whole day?" Jimmy asked.

"It's Jodi," Angie said. "Why do you waste your time with him, Rusty?"

"'Cause anyone who'd play here, I can't afford."

"That sucks, man," Jimmy said. Though Jimmy Saunders had been born and raised in the Keys, he'd picked up the west-coast surfing bug when he was stationed in San Diego in the Navy. "But you ain't been around if you ain't run aground. Hard to find live music on short notice."

"Yeah, well I don't think his grounding has anything to do with his getting around."

A stranger sitting two stools down looked over, a grin on his tanned face. "I'm sorry, but I couldn't help overhearing," he said, with a slight East-Texas drawl. "Did you say you need a musician?"

Rusty looked over at the guy. He'd come in from the parking lot half an hour earlier and had been nursing a couple of beers as if waiting for someone. Rusty guessed him to be a few years younger than himself and half a foot taller than his five-six. Dark blond hair curled past the man's collar, a week's stubble covered his chin, and his clear blue eyes didn't seem to miss much of anything.

Glancing at the man's hands, Rusty could tell he was a picker, at least. The telltale callused fingertips were a dead giveaway. His own daughter Julie had the same callouses. The anchor-shaped guitar tattooed on his upper left arm was a pretty good sign, as well.

"You any good?" Rusty asked. "Play anything besides Texas twang?"

The guy smiled. "I can play anything from Bob Wills to Bob Marley. If you want, I can grab my guitar from the truck and show you."

"You do that," Rusty said. "Meet me out back in five minutes. You'll see where to set your stuff up." As the man went out the front door, two familiar faces came in. Rusty walked out from behind the bar to greet them. "Well, look what the cat dragged in. Wives loose your dock lines early on a Friday for once?"

"Funny," Al Fader said, as he and Bob Talbot shook hands with their old friend. The two men took stools next to Jimmy, greeting him and Angie by name. The Florida Keys stretched more than a hundred miles from Key Biscayne to Key West, and another forty beyond where the road ended in the old pirate town. Made up of about seventeen-hundred islands, Key West had the largest resident population, with about one-third of the seventy-thousand inhabitants who called Monroe County home. Distance didn't dictate friendships in the Keys.

Rusty produced a Dos Equis for Al, and a bottle of water for Bob. Having been a bartender for most of his life, Rusty had a knack for remembering drink orders.

Rufus came in from the back door and approached the bar. "Mistuh Rusty," he said, in his song-song Jamaican accent. "I been needin' to ask you something for a long time now."

"What's that?" Rusty asked.

"Dem fish sandwiches I make," he said, almost bashfully. "Di bread, it not right."

"I can get any kind of bread you want," Rusty said, unsure where this was leading.

"I used to make me own bread, coco bread, from a recipe me mother had."

"I've had that before," Jimmy said. "He's right, it's really good."

"So, where can I buy it?" Rusty asked.

"Yuh don't buy coco bread," Rufus replied, handing a mail-order catalogue to him. "I need me a small oven so I can make me own from Mama Pearl's recipe."

Mama Pearl, Rusty thought. Another little pinch of information. Though Rufus had worked at the *Anchor* for nearly a decade, Rusty still didn't even know his last name. He paid him in cash at the end of the week, and as far as Rusty knew, he might just as well be on the run from Interpol or something. But he did his job, and did it quite well. In the Keys, that was usually good enough, and folks didn't pry. Even if they did, the old Jamaican seemed somehow above it all and locals treated him a little differently.

Rusty looked at the page the catalogue was open to. "Everything in your kitchen's gas-fired," he said, noting the high price tag on the oven Rufus was showing him. "This is electric."

Rufus glanced down. "Sorry, suh," he said, flipping the page. "Dis one is gas, and much smaller."

Rusty looked at the picture, with the description and a very affordable price. "You can make even better fish sandwiches with this?"

"Much better," Rufus replied, showing his gap-toothed grin.

"I'll go ahead and order it, then," Rusty said. "You got room for another appliance out there?"

"It don't take up much space," Rufus said, with a smile. "Thank yuh, Mister Rusty. I got just di spot on di far end of di long counter."

When Rufus left, Angie leaned over to look at the two shrimp boat captains. "How's Nikki and the baby, Bob?"

"She's doing well, thanks. And he's growing like a weed." He chuckled. "I finally found a way to get her to take some time off the boat."

"You know you just been had," Al said.

Rusty eyed him sharply. "What's that supposed to mean?"

Al grinned. "Rufus showed you the expensive one for the sticker shock, knowing you'd like the price of the one he really wanted."

"Yeah, I know," Rusty said. "It's a game we play. So, what brings two of Key Weird's finest skippers all the way up here?"

Forty-five miles wasn't a long way from the southernmost city, but he knew how hard the two men worked. He rarely saw any of the shrimpers until April.

"Had some good runs," Al said. "Filled the holds early."

"We were hoping to get some information," Bob added. "You hear anything about boats from other fisheries hanging around down here and acting strange?"

"Yeah, in fact I have." Rusty glanced out the back window and saw the guy setting up on the little stage, which had been ripped off by a close encounter with a hurricane. Rusty had rebuilt it even better. "But let's go out back; I'm auditioning a Texican. Mind the bar, Jimmy?"

"No problemo," Jimmy replied, looking around and seeing there was nobody else in the place.

Rusty led Al and Bob out onto the deck and over to an umbrella-covered table in front of the stage. A liveaboard couple occupied another table.

"What sound do your patrons lean toward?" the man asked from the stage, as he adjusted the mic.

"Mostly boaters and working-class folks hang out here," Rusty replied. "They like a mix of a lot of stuff, even original."

"I have a few originals," he said, plugging his guitar into the small amp and speaker Rusty had bought. He turned the volume down and spent a minute tuning up.

"I heard about something odd happening up toward Islamorada," Rusty began, leaning in conspiratorially. "A shrimper out of the Port Charlotte area slipped in with some other boats out of Key Largo and anchored up with them during the day. When it started to get dark, the boat just up and left. Kinda weird."

"That's what happened yesterday out on New Ground," Bob said.

"Vessel's name was *Eliminator*, out of Cape Coral," Al added.

"Hmm," Rusty said, thinking, as the man on the stage launched into an upbeat tune that Rusty recognized. "The boat up there wasn't that one, but owned by the same company what owns *Eliminator*. I know the guy and he's not one to fish far from his home port."

"I know that song," Bob said, as the guy sang about becoming a reggae guy. "That's Eric Stone."

"Eric Stone?" Rusty asked, looking toward the stage. "I heard of him, even got a couple of his CDs on the juke box. He played *Dockside* not long ago."

As Eric finished the song, a blond woman carrying a margarita came out of the bar and took a table next to the men. Eric started playing a Jimmy Buffett song, and Rusty gave him a thumbs-up. He was good. Winding up the Buffett tune, Eric placed his guitar on a stand next to the mic and stepped down off the stage.

The blonde stood and walked toward him. "What's going on?" she asked.

He took her by the arm and turned toward Rusty's table. Rusty and the other two men stood as the couple approached.

"This is Kim Hess, my girlfriend," Eric said.

"You didn't say you were Eric Stone. Hell, I got your CDs on my juke, wasn't any need for you to play a lick to get a gig here. But why would you want to play a rundown joint like mine?"

"That's why I asked you to meet me here," he said to Kim. "*Dockside* closed down. Out of business."

"Oh no," she said. "What about the BVI?"

"That sorta depends on this guy," Eric said, turning back toward Rusty with a question in his eyes. "I was scheduled to play *Dockside* for the next few weeks."

Rusty extended his hand, knowing good fortune when it smiled at him. "Name's Rusty Thurman. I own the place. It ain't nothing but windows and Dade County pine, but it's been in my family for generations."

"What do you say, Mister Thurman?" Eric asked. "I need a steady gig for a few weeks. We're planning to head to the Virgin Islands after the first of the year."

Stroking his beard, Rusty wondered how little he could get the talented singer and songwriter for. Some have said that if Kenny Chesney kept waffling between country and trop-rock, the young man standing in front of him was the heir apparent to Jimmy himself.

"I ain't near as big as *Dockside*," Rusty said, playing it humble. "The guy who was supposed to play tonight, I was gonna pay him a buck-fifty. I could go as high as two hundred a night."

"I can do that if you can give me four nights."

"Eight hundred bucks?" Rusty said, thinking it over. If *Dockside* was closed, and it had been shut down a few times in the past, that would mean more locals coming by the *Anchor*, maybe even a tourist or two. The man even had a following, maybe folks from up and down island would drop in. Things had slowed through the summer and an influx of cash, even if it was tourist dollars, would be good.

"Tell ya what," Rusty began. "How about three nights, tonight through Sunday night. And if you bring in the customers, next week we'll do a Thursday night show, too."

"Throw in dock space for our boat?" Kim asked.

Chance favors the prepared mind, Rusty thought. The quote from Louis Pasteur had always been one of his favorites. The empty dock space wasn't earning a cent anyway. Nor was it costing him anything.

"And dock space," Rusty said, smiling. Never one to let another get the last bite out of a deal, he added, "But you gotta pay for electric if you use it. Each pedestal has a digital meter; you pay what the going rate is when you leave."

"You have a deal, Mister Thurman," Kim said, extending her hand.

CHAPTER THREE

"Hey, Jesse," a voice behind me said.

I heard footsteps and turned to see Carl walking toward me.

"Charlie running late?" I asked.

We work in spurts, here on my island. When something needs to be done, we do it. And when there's nothing to do, we enjoy the life moments that come our way, in whatever form they present themselves. Sitting at the end of my pier, I'd been enjoying the moment by watching pelicans dive on baitfish in the distance.

He sat down on the pier next to my dog and gave the back of Finn's neck a scratch. "She just called. The kids are having sleepovers and after she drops them off, she's gonna go have a few drinks with some of her friends. You know her—she'll probably stay at Nancy's rather than run the boat after she's been drinking."

"Devon's working tonight and Kim won't be at the *Anchor* until sunset. I was thinking of diving that hole we found last week once it gets dark. Wanna join us?"

"Could be productive," Carl replied, somewhat vaguely. I could tell he had something on his mind, so I just looked out over the water and waited for him to sort his thoughts while a line of pelicans suddenly rose and banked steeply, all diving like choreographed fighter planes. The sun was high overhead and felt warm on my back.

Carl seemed to be enjoying the moment before speaking. "Living out here, off the grid like we are, has been really good for us. It's let us bond as a family. A lot more so than on the mainland, I think. I just want you to know that."

"Out here, it's kinda like the Keys were when I was a kid."

"I know what you mean," Carl said. "Did I ever tell you my great-grandpa worked down here for a while?"

"No, I don't think you ever mentioned that."

"He fought in the First World War. When he came home, he couldn't find work in Louisiana, so he came down here and hired onto Henry Flagler's railroad crew."

"Must have really been something," I said, "back before the highway and the train, not to mention satellites to tell you the weather."

"He was on Islamorada when the Labor Day storm hit," Carl said. "He was one of the few survivors. He stayed on, taking a job as a shrimper. Dad was born here, but moved to Louisiana as soon as he finished school. He brought us down a few times in the sixties." He turned and faced me. "It's been really nice living here," he said again.

"It's been a pleasure having y'all here," I said, sensing there was more to his statement. "You've more than pulled your weight."

Beside me, Finn lifted his head, looking toward Content Passage. A sound reached my ear from far in the distance—a deep, chugging noise, like a tired old two-stroke diesel boat.

"What the hell?" Carl said, pointing out toward the main body of the Content Keys. The mangrove-covered islands to the northwest that made up the rest of the group hung low on the horizon. "Look, out beyond the Contents, west of the pass."

Looking where he indicated, I could just make out the movement of the outriggers and netting of a shrimp boat. It was moving slowly toward the east. We stood up, and Finn rose and began pacing the tee-dock, ears up and a puzzled look on his face.

"Where do you suppose he's going?" I asked as the boat came into view far beyond the pass. It looked as if it was right on the horizon, most likely beyond the three-mile limit. I went to the little closet where we keep towels and soap for bathing and got a pair of binoculars we kept there.

"No pinks in the bay," Carl said matter-of-factly. "Ain't nothing but trouble the direction he's going."

He was right. Oh, there were shrimp, but not the ones most shrimpers were after this time of year. The big pink shrimp that Key West is famous for is what most skippers would be dragging nets after in December. Besides, the waters to the east of here in Florida Bay had an irregular bottom, not good for dragging nets. And it was covered with small coral heads and limestone ledges, sure to foul nets. And then it got real skinny.

"Maybe he's taking a short cut home," I said, looking at the boat through the field glasses. A short cut didn't seem likely. Shrimp boats draw a lot of water and there were countless shoals, rocks, reefs, and wrecks, any one of which could spell bad news. The time saved wouldn't be worth the risk.

"Charlie wants to move to Louisiana."

"Huh?" I looked away from the passing shrimper. Carl was still staring out over the Gulf, eyes not really focused on anything. "Why?"

Carl looked at me. "She wants family around, Jesse. My folks still live in Slidell, and her mom's just across the border in Gulfport. And my mom can get the kids in a really good charter school. Carl Junior has been having some trouble. I have a brother who lives near my folks and Charlie has a bunch of siblings scattered from the Florida Panhandle to Beaumont, Texas. She thinks the kids need more of a social life, and to get to know their family."

"That's understandable," I said. "I won't talk you out of it if that's what you guys want to do, but I'm gonna miss—"

Just then a white-hot flash caught our attention, causing us both to flinch. Bright yellow flames shot out from the side of the boat's hull, clearly visible, though more than three miles away. A bright orange ball of fire rolled upward for a moment, then the flames just stopped burning, leaving only a gray cloud rolling upward and out around the boat.

A second explosion came from the stern, where darker orange flames rose, igniting the cloud of gas from the first blast. Instantly, everything vaporized in a brilliant flash of bright yellow.

I knelt on the dock and began untying the stern line holding my eighteen-foot Grady-White Spirit to the tee-dock. "You have your phone on you?"

Carl tore his eyes from the burning wreckage, confused. He patted his pockets, looking for his phone. "Yeah," he finally said, moving into action, untying the bow line.

The double boom from the explosion startled both of us. I dropped down into the boat, turned on the batteries, and lowered the engine. It fired up instantly, as Carl pushed the bow away from the dock before stepping aboard.

While he took his cell phone out to call 911, I idled away from the dock and turned on the VHF radio. Plucking the mic from its holder, I spoke into it. "Mayday! Mayday! Any vessel near the Content Keys. There's a boat on fire northwest of Harbor Key Light. Anyone in the area please respond."

The Coast Guard answered immediately. "Vessel calling, this is United States Coast Guard Station, Key West. Please identify yourself."

"My name's Jesse McDermitt," I said, as the engine burbled quietly, idling away from the dock. "I live on an island off Harbor Channel. A passing shrimp boat has exploded three miles northwest of Harbor Key Light. I'm in my boat and heading out there to assist."

"We have a patrol boat in the area," the dispatcher said, her voice calm and succinct. "ETA is twenty-five minutes, Captain."

"Jesse," another voice said over the radio. "This is Dink. I'm fishing off Raccoon Key with a client. Can we help?"

"I don't know yet, Dink," I said, steering the boat toward the quickly disappearing smoke. "Head this way if you can. You'll see me headed north as soon as you clear Content Passage."

"US Coast Guard Key West to all concerned, please go to channel twenty-two A."

Hanging up the mic, I switched channels, not that I'd hear anything more. I slammed the throttle to the stop. The Grady dropped low at the stern and clawed its way up on top of the water in a matter of just a few yards.

The next couple of minutes seemed to drag as I pushed against the throttle repeatedly, trying to coax just one more RPM from the Suzuki engine. At the same time, I had to steer a winding course across the shallows. Most wouldn't dare, but knowing the way through the maze from years of experience, I was unconcerned.

Finally, we cleared the shallows and entered the Gulf of Mexico, still at full throttle. I pointed the nose at the dissipating smoke and trimmed the engine for top speed.

Arriving at the spot where the boat had exploded, I could see that there was little left of the vessel. Just pieces of fiberglass and wood. The hull must have been dragged under. My chart plotter showed that we were in thirty feet of water, more than deep enough to cover the outriggers had the boat sunk completely intact.

I brought the Grady to a stop before reaching the bulk of the debris field; fouling my prop in a shrimp net wouldn't help anyone. If there was anyone left to help. By instinct, I activated the Save Location feature on the GPS. The current would sweep the surface clean in short order and the Coast Guard would want to know where the wreckage sunk.

Behind us, I could hear the high-pitched whine of a big outboard, coming on fast. I looked back and could see Dink, flying across the water toward us in his new skiff. Another man sat on the little bench in front of the console, gripping the hand-grabs tightly. Dink's new Maverick was one of the fastest flats boats around.

"Sheriff's department has a patrol boat on the way, too," Carl said.

Scanning the debris, I saw body parts floating on the surface. Two distinctly different legs, one dark brown and the other white, floated next to each other. Ahead of us floated the torso of a white man. It was missing everything above the armpits. Nothing on the surface moved.

"My God," Carl said, surveying the carnage, retching slightly. "What could have caused an explosion like this?"

There was a strange odor hanging in the air. It mixed with other smells—burning diesel fuel, melted fiberglass, and the sickly copper stench of blood, which coated several floating boat pieces. The strange odor was powerful, like some sort of industrial cleanser.

As Dink approached, I waited until he slowed, then cupped my hands to yell. "It's a shrimp trawler!"

I pointed toward the west side of the wreckage, circling my arm in a wide arc before putting my outboard in gear and turning toward the east. Dink understood and slowed his skiff, steering around the other side, also at a safe distance. Nets are almost invisible underwater and abandoned nets drifting in the currents foul at least five boats a year around here.

I could have sworn one of the severed legs moved when I looked back. I watched it for a second, glancing ahead and all around as I moved the boat slowly around the debris. Suddenly, the water around the leg roiled and it disappeared. Sharks.

I grabbed the mic. "Dink, there are sharks in the water."

Circling the debris, we neared Dink's boat.

"Over there!" Carl shouted, pointing toward the center of the mess.

I looked in the direction he was pointing and saw something move.

"Get up on the bow!" I shouted. "Keep me off anything under the surface."

I turned and headed straight into the debris field. I saw something move and recognized it as a person's arm, weakly waving toward us.

"He's alive!" Carl shouted scrambling forward and kneeling on the forward casting deck, his body out over the forward rail. "Go right!"

I turned the wheel quickly, following his warnings and hand signals, as we made our way toward the injured man. His right arm was bare, though he appeared to be wearing a white shirt. As we got closer, I could see the man's head, resting on a piece of flotsam, his long black hair covering his face. The back of his shirt and his hair were scorched, as was the bare arm.

Suddenly, the shrimper turned halfway around, releasing the floating piece of debris he was hanging on. It wasn't a man at all. The woman's shirt was torn open by the blast, exposing part of a black bra against pale-white skin. The hair on the right side of her head was scorched to the scalp, but she was obviously a woman.

Carl reached over the side rail, as I shifted to neutral and went to help him. He grabbed an arm, just as the woman screamed, throwing her head back. When I reached to grab her other arm, something jerked her under, nearly pulling Carl with her. Her scream ended with a gurgling stream of bubbles.

The splash of a large tiger shark's tail, as it pulled the woman under left no doubt as to her fate.

"I had her!" Carl wailed, dropping to his knees on the deck.

In the distance, I heard the sound of a siren, and far to the east, I could make out the flashing blue lights of the approaching Coast Guard boat. A moment later, another boat with flashing blue lights made a wide turn around Harbor Key Light. It approached quickly, but without the siren.

Things began to happen quickly. They took our IDs, then ordered us away and told us to anchor. Dropping the hook well away from the wreck, I backed down on it, then shut off the engine. Dink idled over and tied off alongside us. "They say how long we'd have to stay?" Dink asked.

He knew the answer as well as I did. As long as it damned well took. He was asking for his client's benefit.

"Not long," I said, as more boats from the Coast Guard, Fish and Wildlife, and sheriff's office arrived. They began the grisly task of collecting what was left of the people who had been on the boat.

Nearly half an hour later, a county boat carrying Doctor Leo Fredrick arrived. He's the lead medical examiner for Monroe County and a colorful character to say the least.

The woman's body, or what was left of it, bobbed to the surface, face up. The right half of her torso from her waist to her ribcage was missing. Small fish continued to dart up, picking at the exposed entrails dangling below the body.

"Divers won't be able to get in the water for a while due to sharks," a Coast Guardsman told us, as he idled up alongside my boat. He'd been the second person to arrive, the first being the sheriff's deputy, who quickly relinquished authority since the wreck was outside the three-mile limit.

"The woman was alive when we got to her," Carl said. "A big tiger yanked her right out of my hands before I could pull her aboard."

"Did any of you see what happened?"

"From a distance," I said, pointing toward my island. "We live on that island and were on the dock watching the trawler go by when it just exploded."

"So you have no idea what started the fire?"

"Never saw a fire," Carl said. He was stressed, out of his element amid the carnage. "I know what didn't cause it."

"What do you mean?" the petty officer asked.

"A shrimp boat doesn't carry anything on board that could cause a blast like I saw."

"How do you know what a shrimp boat would have on board?"

"I own one," Carl said. "I've been a shrimper most of my life."

"Diesel fuel?"

"No, not like that at all," Carl replied, starting to become agitated. "Diesel's slow-burning, creates a dark orange fireball, more like burning black smoke than anything. There *was* a diesel explosion, but it came second."

"You've seen a lot of explosions, Mister, uh—"

"Trent," I said, intervening for Carl. "Captains Trent and McDermitt. And in twenty years of Marine Corps infantry, yeah, I've seen a lot of explosions."

"Something else exploded before the fuel tank," Carl said. "Something that burns a lot hotter than diesel. Something that burns so hot and fast that it sucked the oxygen right out of the air and snuffed itself out. But then the diesel blew, and the flames from that ignited whatever fumes didn't burn in the initial explosion. That's what caused all the damage. Some sort of highly explosive cloud ignited and just flattened everything. It looked like the hand of God Almighty Himself."

The petty officer made some notes on an electronic pad and then handed our identification back to us. "You can go, now. If we need anything more, we can reach you by phone."

Dink and his client quickly untied us, and headed back into the maze of cuts and channels that make up the back-country. I took my time pulling the anchor. The woman's face, though disfigured and burned, had looked familiar. I just couldn't remember where it was I'd seen her before.

We rode in silence back to the island, as the sun was nearing the western horizon. I circled the island and approached the channel.

"Gasoline, maybe?" I asked, as we tied the Grady up to the fixed pier alongside the channel. "At first I thought it sounded like an old two-stroke. Might have been a gas engine."

"You've seen gas explode," Carl said. "Burns hotter than diesel, sure. But still an orange flame. That first explosion was yellow-white. It sucked every molecule of oxygen out of the air in the immediate area and that's what caused it to flame out. Then it hung over that boat, waiting to be reignited, while the people on board were running around."

He was stressing way more than was healthy. I knew only one thing to make him slow down, and that was to get him thinking.

"What burns that hot?" I asked.

Carl stood and stretched his back. "Dunno. Some sort of chemicals maybe. Much too volatile to be any sort of fuel.

Think that trawler was carrying industrial waste out to dump somewhere in the bay?"

"Some people will do anything for a buck," I offered, as we left the dock area and went up the steps to the deck.

"That happened a lot back in the day," Carl said. "But the EPA has cracked down so hard that it's stupid risky now. Someone would have to pay a lot of money to make it worthwhile."

Taking two beers from the cooler under the table, I opened them and handed one to Carl as we looked across the island at the flashing blue lights on the boats out at the wreck site.

"I smelled something out there," I said. "Smelled like some sort of industrial cleanser or something."

"I smelled it too," Carl said, taking a long pull from his beer. "Reminded me of all those damned cats that hang around O'Hare's place."

CHAPTER FOUR

I didn't want to leave right away. Carl and I never got a chance to finish our earlier conversation, but I was already late picking Kim up at the *Rusty Anchor*. So we promised to discuss it more later in the evening.

The tide was falling, so I took the longer route east to Rocky Channel, rather than the maze of shallow cuts south of my island. We'd have to go slower on the return when the water would be at its lowest. But for now, I knew I could run right across most of the flats, and those I couldn't, I knew where they were. While the calm, flat waters in the backcountry might look like you're on the ocean, with islands scattered here and there, the bottom was only inches below the surface in many places.

The sun, red and enormous, painted the clouds in the western sky with a deep scarlet glow, fading to orange nearer the horizon. *Red sky at night*, I thought, aiming the bow at the center of the high arch on the Seven Mile Bridge.

Half an hour later, idling down the canal to Rusty's docks, I could hear music coming from the deck area out back, and the sound of a lot of people. A sloop I'd never seen—a nice-looking Morgan center cockpit—was tied up as I entered the small marina. Several familiar boats were docked beyond it, mostly liveaboards who stayed here through the winter. The dock space at the end of the canal, just before the turning basin, was where locals docked smaller boats, and it was packed.

I spotted Dink's skiff and tossed some fenders over before tying off to his port deck cleats. I was only planning to stay long enough for a beer if Kim was here, two if she wasn't. There was still plenty of room for someone to get past the Grady to reach the fuel dock in the turning basin.

Shutting off the engine, I stepped over onto Dink's Maverick and up to the dock. Finn hesitated for a second, then he also jumped to the skiff and onto the dock before taking off toward the back of the property to mooch food from Rusty's customers.

The parking lot was nearly full, and I recognized most of the cars and pickups. Rusty must have been celebrating something.

I opened the door to the rustic old bar and stepped inside. There was definitely some kind of celebration going on. The *Rusty Anchor* was usually a quiet place where liveaboards and locals hung out, fishing guides met with their clients, and sea stories were swapped by all. Being small and out of the way, Rusty didn't get as much in the way of tourist business as some of the larger places in Marathon, like *Dockside* or *Brass Monkey*, did.

Dink was sitting at the bar telling a gathering crowd about the explosion. It was fortunate that he was sitting.

Dink was kind of accident prone—but only on land. He had perpetual sea legs and would trip over an ant on land. And you'd have had a hard time finding a politer man; he was the sort that would apologize to the ant.

Looking around, I didn't see Kim, so I went to the end of the bar against the wall, weaving through the tables to avoid the crowd at the other end. Rusty put a cold Red Stripe on the bar before I got there. The last two stools didn't have a view of the TV over the bar and a wall blocked the sight of the deck out back, so they were usually empty, which suited me fine. I prefer having my back to a wall.

"Hey, Jesse!" Dink shouted, pointing at me. "He was there, y'all. He saw the explosion."

As one, the crowd of people who had been listening to Dink turned toward me, several asking questions at the same time. I don't like crowds and I really don't like being the center of attention.

"I didn't see much," I said. "Wasn't looking at it when it exploded. Dink and his charter got there about the same time I did."

I turned toward the bar, and most of them got the hint. They all had familiar faces, though I barely knew half their names.

Hearing the door open, I glanced over and saw my daughter come in. At nineteen, she was in her second year at the University of Florida up in Gainesville. She'd graduated high school a year earlier than her peers and then took nearly a year off before enrolling in college.

"Can't stay," I said to Rusty.

Rusty and I know one another better than brothers. He nodded and said, "We'll catch up Sunday morning."

Kim scheduled all her classes Monday through Thursday, except for a morning sociology class on Friday. Every other weekend, she makes the seven-hour drive down here and stays with me on the island. She usually leaves before noon on Sunday to have time to catch up on her studies before returning to classes on Monday.

I liked to believe it was to spend time with me, but the truth was, she liked the island lifestyle as much as I did and needed the time here to decompress. Then there was the matter of her boyfriend, who lived on Little Torch Key just down island from Big Pine. Lately, I hadn't seen a lot of her during her weekends home. I understood, though. I remembered being nineteen.

"Hey, Dad," she said, giving me a big hug. "Hi, Rusty, what's the celebration about?"

"Celebration? Oh, you mean all these folks drinking and having a good time? *Dockside* is closed up again. This time it sounds permanent. I kinda feel bad about it, but not a whole lot."

"Really?" I asked.

"County-ordered," Rusty replied, sliding a beer down the bar to Jimmy. "Egghead engineers are saying it could slide into the water any minute. Place's been that way for years."

The back door opened just as the singer out on the deck started a new song, which brought a chorus of shouts and applause from everyone on the deck.

"Who's that?" Kim asked, nodding her head toward the little stage.

"Eric Stone," Rusty replied. "Originally from Texas, but been hanging around down here a few years now. He was supposed to play *Dockside* this weekend, but now I got him.

I guess word spread." He pointed to a rack of CDs. "He's got a lot of original tunes."

Kim went over to the rack and looked through them, returning with a CD and pulling a ten-dollar bill from her purse. "I'll take this one—Boat Songs Number One, Songs for Sail."

Rusty quickly made a tick mark on a notepad next to the CD title, and put the bill in a box under the bar. Outwardly, his accounting methods were very simple—he carried a small notepad in his pocket, in which he recorded all the running bar tabs—but I knew that in his office he had a desktop computer with all the latest accounting software. He, or I should say we, since I'm part owner of the *Anchor*, probably made a dollar from that sale and I had no doubt that every cash transaction was recorded back in that office and declared as income. Rusty didn't cut corners where the IRS was concerned. Come to think of it, he didn't cut corners on much of anything at all, that I knew of. He conducted business in person, with a handshake.

"We can listen to it on the way home," I said, tilting my bottle for the last swallow. "Is Marty coming for supper tomorrow?"

Deputy Martin Phillips and Kim had been dating for a couple of years now. Being a deputy meant working odd shift changes and weird hours. I knew that he went up to Gainesville when he had time off, and I was pretty certain he stayed with Kim in the apartment she shared with a friend. But when she was here on the island, he always seemed to have an early shift the next day.

"Yeah," she replied. "If it's okay with you."

I put my arm around her shoulder and pulled her in close. "Your friends are always welcome."

Jimmy and Al Fader slipped away from the group and joined us as Rusty leaned over the bar to talk conspiratorially. "Your shrimper ain't the only weird incident. Al here saw something unusual and I heard about something up island a lot like what he saw."

"What do you mean?" I asked.

"Yesterday morning," Al began, "we were anchoring up on New Ground and a shrimper from out of Cape Coral anchored with us."

"Happens a lot this time of year," I said. "Pinks are running."

"Yeah, but he never wet his nets," Al said. "Come nightfall, when the rest of us were readying to make our last trawls for the week, he pulled the hook and headed back north."

"Same exact thing happened two nights ago," Rusty offered. "Up near Sprigger Bank. I called Justin Creech this morning. He owns *Instigator*, the boat that anchored up with the Islamorada fleet. Or he used to. Sold three of his boats a couple of months ago, *Alligator*, *Instigator*, and the boat Al saw, *Eliminator*."

"Why would they come all the way down here and not fish?" Kim asked, putting a voice to my own curiosity.

"No idea," Al replied. "Bob Talbot and I, along with Charlie Hofbauer and one of my crew, went over to *Eliminator* to tell them they weren't welcome. One of their crew said they had no intention of fishing. I circled around their boat to see where they hailed from, and when I was downwind, it stunk to high Heaven."

"A smelly shrimp boat ain't too unusual," Jimmy said.

"No, not the usual stink," Al said. "I'm used to that. This was some sort of industrial smell, like a chemical plant."

"I smelled the same thing," I said, still trying to place the odor in my mind. "Out on the wreck this morning. Like a solvent or something."

Kim's eyes went wide. "Wreck?"

"A shrimp boat blew up out on the Gulf this afternoon," I said, rising from my stool. "I'll tell you about it on the way."

I knew Dink would be retelling the story soon for anyone who bought him another beer. I also knew that, as with all sea stories, the retelling would become more grandiose. Kim didn't need to hear all the gory details, especially when the details become elaborated with drink.

We said goodbye to our friends and Jimmy followed us out. "Got a sec?" he asked once we were away from the noise.

"Go on ahead, Kim," I told my daughter. "See if you can round up Finn. He's probably out back, begging for scraps."

After she'd walked away a bit, Jimmy turned to me with a serious expression that belied his typical laid-back demeanor. "You and Al both mentioned a strong smell. Acetone maybe?"

"On a shrimp boat? What for?" I considered it a moment. "Yeah, might have been acetone."

"It's used to make methamphetamine, man."

"What's that?"

"Doesn't surprise me that you don't know," he said. "Never did it myself; it's a synthetic drug, super addictive, and dangerous to make. There just ain't no good reason to have acetone on a commercial fishing vessel."

"Dangerous how?" I asked, as I watched Kim coming back around the side of the building, Finn trotting and jumping alongside her.

"For one thing, the fumes created when they cook meth can kill you, and some of the chemicals used are explosive. If real methylamine is used, combined with acetone on board, a fire could cause a massive blast."

"Like the kind of explosion Carl and I saw?"

"Yeah, a white-hot flame, man. If they were cooking meth on a boat, they were freaking nuts. Bouncing around would be bad news."

"Any idea how long it takes to make?"

Jimmy looked out over the marina. "I don't know for sure. Like I said, I don't mess with synthetics. Eight or ten hours? I don't know."

About the same amount of time that a shrimper lays at anchor during the day, I thought. Almost instantly, my mind changed gears as Finn came trotting ahead of Kim. Not my circus, not my monkeys. I live in the now.

"These people are dangerous," Jimmy said. "The manufacturers only care about the money, and the tweakers only care about where they get their next fix. And both would kill to get what they want. *Cuidado, hermano.*" Then changing the subject as Kim approached, he added, "We need to get out for some wahoo one day."

"Thanks, Jimmy," I said. "Let's do that. You free on Wednesday?"

"Sure am," he said, clapping me on the shoulder as he turned.

He went back toward the bar and I started toward the dock, Kim angling to intercept. "What did Jimmy want?"

"Said the wahoo bite is on," I replied. Completely true. Some things, you have to shield your kids from. "We're going fishing Wednesday."

"Can we go tomorrow?"

"Hey, Jimmy!" I yelled, catching him as he was reaching for the door. "Wanna go tomorrow?"

"Sunrise?"

"Make it an hour after," I replied.

"I'll be here," he said, waving, and stepping inside.

"Wahoo!" Kim cried out, dancing in circles. "You really live the life down here." She stepped across the forward casting deck of Dink's skiff and loosed our bow line.

I started the engine and untied the stern. "I'm getting used to it."

CHAPTER FIVE

C edric Harper paused before getting out of his car. He'd parked in front of a building on the outskirts of Fort Myers. The warehouse in front of him looked like a dozen other upscale commercial and industrial buildings in the area. And for the most part, it was.

The business manufactured a line of time-release deodorizers in cans and strips meant to be placed inside the return air ducts of air conditioning systems. They shipped the scented canisters and strips all over the world. Cedric wasn't part of that business, but he worked for the man who owned it.

Pulling the handle, the hinges creaked as the door on the old Toyota Corolla swung out and drooped slightly. Everything about the car seemed to sag, from the headliner, to the suspension, to the driver.

Cedric got out of the car and looked around nervously. It was dark, but the orange glow of the sodium-vapor lights mounted on the front of the building and out on the street illuminated his surroundings, casting an orange glow and creating long shadows from the trees and buildings. A tall security fence surrounded the building, save for the parking lot where his car was parked. It was the only car in the lot, but Cedric knew the building was occupied.

Approaching the entry door, he looked up at the camera mounted above it. The thing always made him a little jumpy; the tiny red light above the lens was like some sort of unblinking creature of the night, staring coldly at him.

He pushed the button beside the door and heard a faint buzzing sound from inside the building. After a moment, there was a click and another, quieter buzz from the locking mechanism. Cedric pulled the door open and went into the expansive lobby.

The ceiling was a good fifteen feet above his head. During the day, the lobby was bright and airy. Potted plants flanked comfortable-looking leather chairs. A desk was centered on the far wall with a large painting of an old schooner under full sail in heavy seas hanging above it. Hallways extended at right angles from there to the many business offices.

The chair at the receptionist's desk was empty, as it always was when Cedric came in. The woman who occupied it left every weekday evening at exactly five o'clock; never a minute early nor a minute late.

Turning left, he walked down a long hallway with closed office doors on the left and a wall of framed photographs on the right. Eugene Ballinger, the owner of the business, was featured in most of the pictures, usually on one of his boats, and almost always with scantily clad women surrounding him and whatever rock star or actor he was with. Ballinger had friends in high places and money to burn.

At the end of the hall, he pushed open a steel door on the right and stepped out into the huge warehouse. A number of box trucks were parked diagonally in two lines, extending from the big rollup door at the far end of the warehouse. They were used to deliver the scented air fresheners to shippers and distributors. Machines to package the products, and pallets loaded with boxes filled the rest of the area; finished products were on one side and incoming supplies to make them were on the other.

Turning left, Cedric made his way around several pallets stacked with boxes, wrapped in plastic, and ready to ship. He continued to the corner of the warehouse where another door stood open. A shaft of light from the doorway illuminated the concrete floor in front of him and he stepped through it into another hall, much shorter than the one he'd just come through.

Stopping at the first door, Cedric paused and took a deep breath, before turning the knob and pushing the door open to the man's inner sanctum.

"What did you find out?" Ballinger asked, not looking up from the laptop screen in front of him nor wasting time on pleasantries or idle chit-chat. "Where did they go?"

"It's not good, Mister B," Cedric replied as he nervously approached the man's desk. "In fact, it's really bad."

The man's head came up and he looked over his reading glasses, his small, amber-colored eyes holding Cedric motionless, like a deer caught in the headlights of a fast-moving truck. He was slightly taller than Cedric's five-eight and a few pounds heavier. Though in his mid-forties, he looked to be in good shape, tanned and fit, with dark blond sun-streaked hair that always looked wind-blown.

"It blew up."

"What?" Ballinger shouted, pushing away from the desk. "How the hell did that happen?"

"The boat just exploded, Mister B. It went down in the Gulf, taking everything with it. The word I got is that there weren't any survivors."

"None?"

Cedric hesitated a moment, knowing what the man was asking. "I'm sorry," he said, looking down and shoving his hands in the pockets of his jeans. "She was on board."

"Killed in the explosion?"

Cedric was reluctant to tell his boss what he'd heard, but knew better than to lie or omit anything. "I heard from a very reliable source that she survived the blast but was killed by a shark."

Ballinger stared intently at the younger man. Finally, he blinked and nodded. "Thank the gods for small favors. She needed to go, anyway. What happened?"

Cedric fidgeted, realizing that he'd never known anyone with such a cold heart. The woman had been his boss's mistress for over a year. She was the one who convinced him of the money that could be made in his current side business. A woman of some means, she'd put a good bit of her own money into the new venture.

"I heard that a couple of do-gooders saw it happen and went to help. They called in the cops and the Coast Guard. They told the cops that it just exploded while underway." Cedric paused for a second. "Mister B, if they dive on it, they're bound to find something."

"If?"

"Yeah, well, it happened just before dark. The shark that killed Miss Richmond wasn't the only one in the area. They'll probably dive it tomorrow."

Ballinger thought it over for a moment. "Do you know exactly where my boat is?"

"Well, yeah," he replied, knowing the boat's last position was stored on his tracking software. "But it sunk in thirty feet of water."

Ballinger stood up behind the desk and walked over to a window, which looked out over a retention pond. "So, we have what? Ten hours?"

Cedric gave his boss a puzzled look. "Ten hours for what?"

"To move it."

"Move a sunken boat?" Cedric asked, still puzzled.

"The name and home port are on the stern. That'll connect the boat to me. Not good, if they recover the equipment on board. Contact whichever boat is nearest and have them drag the wreck at least a mile from where it went down."

"Drag—you mean the whole boat? How?"

"It's a trawler, Cedric," Ballinger said, turning to face him. "Those big things that stick up in the air with all the ropey looking stuff hanging off? Those are nets meant to drag the bottom. They can snag the wreck and drag it and any debris away. But they gotta get it done before daylight. Which boat is closest?"

Cedric pulled his cell phone from his pocket and opened an app that displayed a map of the southwest Florida coast, the Keys, and a big chunk of the Gulf of Mexico.

"The *Alligator* is twenty miles northeast, just off Cape Sable, and *Eliminator* is halfway home. *Alligator* had to work late to finish up, and will be getting underway pretty soon."

"How long before they can reach the wreck?"

Cedric studied the tiny chart in his hands. "Three, maybe four hours, I guess."

"Call the captain on his satellite phone," Ballinger said. "Tell him to go to the wreck and move it at least a mile away and record the position so we can recover the equipment. And be careful how you word it; the government can snoop on anything."

"I doubt anything will be salvageable," Cedric said.

"We still have to retrieve it. Lobster divers could stumble on the location and find what's aboard." Ballinger stepped closer. "Show me where the wreck is."

Cedric nervously fiddled with the device, zooming in on a spot marked with a red dot, then zooming out again to get a reference of the location.

"It went down here," he said, pointing at the red dot. "About three miles north of this group of deserted islands, maybe ten miles north of Big Pine Key."

"Those islands have names?"

"I don't think they have individual names," Cedric replied. "The group is called the Content Keys."

CHAPTER SIX

When we arrived back at the house, Carl already had the big center console out. *El Cazador* was tied to the fixed pier, looking eager to be on the hunt. Thirty feet long with a wide beam and single inboard diesel, the Winter Yachts fishing boat made an ideal dive platform. Lots of room to move around, fixed tank racks, and plenty of seating. With its big Carolina-style bow flares and sharp entry, it made for a very comfortable and dry ride in any sea conditions.

"We're going diving?" Kim asked excitedly.

"I found a deep hole about a mile off Sawyer Key," I replied, steering the Grady into the dock space under the house. "Some kind of sinkhole opened up recently. It's small, but deep, nearly eighty feet. You okay with that?"

"I've been deeper."

"Yeah, but this is vertical diving," I cautioned, maneuvering the Grady into position behind my skiff. "The sink is only about fifteen feet across at the surface, layers of limestone restrict horizontal clearance below that in a couple of places. Kinda like a vertical cave with stalactites going sideways."

"Marty and I have been doing some cavern diving up in Ocala, Dad. I'm good with it."

As we tied up to the dock, I noticed that Charlie's boat wasn't back yet. I'd given Carl and Charlie a slightly larger Grady-White when they came to work for me. It had been a wedding gift from my friend Deuce Livingston and had belonged to his murdered father before that. Charlie's drinks with the girls must have gone into overtime.

"I put six tanks aboard," Carl said, coming through the door to the outside. Finn took advantage of the opening and bolted outside to find a tree. "You don't plan on more than a couple of dives, right?"

"Two's good," I said. "Charlie's not back yet?"

"She called and said she's gonna spend the night with Bob and Nikki, so I don't have a curfew."

"Give me five minutes to get changed," Kim said, as she grabbed her overnight bag from the forward storage box and followed Finn.

"I loaded a cooler with sandwiches and fruit," Carl said. "Didn't know if you guys ate at the *Anchor* or not."

"Thanks," I said, as we walked out onto the fixed pier toward *El Cazador*. "We came straight back as soon as Kim arrived. Not sure if she ate on the way, but I can always eat."

Three dive bags sat on the pier next to the boat. I grabbed mine and stepped down into the cockpit, placing it next to the large fish box built into the deck. Knowing Carl, there was no need to check the lights, and I knew my own gear was in perfect order. I lifted the hatch and put my bag in, then added the other two as Carl handed them to me.

"I'm all set," Kim said, coming down the steps to the pier.

"Then let's go blow some bubbles," I said, turning the key in the ignition switch. The big Cummins diesel roared to life, then settled into a quiet, burbling idle.

Raising the electronics panel in the top of the console as Carl and Kim climbed aboard, I took my wallet out and retrieved the GPS numbers I'd saved when I'd found the spot in the Grady.

We idled down my short channel and turned left into the deeper water of Harbor Channel. The sky was clear, and the moon and the stars were shining bright as I nudged the throttle up. *El Cazador* came up on plane easily, with plenty of throttle left, nosing its way toward deeper water, befitting its name, The Hunter.

Carl went forward and sat in the big double seat in front of the console and Kim joined me at the helm. "Looks like the tide's dead low."

"No more than half an hour ago," I said, turning toward the shallows to the north that separated my island from its nearest neighbor.

Three times a week, I swim out to that island and back. The shallows between the two islands is never less than two feet. *El Cazador* has a recessed prop tunnel, with moderate deadrise at the transom, giving her great shallow-water capability for her size. On plane, she barely draws a foot of water.

The ride was less than ten minutes. As we neared the waypoint on the GPS, I slowed to an idle and began watching the depth finder.

"Is that it?" Kim asked, as the red and yellow contours shown on the GPS started to fall away to deeper water in a steep slope.

"Not yet," I replied. "But it's coming up."

Carl went up to the pulpit to ready the anchor.

"There," I said, as the bottom dropped sharply away.

I reversed the engine and brought the boat to a stop. The depth finder showed a deep hole below us, with a lot of clutter. I allowed the boat to drift while watching the screen. We were drifting sideways in the current. When the edge of the sink came up on the screen again, I waited a few seconds longer, until I was sure the bow had drifted away from the deep fissure.

"Drop it," I told Carl.

He released the anchor with a splash, letting the braided nylon rope slide through his hands until the anchor reached the bottom. After we'd drifted for a moment, he tugged on the rode, turning the anchor in the proper direction before pulling more line from the small anchor locker, until he reached the red tape wrapped around it at one-hundred feet. He then measured off another fifty feet by extending the line between his outstretched arms eight times, measuring out roughly six more feet each stretch, and then tied it off to one of the deck cleats on the bow.

"The anchor should be about ten or twenty feet down-current from the edge of the hole," I said, switching on the LED spreader lights, as Kim began pulling our dive bags out of the fish box.

I backed down on the anchor, satisfying myself that it was holding. "We'll follow the anchor line down," Carl said. He was always prone to voicing the plan, though we'd dived together many times. "I'll clip a tethered strobe to the anchor, in case anyone gets separated. From there, we only need to swim against the current a few feet to the edge of the sinkhole. Let's group there before descending."

Carl removed the rigid blue-and-white international dive flag from the overhead and secured it to its six-foot mast, then inserted the mast in a vertical rod holder in the transom. I switched on the spreader lights mounted wide on the aft end of the T-top to illuminate the flag from both sides. With no wind, it swung back and forth as the small rollers rocked the boat.

From a storage rack on the gunwale, I removed the diver-down light pole and telescoped it out to its full ten feet. When I plugged it into the anchor-light receptacle, the alternating red and white lights illuminated the whole boat and could be seen for miles.

The three of us began to suit up. Carl and I don't usually wear wetsuits; the water temperature in the Keys rarely gets cold enough, except in January. Even then, it's close to seventy degrees. The GPS showed the current water temperature to be near eighty. But Kim was pulling on a light-weight, one-piece Lycra suit.

While I've never read any sort of research on the subject, as a dive-boat operator, I see a lot of divers; I've noticed that women are more likely to wear wetsuits, sometimes even in the summer. Maybe they lose body heat faster and were more susceptible to hypothermia than men. Or maybe men are just more stubbornly macho. I get a little cold toward the end of a long dive, when the water is below seventy-five or so, but not enough to warrant the struggle to get the damned things on and off again.

When we were all ready, Carl moved first to the stern and sat down, carefully swinging one leg at a time over the transom to stand on the swim platform. Unlike the *Revenge*, there wasn't a transom door on *El Cazador*. It didn't have a swim platform when I got it, but I added a small one, along with a telescoping ladder to make it easier to get back aboard from the water.

Kim checked my gear from behind before joining Carl on the swim platform. With their backs to me, I quickly made sure their first stages were secure and the air valves were open before stepping over the transom to join them.

We entered the water one at a time, me going first. Once I'd moved away slightly, Kim made a giant stride entry and came to join me, allowing Carl room to step off.

Each of us had powerful dive lights tethered to battery packs on our waists with a curly cord, like an old telephone receiver. We also had backup flashlights, one in each pocket of our buoyancy compensators.

Leading the way, I finned around the boat to where the rode entered the water at the bow. There weren't any instructions needed; the three of us had dived together dozens, if not hundreds of times, and Carl had already hit the high points.

I took hold of the anchor line and raised my BC's purge valve, depressing the button on the end. The air quickly bled out and I began to descend, following the yellow, braided-nylon anchor line.

Shining my light ahead and toward the bottom, I could clearly see the rode almost all the way to the anchor, the bright yellow line a sharp contrast to the inky blackness around me. The ten feet of chain on the end connecting the line to the anchor was absorbed by its surroundings. Visibility was limited to the dive light's ability to pierce the inky black water. Still, I could just make out where the rode reached the anchor, more than a hundred feet ahead.

I slowly finned against the slow-moving current, following the rode toward the new fissure. Looking back, I could see Kim right behind me, with Carl just descending from the surface.

I equalized the pressure in my ears and continued. The sound of our breath intake and bubbles was accentuated, along with the night sounds of the sea; clicking noises, and the occasional trill of a fish. The ocean isn't a quiet place. Not even at night.

We reached the anchor and I made sure the flukes were sunk deeply in the sandy bottom before turning toward the drop-off. Carl quickly attached the strobe to the end of the five-foot chain the nylon rope was attached to and turned it on, letting it float a few feet above the bottom. At the edge of the hole, we stopped and looked down, hovering in place by slowly finning into the current.

The contours around the edges were more rounded than they were when I found it last week. The constant movement of the current carried sand away from the edge on one side and pushed it into the abyss on the other. Several feet down, a jagged limestone outcrop jutted out into the hole a few feet and the antennae of several lobsters were visible in the crack between the ledge and where it disappeared into the wall.

Pointing my light at the wavering feelers, I glanced over at Kim. She was grinning behind her second stage. I held up three fingers, then pointed down into the crevasse, and she nodded her understanding that we would try to catch three on the way down.

She raised three fingers in return, then gave a jerking thumbs-up, followed with a V-sign. I grinned. She wanted to catch three on the way up, too.

I nodded, then looked over at Carl. He pointed to his chest, then to Kim, and finally to me. Kim and I nodded our understanding, and he kicked a few times to move out over the center of the hole where he doubled his body over, and descended. Kim jackknifed her body and dove after him without hesitation. Moving out over the center of the hole, I followed them down.

We moved slowly, so as not to disturb the lobster. Soon, they'd be leaving the hole to forage across the grassy flats all around us. It only took a couple of minutes before we had three good-sized bugs in the bag Carl was carrying.

I was carrying a pole spear, which is nothing more than a five-foot aluminum rod with a length of thick surgical hose attached at one end and a threaded spear tip with butterfly barbs on the other. With my right arm through the loop, I adjusted it, so the rubber hose was around the inside of my bent elbow, but held loose, with no tension on the hose. If there was a big grouper down here, I wanted it and a pole spear is easier in a confined space than a spear gun.

Checking my gauges, I saw we were at forty feet and I still had plenty of air. So we descended further. Once we were past the limestone outcrop, the sinkhole opened to a good thirty feet wide.

The whole Florida peninsula is built on a limestone base, with crevasses and underground rivers carving a network of tunnels and caves in the soft rock. In the northern part of the interior there are vast networks of these underwater caves and rivers that extend for miles and probably connect to others. It was this network of caves and caverns that Kim had mentioned diving with Marty.

I'd done my share of cave and cavern diving. I remember a slime-covered pond that an old friend knew about. It was on a farm just outside of Ocala, and no more than twenty feet across. Like surface rivers, underground rivers will change course sometimes and the pond was a remnant of such a change.

Russ Livingston, Deuce's dad, had brought me there without telling me what we'd find. Just that I'd get a kick out of it. We'd waded into the algae- and hyacinth-covered pond, carrying our tanks and BCs. The water was deceptively deep, and we'd had to use lights immediately after submerging. Russ had led me to a small crack in the bottom, where I realized why we had to drag our gear. He'd gone first, pushing his rig ahead of him through the opening. I remember shining my light into the narrow opening and seeing him don his gear ten feet below.

Once I'd joined Russ on the other side of the opening, I saw just how large the cavern was. From the opening, it flared out kind of like an inverted funnel, and at thirty feet it was at least fifty feet across.

We'd dived to nearly a hundred feet that day, reaching the sandy bottom where a narrow tunnel stretched away to one side, but was much too narrow to get through. I knew it to be one of the many subterranean rivers that had changed course, finding a shorter way through the limestone. Over time, sediment had filled and restricted water movement in the upstream side, and the river had become dormant.

Russ had sifted through the sand at the bottom, found something, and began to dig around it, shaking it loose from the sediment. Slowly, a grayish rock began to appear. Not knowing what it was, I started to help him. After a minute, we got the thing loose, and the sand fell under it, exposing the giant skull and tusks of what could only have been a mastodon.

Later, sitting on the tailgate of Russ's old pickup, he explained that most of the other bones from the ancient fossil had been removed by treasure hunters, but the skull was too big to fit through the rock opening. He told me that in ancient times, when sea levels were lower, some of the underground rivers had been on the surface. He'd told me about some of the caves he'd explored and all the animal bones he'd found in them and hypothesized that an animal, or even an early human, could be caught up in a fast-moving stream and swept into the subterranean portion.

Glancing at my gauges, I continued to descend, Kim and Carl right with me. At sixty feet, I happened to glance to my left and saw two very large hogfish resting in a hollowed-out spot in the side of the sink. I froze in place and could sense that the others had also stopped, reading my body language. Moving very slowly, I reached up with my left hand and took hold of the pole spear near the tip. I pulled it back, stretching the rubber hose behind my elbow, until I could grip it near the tip with my right hand. The pole spear was cocked and ready, and the two hogfish hadn't yet paid much attention to the intruders of their watery domain.

Using only my fins, I slowly turned my body, moving slightly to my right for a better shot. Unbelievably, the nearer hogfish moved slightly forward, directly beside his partner, as if shielding the other fish. I slowly raised my arm, extending the point of the spear, aiming for the sweet spot just behind the long sloping head of the first fish.

When I released my grip on the pole spear, it shot forward, skewering both fish, one in the kill spot and the other just behind the gills. The first fish twitched once and was still. The second one kicked its tail a few times, before it died too.

Carl dropped down next to me, carefully opening his catch bag so the lobster didn't escape. I removed the threaded tip of the spear and slid both fish off and into the bag. We'd been in the water less than twenty minutes, and we'd caught enough food for five people. More importantly, we'd caught exactly what we wanted instead of whatever took our bait. Fishing is fun, but diving for food is just all around better for the fishery, since there's no unwanted by-catch.

Slipping past me, Kim continued down, examining the jagged walls of the sinkhole as I threaded the tip back onto the spear. The hole had probably opened up more than a week before, and with the twice-daily change in direction of the current, any loose sand or rocks were likely already dislodged. Over the coming months and years, it would gradually be filled in with the detritus of the sea.

Dropping down alongside her, I checked my pressure and depth, then followed her gaze. We were at sixty-five feet, more than thirty feet below the seafloor, and directly ahead I could easily make out the remnants of a long-dead coral reef. But there was something a little off about the symmetry. One branch of the ancient coral grew perfectly straight, disappearing at nearly a forty-five-degree angle into the limestone just above the now-exposed reef.

Digging into her pocket, Kim produced the GoPro camera she always carried and using her tethered dive light to illuminate the old coral formation, she took several pictures before looking at me excitedly. She was breathing faster than normal.

I tapped my gauge cluster and pointed at hers. She lifted it and looked at the reading, then held up eight fingers. It was time to surface. She'd gulped down air faster than normal and was down to just eight hundred pounds of pressure. That could be burned up quickly at our current depth. In this hole, we were under more than three atmospheres of pressure, so each breath from our regulators consumed three times as much air.

I jerked my thumb upward and she nodded. Slowly, we finned toward the surface. Carl was still hanging out where we'd bagged the hogfish, considering a deep slit in the side of the sink, and shining his light into it.

Tapping him on the shoulder to get his attention, I gave him the surface signal and he nodded. Together, the three of us continued upward, rising slower than our air bubbles. We had to go single file past the limestone outcrop, and once clear, I waited for Kim, to check her pressure once more. Down to six hundred pounds. She was still breathing way too fast.

Once we reached the seafloor, we finned toward the flashing strobe and Carl turned it off, untied it, and pocketed the marker. From there, we followed the anchor line upward toward the boat. At fifteen feet, I stopped and checked Kim's gauges again. Her breathing was back to normal and her pressure was at five hundred pounds. Enough for a ten-minute safety stop and still leave her enough air to get back aboard with a hundred pounds.

Finally, we started for the surface, letting the current carry us under the boat to the swim platform. At the stern, I inflated my BC and shrugged out of it, to make it easier to get aboard.

CHAPTER SEVEN

Kim started chattering excitedly as soon as she pulled the second stage out of her mouth. "Did you see that? It was a coral reef! More than thirty feet under the sea floor."

"That was worth the price of admission alone," I admitted, lifting my gear over the transom and reminding myself once more that a door would make a nice addition to *El Cazador*.

"During the last ice age," Carl began, as he helped Kim out of her BC and handed her rig up to me, "sea levels were much lower than today. What you saw was the old sea floor, buried by centuries of sediment."

"How old do you think it was?" Kim asked, climbing up the ladder to stand with me on the swim platform.

I shrugged. "No idea, but it was a heck of a find."

"The most recent ice age was over ten thousand years ago," Carl said. I gave him a questioning look and he shrugged his shoulders as he hung onto the ladder. "So I'm an internet junky."

"Ten thousand years?" Kim said in awe. "Do you know when the first Indians were in this area?"

Climbing the ladder, Carl had a questioning look on his face. "The first Indians?"

"Yeah," she said, stepping over the transom and opening a drawer where clean towels were stored. She began wringing seawater from her hair. "There was a spear, or something stuck in the coral."

I grinned at my daughter. "I doubt that was a spear. I don't think there were any people around here that long ago."

At the helm, I flipped on the radar out of habit. Night diving is dangerous, but most of the danger isn't from the dive itself. Night collisions with anchored boats happen all the time. It's always a good idea to see what's around you. Head on a swivel, or in this case, a radar beam. After a moment, the screen came on and the unit showed the radar echo of a boat that was approaching our position from the northwest. But it was four miles off and moving slowly; nothing to worry about.

"Don't be so sure," Carl said. "The first inhabitants came over a land bridge from Asia during that same ice age. I read somewhere that artifacts have been found in north Florida dating back twelve thousand years. What'd it look like, this spear?"

Kim went to her dry bag in the starboard fish box and returned holding a small tablet computer. She plugged the cord dangling from it into the GoPro. One of the pictures she'd taken instantly appeared on the device's screen.

She scrolled through several, then stopped. "There," she said, pointing at the screen. "That shaft is perfectly straight."

"Could be a spear," Carl said, studying the picture. He grinned. "I know one sure way to find out."

"Okay, let's rest a bit," I said. "Eat something and go back down."

Kim had a worried expression. "I'd hate to destroy the coral formation to dig it out."

"By this time next month, sand will have half-filled that hole," I said. "And by spring, there won't be any evidence that it ever existed."

She considered that a moment. "Then I want to collect a couple of pieces of that coral," she replied, putting her little computer away. "It's ancient sea life."

We went up to the bow and Carl pulled a cooler from under one of the bench seats and opened it. "I got conch salad sandwiches, mangos, some sliced pineapple, and grapes."

"Pineapple?" I asked.

"I don't think it was completely ripe, but I couldn't wait anymore."

Two years ago, Charlie planted a bunch of pineapple tops on the little island partially connected to the north side of my main island. They grew slowly, and this past summer and fall, they began to flower. Several of the plants had produced suckers the first year, which she cut and replanted. Now we had dozens of them growing.

"I'll have a sandwich to start," Kim said, pulling her wetsuit down and tying the sleeves around her waist.

"I'm sorry," I said. "I figured you ate on the way."

"I did," she replied, taking a bite of the sandwich Carl handed her. "But that was like three or four hours ago."

The pineapple was sweet—not quite as juicy as it would have been if Carl had left it another week or two, but it's the best snack after a dive and we were going to be eating a lot of them soon. And maybe a few piña coladas, too.

After eating, I sat back against the combing and let my head fall back, staring up at the stars. Miles from the nearest light source, and with a sky clear of any clouds or even water vapor, there were more points of light than dark spots.

Kim leaned back next to me and gazed up at the heavens, too. "Will it always be like this, Dad?"

"Like what?"

"Quiet and peaceful."

She'd no more than said the words when a deep reverberation reached my ears, like the sound a really big dog makes deep in his chest when he's warning you not to come any closer. It grew louder, but way down in the lower pitch range.

"Somebody's pulling hard," Carl said, standing and looking off to the northeast.

I stood up too, straining my eyes to see the lights of a boat. "Big engine."

Carl went to the helm and switched the radar back on. Joining him, we waited for the system to warm up and when the screen activated, we could clearly see the radar signature of the boat that was approaching earlier. Only it was now stationary.

"Treasure hunters using mail boxes?" Carl asked.

A mail box is nothing more than a big ninety-degree elbow mounted on the back of a large boat, which redirects the propwash straight down. They work great at blowing the sand off the bottom to uncover a wreck site or lost treasure.

I clicked the button to zoom out and took my bearings from the island cluster of the Contents and Upper Harbor Key.

"They're on the spot where that shrimper blew up," Carl said.

He was right. If they weren't on top of the wreck, they were very close to it.

"I don't think they're using a mail box," I said. "Look at the range. It's slowly moving to the north. Less than a knot, but moving."

"Less than a knot?" Kim asked. "The engine sounds like it's at full throttle."

Sound carries well over water, and although the boat on the radar screen was more than two miles away, we could hear it easily. Another sound reached my ear. Twin outboards, coming up from the southwest.

After a moment, I could see the green and red bow lights of a fast-moving boat coming out of Cudjoe Channel, and turning toward us.

These islands have been a waypoint and hiding place for pirates and smugglers for centuries. I didn't like the looks of things.

Just as I reached inside the overhead box mounted above the helm and felt the familiar grip of my Sig Sauer, a blue light flashed from the top of the speeding boat.

"Everyone have their fishing licenses?" Carl asked, as I closed the box again.

The boat slowed as it grew nearer, and then dropped down off the step and idled toward us. "Is that you, Captain McDermitt?" a voice I recognized called out.

Kim stepped out from behind the helm, smiling at the approaching sheriff's patrol boat.

A moment later, we had the two boats lashed together and Deputy Martin Phillips stepped over, in uniform.

"Working late?" I asked.

Marty gave Kim a hug, then shook my and Carl's hands. "Sort of. I'm technically off duty in about thirty minutes. But I brought food, water, and bug spray to stay out all night. I wanted to keep an eye on...."

He stopped mid-sentence, hearing the sound of the far-off diesel.

"What the heck's going on out there?" he asked.

"We were wondering the same thing," I said, pointing at the radar screen. "That boat just came down from the northwest."

"Yeah, I saw it on radar from Cudjoe Basin."

"Think it might be aground?" Kim asked.

"Only if it draws more than twenty feet," Carl said. "He's out beyond the three-mile limit. Nothing shallow enough out there for a boat to ground on."

"It's definitely straining," Marty said.

I looked off toward the sound. "And it's damned near on top of that wreck from earlier this evening."

"I'd better go check it out," Marty said.

"You can't, Marty," I said, putting a hand on the young man's shoulder. "The wreck is outside your waters."

"Well, something's going on out there."

"Why don't you drop your hook," I offered. "You said yourself, you're almost off-duty. I have a small night-vision spotting scope. We can get close without being seen and see what they're up to."

Marty agreed and stepped back over to his boat, tossing off the lines. Carl went forward, and I started the engine. Once we had the anchor pulled, I maneuvered toward Marty's boat now anchored a few yards away. He stood on the gunwale, steadying himself with one hand on the T-top rail.

Once he was aboard, I turned toward the northeast. "That scope is in my bag," I told him. "Under the starboard seat in the bow."

Retrieving the small night-vision scope, he sat down on the big seat in front of the console with Kim, and I bumped the throttle up, dowsing all the lights. It's against the law to run without lights at night, but I figured with a cop on board, it'd be okay.

I wasn't worried the other boat would hear us. With the sound of their engine, I doubted anyone on board could hear someone talking right next to them. But I slowed when we were about a mile from it, the GPS showing that we were almost to the three-mile limit. I shifted to neutral and killed the engine.

If they had their radar unit on, they could see us. But being blacked out, they couldn't make out anything at all.

"What do you see," I whispered, unnecessarily.

"It's another shrimper," he said, looking intently through the scope from the bow. "Name on the stern is *Alligator*. Out of Fort Myers." Marty lowered the scope and looked back at me, puzzled. "And he's trawling with no lights on."

"Trawling?" Carl asked. "That skipper's nuts. There's too much out here to snag on."

Eliminator, Instigator, and Alligator, I thought.

I went forward and stared in the distance where the sound was coming from. We were close enough to see it with the naked eye if he had any lights on, but all I could make out was stars down to the horizon. "Maybe he's not dragging for shrimp."

Carl looked over at me. "What else would he be trawling—?"

"He's snagged on the wreck," Marty interrupted. "And trying to move it."

Going back to the helm, Marty joined me, and I zoomed the radar in to a one-mile radius. The boat was just on the edge of the screen. Slowly, it moved away to the north.

"No wind," Carl said, looking over my shoulder. "Current's west-southwest at one knot."

"That boat's moving north," Marty mumbled. "Barely moving, but definitely making some headway, and not with the current."

I looked at Marty, still studying the screen. "Still at just one knot. For at least thirty minutes."

"Why would he pull so hard if he was snagged?" Kim asked.

You can only protect your kids so much. "He's not snagged. He's trying to move the wreck."

"Why would he want to move it?"

"To hide the evidence," I replied, putting the boat in gear.

"Evidence?" Carl and Marty asked in unison.

"What do you know about manufacturing methamphetamine?" I asked Marty.

"It's dangerous at best," he replied, looking up from the screen. "We've busted up a lot of small-time meth labs in the county. Another one springs up the next day. Thousands are killed every year in explosions—wait, you think that boat exploded because one of the crew was cooking meth?"

"Don't know much about it," I replied, turning the wheel and bringing *Cazador* up on plane. "First I ever heard of the stuff was this evening. About all I know is that acetone is used to make it, and acetone is extremely flammable— burns white hot."

"Where are you going?" Marty asked.

"I want to get a little closer and get the moon behind us. We can watch from a safe distance to the west and see what they do."

"What if they see us on their radar?"

I pondered that a moment. I didn't relish putting my daughter or Carl anywhere near danger. "Pull the rods out and put them in the stern rod holders and put the outriggers out. We'll idle a safe distance away and look like just another fishing boat. They damned sure can't chase us down."

After about five minutes, steering mostly by the radar screen, I slowed the boat and shifted to neutral, shutting off the engine. We were less than half a mile off the shrimp boat's port side.

After my eyes adjusted to the darkness, I could make out the boat easily by the light of the moon, now halfway to the western horizon. It had both nets in the water, but the lines seemed to be hanging loose from the booms. I took the scope from Marty and looked closer.

"The nets are tied off to the stern," I said. "They're definitely pulling something really heavy."

Over the sound of their engine, I could barely make out shouting voices. Not excited or angry voices, just someone yelling to be heard above the engine. However, the voices were indistinct, and I couldn't make out anything they were saying. Two men were on the aft work deck, looking down at the water behind the boat. Another man was leaning out of the pilothouse, also looking back.

"Can you describe the explosion you saw?" Marty asked.

"There were actually three," Carl said. "They happened fast, one on top of the other. The first one blew most of the aft deck off and yellow-white flames shot up and out of the starboard side. But the flames only lasted a second and went out, leaving a heavy black smoke cloud billowing up. That's when the diesel tanks exploded. When the diesel flames reached the cloud above the deck, it flashed white hot, blasting the boat into so much confetti. When Jesse and I got to it, there wasn't anything floating bigger than a life ring, except for the woman's body. What was left of the boat had already sunk to the bottom."

Kim glared at me. "You didn't say anything about a body."

"So sue me," I said. "I've seen a lot of ugly that I'm never gonna tell you about."

"An explosion like Carl described," Marty said, "could have been acetone, but the size of the blast he described is way bigger than the small, homemade meth labs we usually encounter. Most people make meth for their own use; scrounging ingredients from drug stores and wherever, and substituting nail polish remover and brake fluid, even using plastic bottles to make it in. If they had a meth lab on board and that was the cause of the explosion he described, it would have to be a big one. Not something a crewman could hide from the captain."

We drifted in silence, speaking occasionally. I started the engine and moved farther north a few times, staying about half a mile west of the shrimper. They didn't seem to acknowledge we were there, so I assumed they had their radar off, not wanting even the screen's glow to give away their position.

"How long do you want to do this?" Carl finally asked. "It's nearly two o'clock."

"Just a little longer," I said.

"I really need to get back to my boat," Marty said. "I should call this in, but I don't have a cell signal way out here."

Just then, everything went quiet. Relatively quiet, that is. The engine on the trawler was still running, but at an idle now. I looked through the scope and watched the men at the stern working to untie the lines to the nets. They seemed to be having a hard time with them. No doubt the heavy pull of a sunken boat had tightened the knots.

The guy in the pilothouse stepped out and I could clearly hear his voice. "Just cut the damned things loose."

The other two men did as they were told and a few minutes later, the trawler began to move off toward the mainland at normal cruising speed.

"They just dumped the nets," Carl said, perplexed.

Engaging the transmission, I noted our latitude and longitude and took a bearing on where they'd cut the nets loose. Slowly, we idled toward that spot, half a mile away.

"What are you doing now?" Kim asked.

"Get up on the bow," I told her by way of reply. "If you see anything in the water, let me know. I want to have a look at whatever's down there."

Kim went forward, and Marty whispered, "I'm gonna have to go down there with you."

"Wouldn't have it any other way, Deputy."

I turned the helm over to Carl, so Marty and I could swap out both Carl's tank and mine for fresh ones. I didn't want to anchor and take the chance of getting the ground tackle snagged on whatever was down there, so I was glad to have Carl aboard.

"My Sig's in the overhead," I told him. "If you need it."

"I can take care of myself, Dad."

"I know you can. But just help Carl out, okay?"

Truth was, Kim was very good with a pistol and Carl was a relative novice. But if it came to using it to defend the boat, I was sure Carl would have less hesitancy and less emotional baggage afterward.

When Marty and I were suited and ready, we sat on opposite sides of the boat. Carl used the forward-scanning sonar to locate the wreck and then made a turn and slowly idled past it. He shifted to neutral and gave us the go signal. Marty and I rolled backwards off opposite gunwales as the boat continued to drift forward under its own momentum.

"Clear!" I shouted, when we were a safe distance.

"We'll be on-station down-current from the wreck," Carl shouted back as Marty and I dumped the air in our BCs and submerged.

Using the high-powered dive lights, the wreck was easy to find. In fact, Carl had probably missed fouling the nets in the prop by only a few feet. The nets were tangled with the twisted wreck of the trawler. The vessel looked to be seventy or eighty feet in length.

The pilothouse was snarled up in one net and the pulpit and forward deck equipment were hopelessly snared in the other. The house had been practically pulled loose from the deck, or was blasted loose, and the booms and rigging were nowhere to be seen. Maybe they were blown off in the explosion, or more likely, the dead boat's nets were tangled on the bottom and the whole rig was dragged off.

Getting Marty's attention, I circled my hand in an arc going up-current, stopping at what was left of the aft deck. If we were going to find anything, that'd be the place to start looking.

He nodded, and we gave the nets a wide berth as we finned against the slow-moving current, then angled into it toward the stern of the wreck as we descended to the bottom.

It was a mess. Ragged beams and planking jutted out from the middle of the work deck. Knowing shrimp boats a little, I knew the engine and fuel tanks were located further forward, beneath the galley and dining area, with the living quarters below that and forward.

It looked like the holds themselves had been the source of the explosion, but how? Shrimp isn't combustible. The deck was blown almost completely off, and there was a massive hole in the side of the hull, below the water line.

We reached the bottom, where my depth gauge showed thirty-eight feet, and approached the breach in the starboard side of the wooden trawler. In my head, I pretty much discounted the earlier dive, since I'd been out of the water for a few hours, and knew instinctively that our bottom time was limited only by our air supply on this dive.

The heavy planks that once created a fair curve along the hull were broken outward, shattered wood looking like the teeth of some giant beast. The hole extended all the way up to the gunwale where the deck was ripped back, exposing the inside of the starboard hold. Or what was left of it.

The explosion was obviously enormous. Shining our lights inside, we could see another breach in the hold on the bottom. The boat had two holds, one on each side. The one we were looking in was about twenty feet in length and half the beam width, maybe eight feet wide, with room for a man to stand inside. A serious shrimp boat. The bottom of this hold held a lot of sand and coral, which I assumed was scraped up from the seabed as the boat was dragged for two miles.

The beam from Marty's light stopped moving, fixed on a single object inside the hold. It wasn't anything that had been dredged up, but it definitely didn't belong in a shrimp hold. It appeared to be a metal cylinder of some kind, either aluminum or stainless steel, about two feet in diameter, and only a portion of it was sticking out of the sand.

Marty tapped me on the shoulder. When I looked over, he pointed at himself, then at the cylinder trapped in the sand. I nodded and moved away from the opening enough to allow him to gain entry. I held my light on the object while I looked around at the rest of the hold's interior. On the forward bulkhead, about a foot below deck level, a metal pipe was imbedded in the aluminum lining of the hold. It looked like the pipe had been broken off; the visible end was twisted and jagged, with some sort of gauge mounted on it.

Marty was struggling with the cylinder, trying to get it out of the sand, but he didn't seem to be making a lot of headway. So I swam into the hold and approached him. Together, we started digging sand away from whatever the thing was. When we'd cleared more than a foot of it, I saw why he'd been unable to move it. The thing was mounted on a metal stand, which was in turn bolted to the bottom of the hold, its mounting brackets bent and twisted toward the stern so that the cylinder was sitting at an angle.

There was no way we were going to get it loose without tools. Getting Marty's attention, I shined my light on the pipe imbedded in the forward bulkhead and we swam the short distance to it. Along the way, I noticed other things that shouldn't be in the hold of a shrimp boat. Electrical wires dangled from the overhead and there were several spots where something had been bolted to the bulkheads, but the bolts had been ripped out of the thin aluminum.

The hole in the bulkhead that the pipe was sticking out of was much bigger than the pipe itself. I figured there was something bolted to the end of the pipe that was larger. Whatever the pipe was attached to might be something we could take back and hopefully help us determine what caused the explosion. The blast was so powerful, whatever was attached to the end of the pipe had been forced through the aluminum bulkhead.

Marty took hold of the pipe and it moved easily. Slowly, he pulled on it, drawing it out of the hole.

Something dark with long threads hung off the end of the pipe, like a mop head. When I shined my light on it, Marty jumped back, an audible scream coming from his regulator.

He quickly composed himself as we stared down at the pipe, which had fallen to the bottom of the hold. Impaled on the end of it was the large object that had made the big hole in the aluminum lining of the hold; a mangled face was staring back up at us. Or it would have, if the eyes in the severed head hadn't been pushed into the back of the skull by the pipe.

Suddenly, I heard the distinctive sound of a klaxon horn, the diver recall system I'd installed on both the *Cazador* and the *Revenge*. The underwater speakers broadcast the sound, which could be heard underwater at a great distance.

Marty dug into the cargo pocket of his shorts, pulling out a large plastic bag. Several smaller bags fell to the bottom, and I scooped them up while he worked the big bag around the head of the dead man.

A moment later, we exited the hull and swam around the stern of the trawler. I could only think of one reason Kim would activate the recall. Another boat was approaching.

We moved with the current, both of us pointing our lights upward to give Carl a visual on us. I could hear the low idle of *Cazador's* engine, but couldn't tell where it was coming from. I could also hear the rhythmic beating of another engine, slowly growing louder.

A light appeared above us, and the sound of *Cazador's* engine died. We swam slowly upward, toward the illuminated surface, keeping our own dive lights trained on either side of it. I knew from experience that they could see our lights quite clearly.

Recovering divers in open water at night can be dangerous, but Carl and I have made many night dives and I was confident in his knowledge and ability.

We surfaced at the transom, both of us inflating our BCs and handing up our weight belts. Kim was standing on the swim platform.

"Carl," I called out. "Come take this bag from Marty and put it in the forward fish box."

He appeared at the transom and reached down to take the bag from Marty. "What's in it?"

"Never mind that," I said. "Don't open it. Just put it in the port fish box. Why the recall?"

"That shrimp boat is coming back," Kim said. "It's about a mile away now and closing fast."

Fast was a relative term. A trawler that size could probably muster ten knots, so it was still a good five minutes away. *El Cazador* could change that distance to two miles in that time.

Still in the water, Marty and I shrugged out of our BCs, handing them one at a time to Kim, who lifted them up to Carl. When we were finally on board, I could see the shrimp boat clearly. It wasn't running without lights now. In fact, a large spotlight was trained in our direction, but I doubted they could make anything out just yet.

"Douse the lights," I said, climbing over the transom. "Let's get underway."

Carl moved quickly to the helm and restarted the engine as Marty climbed aboard. "Go west, Carl, and angle away from them. Don't let them get a look at the transom."

El Cazador increased speed, climbing up on top of the water. I joined Carl at the helm, Marty and Kim taking up positions on either side of us.

The trawler began to turn after us as Carl steered a course to the west-northwest, keeping the name on the transom at an angle to the approaching boat. We had a huge advantage in both speed and maneuverability. The trawler would be lucky to maintain ten knots and *Cazador* doesn't even plane until sixteen knots. I could easily triple the bigger boat's speed.

At full throttle, running at more than thirty knots, we soon put a few miles between us and the shrimper. Checking my watch, I saw that it was after three o'clock.

"Turn toward Sawyer Key," I said. "Make them think we bugged out into the backcountry. Close to the islands, we can get lost in the back scatter and then use Marty's boat to block their radar, so we can get back out to it."

"If they come inside the three-mile limit," Marty said, "I'll be obligated to respond, off-duty or not."

Out of range of the boat's spotlight and hopefully any binoculars they had on board, Carl turned due south, heading toward the marker showing the entrance to Cudjoe Channel. I kept an eye on the sonar and when we reached ten feet, I said, "Okay, turn east now, the back scatter of these islands will cover us."

The radar screen showed Marty's boat, floating at anchor where we'd left it. It also displayed the larger trawler, now approaching the three-mile limit. When the two echoes lined up with our position, Carl turned and kept Marty's boat between us and the trawler.

"He's turning," Marty said, watching the radar.

Sure enough, the trawler had begun a slow turn to the west and then north, heading back the way it had come, just before crossing the line. We slowed as we approached Marty's patrol boat, and Carl turned the helm over to me so he could put fenders out.

Kim joined me at the helm. "What's in the bag that you don't want me to see?"

"Some things are just as bad knowing as seeing," I replied.

Once Marty was aboard the patrol boat with his grue-some find, he called it in to his dispatcher. "Y'all probably want to get out of here," he said, untying the lines. "I vio-lated strict orders to not do what I just did, and I'll get into a lot of trouble if my boss finds out I involved civilians."

Kim went to the rail and hugged Marty tightly across the gap between the boats. I started the engine and turned east toward the flashing light at Harbor Key Bank.

As we made the turn into Harbor Channel, I asked Carl, "When do you think you'll move?"

It seemed like a lifetime ago that we'd started the con-versation, but it hadn't even been a full day yet.

"Charlie wants to take advantage of the Christmas break," he replied, uneasily. "She doesn't want the kids to miss any school."

"That soon?"

"I could stay on," he said. "I don't want to leave you in any kind of a bind or anything."

"No, that's not what I meant. It's just, well, I'm gonna miss you guys."

Slowing for the turn into my channel, Kim rose from the front seat and joined us. "You're moving?"

"Yeah," Carl replied. "We don't have any kin here, except Angie. Both our families live up in Louisiana and Missis-sippi."

Punching the button on the key fob, the doors below my house started to swing open. We were tired, but I took the time to spin *El Cazador* around, using the bow thruster, and backed into her berth. You never know when you might need to leave in a hurry.

Finn came trotting down the steps, barking and running back and forth on the pier until we'd docked.

I took the catch bag from the forward, refrigerated fish box. "Just leave everything else," I said. "It's nearly four o'clock and we're all bushed. We can clean everything up in the morning."

The truth was, Marty's evidence bag had leaked and there was blood and brain tissue in the aft fish box, and I didn't want Kim to see it. Finn nearly melted down, when I opened the outside door. I rubbed his neck for a moment, while I said goodnight to Carl and Kim.

We each went to separate houses, me to my stilt house, Carl to the one he and Charlie had built, and Kim went to the western bunkhouse.

After putting the fish and lobster in the fridge, I set up the coffee maker, but didn't set the timer. I planned to wake before sunrise, but I also planned to roll over and go back to sleep after calling Jimmy.

Stripping down, I took a quick shower, and set my alarm for two hours later. I didn't want Jimmy to get out of bed if he didn't need to. And the fishing trip was off for the morning.

CHAPTER EIGHT

When I woke for the second time, it was late morning. Jimmy had asked a bunch of questions when I'd called him just before sunrise. But I'd only told him that a night dive had taken a turn and we'd stayed out much longer than anticipated.

While pulling my shorts on, I had a sudden moment of clarity, as the face of the woman who'd been killed by the shark entered my mind. I remembered where I knew her from, and the realization stopped me in my tracks. We'd met briefly, about seven or eight years ago, and I'd become involved with her sister, Savannah.

Charlotte Richmond had been nothing like Savannah, except that both women were beautiful, just in different ways. Where Savannah was fair-haired and dark-tanned with deep blue eyes, Charlotte was fair-skinned with chestnut hair and dark brown eyes. They were polar opposites in temperament, too. Savannah had been adventurous and outgoing, while Charlotte seemed to need a manicurist within ten miles at all times. Nobody who met the two would ever guess they were even distantly related.

Could that have been Charlotte? I thought, continuing into the living room of my two-room house. The image of the woman's face stuck in my mind. Older, with dyed black hair, but it was definitely her. Why would Charlotte Richmond be involved in whatever was going on aboard that shrimp boat?

Letting Finn out, I switched on the coffee maker and stood at the large, south-facing window. Staring out across the water to the narrow gap between Howe Key and the Water Keys, I thought about Savannah. I was still living aboard the *Revenge* at the time, tied up in a slip at *Dockside*.

We'd been good together, and were rarely apart. Right up until the morning I woke to find the other side of the bed empty. I'd then gone outside and found her boat was also gone. The very next day, I'd come out here. My island was nothing but overgrown mangroves, sea grape, scrub oak, and a few trees then. I'd spent the rest of that summer and fall working, clearing the underbrush and trimming back the jungle to build my house. Her leaving and the deceit had hurt deeper than I'd cared to admit.

Charlotte had left early in the summer, after Savannah had told her that she wanted to stay on in Marathon for a while. They'd come to the Keys aboard the family yacht on some kind of a vacation getaway, dodging responsibilities while their parents were abroad. Savannah had told me she'd gone through a nasty divorce, which was a lie.

The Richmond family was wealthy, the old school way. Her father was a fisherman from up in South Carolina and had retired owning a whole fleet of commercial fishing vessels, which he'd sold. Maybe that was the connection to Charlotte being on a shrimp boat.

A sound interrupted my thoughts. Far off, I heard an outboard and went out on the deck to see where it was coming from. Looking first to the island's interior, I saw nothing to indicate that Carl or Kim were awake yet, and Finn was lying beside the door to the western bunkhouse, where Kim was probably still asleep. The sound of the boat was coming from the south.

The water in that direction was dangerously shallow, with a winding system of cuts and natural channels which drained the backcountry into Harbor Channel twice a day. None were marked, so anyone coming up from that direction would have to be good at reading the water, or already know the way.

Standing on the deck near the top of the stairs, I listened. The boat was moving slow, still half a mile away, if not more. I went back inside and poured a cup of Hacienda la Minita coffee.

Outside again, I could hear the boat accelerate. A moment later, it came into the narrow gap from behind Howe Key. I didn't know the boat, but easily recognized the man at the wheel and the woman sitting next to him.

Hearing a creak from behind me, I turned to see Carl coming up the steps. "That sounds like Angie's boat."

"It is," I replied, as Carl strode across the deck to join me. "Jimmy's with her."

Carl and I walked down the steps to the pier and a moment later, Jimmy turned into my channel, slowing the boat to idle speed.

Carl caught the line that his daughter tossed and tied it off. Jimmy reversed the engine, backing the eighteen-foot Dolphin flats boat snuggly up to the dock.

Angie stepped up on the pier and gave Carl a hug. "Hey, Dad. I ran into Charlie; she should be here shortly."

"What brings y'all up this way?" Carl asked. "Not that I don't like you visiting."

Jimmy stepped up beside me, after tying off the stern line. "I have information you need to know, man."

"Want some coffee?" I asked, sweeping a hand toward the stairs.

"Only if it's the same kind Rusty has," Jimmy replied. "I'm kinda spoiled."

"It is. What's this information you're talking about?"

Carl led the way up the stairs, but Jimmy hung back. "The wreck yesterday. Word is that the woman on the boat was—"

"Charlotte Richmond," I said finishing his sentence.

"You already know?"

I turned to follow Carl and Angie up the steps. "Carl and I almost had her aboard, when the shark took her. I only remembered where I knew her from this morning."

Jimmy's shoulders shuddered. "No worse way to go, dude."

"There's a good way?"

"I want it to be while I'm stoned to the gills on some primo weed, napping on the beach, man. Anyway, there's more to the story than just who she was."

I went inside and brought out a tray of mugs with the pot in the center. Angie took the tray from me, and placed it on the table, pouring three cups full.

"From what I heard, Charlotte Richmond had some kinda falling out with her folks," Jimmy said. "About a year or so ago. She'd been playing around with different drugs and got arrested for trafficking coke."

That couldn't possibly be true. Charlotte was the quintessential charming Southern belle, finishing school and all. "Doesn't sound like the woman we met way back then."

Jimmy shrugged. "Just some things I picked up. Not sure if it's true or just gossip." He grinned. "I haven't told you the best part. Her sister's supposed to be on her way here to claim the body."

Savannah?Coming here? I thought. She'd left, leaving little more than a note, telling me that she'd lied about being divorced. I've only seen her once since then. We were both called as witnesses to testify against Earl Hailey up in Miami.

Kim came up the steps, picked up the coffee pot, which only had about a cup left in it, and disappeared inside the house without saying a word. Like me, she needed that jolt to her system to be sociable.

When she came back out, she had a mug in her hand. "I put on another pot. What are you guys doing up here, Angie?"

I caught the questioning look Angie gave her father, as well as the subtle nod he returned. "We want to come and work for your dad," Angie replied, matter-of-factly.

"You already work for me, Jimmy," I said, sensing a conspiracy.

"Angie's boat is nickel and diming us to death," Jimmy said. "No matter how much money we pour into the thing, it doesn't displace the bilge water. And renting a trailer wouldn't leave much of what the two of us make."

"What about the school?" I asked.

Jimmy worked part time for me as mate on charters and worked as a guide and instructor for a school I helped create, also. It was the realization of a dream my late wife had.

"That's just a part-time gig, man. And you don't do enough charters anymore to keep me busy enough. So I'm looking for a third job."

"And since Carl and Charlie are moving, you think I need help out here?"

"You do," Carl said. "You won't last a month out here by yourself."

My mind was still on Savannah, which it shouldn't have been. Devon and I have been together for several months, and aside from her odd schedule as a detective with the Sheriff's Office, we had a pretty good relationship going.

Bringing my mind back into focus, I considered what Jimmy said. He was a hardworking man, of that I had no doubt. And he was as reliable as the day is long. Both are qualities that are difficult to find. And Carl was right; I'd go nuts out here completely alone. My nearest neighbor was Mac Travis and Mel Woodson. They lived on an island several miles away and Mac was probably more reclusive than me. Many weeks ago, I'd dropped him in the middle of the ocean from my plane, with nothing but a pair of pliers and two screwdrivers to salvage a derelict Cuban refugee boat. He'd promised to stop by and fill me in, but as far as I can tell, he and Mel haven't left his island.

Devon wasn't real crazy about boats or islands, though she lived and worked on one. So it wasn't likely she'd move out here any time in the near future. The work on the aquaculture system would certainly suffer. Not that I needed the income, but a lot of restaurants relied on us.

"You're hired," I said. "Again."

How he'd work around my hard and fast rule against pot, I didn't know. But I trusted him to do it and he knew it applied here as well as on the boat. So there was no need to bring it up.

"What are you going to do with the houseboat?" Kim asked.

"I know someone who wants to buy it," Angie said. "It's not much, but he doesn't have a place."

"Won't it nickel and dime him, too?" I asked, grinning at Jimmy.

"Yeah, well, I guess it floats fine," Jimmy admitted. "It's just that your place here takes three."

He was right. And he was no doubt coached by Carl and Charlie. Living here was very comfortable, though we had little of the amenities of the mainland. Our lifestyle was about as laid-back as one could imagine. But we did in fact work every day. Last night was work. We got most of our food from the sea or the aquaculture garden. What we didn't eat, we sold.

The sound of yet another boat reached my ears. In the past twenty-four hours, we'd had more boats within sight of my island than I can remember having seen since the lobster mini-season. This sound I easily recognized. It was Charlie, returning with the kids from their sleepovers.

Kim took Angie and Jimmy to show them the island that they'd soon be living on. Jimmy'd been here a few times, but Angie had only been out once. Carl and I went to the dock to help Charlie. Living on an island meant trips to the mainland were a hassle, and she never returned empty-handed.

Before Charlie even got the twenty-one-foot Grady-White backed in next to my seventeen-foot Grady, the sound of twin outboards could be heard out on the Gulf side.

"You might think about installing traffic lights," Carl said, as the kids took off to play with Finn.

Charlie hugged her husband and told him of their friends in Key West who'd told her to say hi. She only had a few bags and we carried them up to the deck.

Carl and Charlie had been living here for nearly three years. It was going to be difficult to adjust to them not being here. But he was right. A parent's first responsibility is to their kids, and living alone on an island in the middle of nowhere wasn't the best way to raise them. They needed to be around other kids, and not just at school. They needed cousins, aunts, uncles, and grandparents.

I was an only child, as was my dad, so I had no siblings, aunts, uncles, or cousins on that side. I had two uncles and an aunt on my mom's side. One uncle was gay and the other a die-hard bachelor. Aunt Beth was unable to have kids, so I had no cousins on that side, either. I hadn't seen any of them in decades. The only family I had around when I was growing up were my parents and grandparents. I kind of envied the Trent kids; it sounded like they were going to have a lot of extended family around.

Across the flats to the north, I spotted the sheriff's patrol boat as it came past Content Passage. Carl took the bags I was carrying and followed Charlie down the back steps. Marty was at the helm of the patrol boat and Devon was beside him. She usually didn't get off work until late in the evening and it was barely after noon.

With the tide at its fullest, Marty turned across the flats between my island and the next one to the northeast, staying on plane all the way. He was very familiar with the water around my island, spending a lot of his free time here every other weekend. He slowed when he turned into Harbor Channel just before the cut leading up to my house.

"You're early," I said, catching the line Devon tossed as Marty brought the boat to a stop behind Angie's.

"Got another girlfriend you need to run off?" she asked, grinning at my discomfort. I often worried that I was too readable, and that my thinking about Savannah earlier would be tattooed on my forehead.

"That's Angie's boat," I said. "Carl's daughter. Is everything okay?"

"Just wrapped things up early," Devon replied, stepping up onto the pier and then into my arms. "Can't say the same for Deputy Phillips."

Marty looked down at the deck under his feet. There was a mixture of emotions on his face. Anger, tempered by strong indignation and embarrassment.

"What happened, Marty?"

"Got royally chewed out," he replied, looking around. "I'm on suspension."

"What the hell for?"

"Disobeying orders," he replied, finally meeting my gaze. "My sergeant took my report and the evidence, then lit into me for being out there last night."

Something there wasn't right. I'd known my share of officers and NCOs in the Corps who were the "by-the-book" types. Those who put the implementation of policy first and overlooked the results of their troops' initiative. Those NCOs under me, I straightened out quickly. Officers appointed over me, I could only advise. The good ones took the advice in the spirit intended, some didn't.

I felt bad for the kid. "Well, since you're off duty, stay for supper and we can have a couple beers to hash it out."

Kim came down the steps, as we were starting up. "Hey, Devon."

"Hi, Kim. How was the night dive?"

Marty looked alarmed for a second, and Kim caught it. "It was great. We found an ancient coral formation deep under the sea floor."

By Marty's expression, I assumed that Devon didn't know the details of what happened last night.

"Go ahead and get settled," I told her. "Me and your deputy are gonna get a beer down at the fire ring."

Devon opened the door to my house, and carried her bag inside. I knew she'd be a few minutes, showering and changing out of her detective suit and into proper island attire.

Sandwiching myself between the two youngsters, I herded them down the back steps. Marty started to say something, but I squeezed his shoulder.

"Kim, you mind taking Finn for a swim?" I said. "He's been cooped up in the house all morning."

"But—"

"Marty and I want to talk about you behind your back," I interrupted.

"Dad!"

"I'm just kidding," I said with a wink.

"You want to talk about the wrecked shrimp boat."

"Indulge an over-protective father?"

She smiled and turned toward the Trents' house, where Finn was playing with the kids.

"I really can't tell you much," Marty said, walking beside me toward the tables. "It's an ongoing investigation as far as I know."

I just nodded, and kept walking. Stopping at the tables, I lifted the lid on the cooler. There were several bottles of water and three beers floating in about six inches of water, with a few translucent ice cubes. I took two of the Bahamian Kaliks and continued toward the fire ring, offering one to Marty.

"Um," he hesitated. "I don't know if I should be drinking, sir. I still have to get back home."

Tossing a couple pieces of driftwood onto the coals from the previous fire, I stirred and poked at them with a stick.

"There's a lot of room here on the island."

He hesitated, then pulled the tail of his uniform shirt out of his shorts and took it off. He removed his vest and lay it on the ground, folding his shirt and placing it on top of the vest. "Thanks," he said, taking the beer.

I've known Ben Phillips, Marty's dad, for some time. He was a guide out of Ramrod Key and a stand-up guy. To me, the fact that it bothered Marty to drink in uniform spoke volumes about the young man's character and reflected on his upbringing.

"I also know Kim's had a beer or two."

His eyes went wide.

"Don't worry about it," I said. "Her mom was younger than me when we met, and I snuck her a few beers. People are gonna do what they do. Just don't let her get drunk, okay? Now, tell me about this suspension."

"Not much to tell," Marty said, sitting on an old fallen palm log. "Sergeant Brady, he's my shift supervisor; he's a real pain. Everything has to be by the book."

"Sometimes that's necessary. Did he read your report?"

"Glanced at it is about all."

Pulling a chair closer, I sat down. "What about the head? Take it to the morgue?"

"I was going to," Marty said, after taking a pull from the beer. "I filled out the form early this morning, after y'all left. I was heading to the sub-station to file it, but Sergeant Brady contacted me as I was heading in and told me to report directly to him when I got to the dock. He was waiting at the slip when I got there. After chewing me out and putting me on three days suspension, he said he'd take care of the evidence."

"But he let you take the boat back out?"

"Most of us do," Marty said. "We're spread pretty thin in the Middle Keys and none of us have to share a boat. We usually take them home so we can respond faster if we get a call and we're off duty."

I considered what he said a moment. "You're spread thin and he suspended you?"

"Like I said, he's strictly by the book. It's probably written in there somewhere, that if you find a head doing what you're not supposed to be doing, it's three days without pay." Marty took another drink from his beer. "At least two of those are weekend days."

"What all was in the report, Marty?"

"My boat's not equipped with dive gear," he said. "I had to put it in the report that you and I found the head together."

It didn't bother me that my name was on some report. Not much, anyway. But I really didn't want Carl or Kim involved, if it wasn't necessary.

"Just my name?" I asked.

"Yes, but if I'm asked—"

"You'll have to answer," I said. "We'll burn that bridge when we get to it." I took a long pull from my own beer, before broaching the next subject. "Now, about your sleeping arrangements when you go up to Gainesville."

Over my twenty years in the Marine Corps, I've had to have some difficult conversations. With men who worked under me when they screwed up in their private lives, and occasionally with officers appointed over me who were behaving badly. I've also had to talk to more than a few grieving parents and widows. Those were the hardest. Emotionally hard.

Without a doubt, a conversation between a man and his daughter's boyfriend about sex is a lot more uncomfortable.

After Marty left to find Kim, I sat on the log and continued poking the fire. Devon came over and sat down beside me, her bare thigh against mine. She'd changed into shorts and a tee-shirt, but had one of my work shirts over it.

"He didn't tell me anything about what happened," she said. "And it's not my place to pry."

I continued stirring the coals. "He came out to where we were diving last night. We had a run-in with another shrimp boat."

"A run-in?"

Pointing beyond the bunkhouses, I said, "The trawler that blew up yesterday? It's not there anymore."

"I heard something about it," she said. "The Coast Guard took it because it was outside territorial waters. What do you mean it's not there anymore?"

"Another shrimp trawler came out of the north late last night, dropped nets on it, and dragged it two miles to the north."

"What the hell for?" she asked. I could practically see the hair on the back of her neck stand up. Like me, Devon has a very narrow view of the line between right and wrong. Moving the trawler was tampering with evidence. Even if it wasn't her case, I knew it rankled her.

"Marty got the GPS numbers where they dropped it. He and I dove on it before we came back in late last night. Actually, it was more like early this morning, about zero three hundred."

"And you found something?"

"A body part that didn't float up with the rest," I replied. "A man's head, probably Hispanic."

"And Marty took it to the morgue?"

"Turned it over to his supervisor along with his report, early this morning." I tossed the stick in the fire and looked Devon in the eye. "I think these guys are manufacturing methamphetamine."

"That's what's got you so introspective?" she asked. "Drug dealers in your backyard?"

I put an arm around her and pulled her close. Her hair smelled of shampoo, with a hint of coconut.

"No, that's not it," I said, breathing deep the scent. "I just gave him the green light to spend the night with my daughter."

Devon smiled. "Like he needs a green light. They've been sleeping together for over a year."

"Yeah," I said. "But not here on my island."

CHAPTER NINE

The sun was high overhead as Cedric waited in the parked car. Most of the vehicles in the lot looked worse than his old Corolla. His car didn't look like much, and the chances of it starting at any given moment were about fifty-fifty. Not that it only started half the time, because it did start most times—but it also hadn't started and would occasionally quit running for no reason. So any time he stuck the key in the ignition, it was a gamble.

Running back and forth across the state wasn't something the Toyota was up to, so Cedric was driving one of Ballinger's cars—a late-model, black Lexus. The car had once been driven by one of the boss's salesmen.

He ran the car's engine to keep the air conditioner on. The A/C was cold. It had to be, the car being black and in south Florida. Keeping it on, he wasn't forced to put the windows down. That meant that he wasn't assaulted by the smell of decay that seemed as much a part of the old marina as the water.

The marina was a remote commercial dock on the Caloosahatchee River, on the outskirts of Cape Coral. The place was filthy, rundown, and smelled of dead fish.

He watched the green arrow that represented the shrimp boat on his phone's screen as it neared the marina. It was arriving later than he'd figured on and he'd had to wait longer than he liked. He'd been tempted to call, but that was too risky. Besides, the app told him they were moving, and the boats were so slow; he hadn't needed to rush. He just liked driving the Lexus.

Ballinger wanted the GPS coordinates of the wrecked boat. He wanted to send his own crew of divers to remove anything that might be on it. They were standing by, waiting for the captain to take them out.

The ugly shrimp boat turned into the short creek and approached the dock. Cedric waited until they were tied up before he got out of the car. Just being around this place made him nauseous, never mind helping with the lines.

As he approached the boat, he looked around nervously. Ballinger said he had the cops in his pocket, but you just never know.

The captain of the boat came out of the wheelhouse and vaulted the side of the boat, landing easily on the dock.

"What took so long?" Cedric asked.

The captain was a redneck from Texas, and Cedric didn't like him. He was big and rough-looking. But the man feared his new boss and Cedric was an extension of him.

"Ran into a little trouble during the tow," Darrel Taylor replied. "Some guys in a fishing boat was skulking around. Looked like they were just trolling. So we towed it farther out."

Cedric absently lit a cigarette, as the men on the boat unloaded plastic containers onto the dock. Cedric knew the bottom one of the first stack of four crates didn't have shrimp in it. The ones on top did, but he had no idea if the shrimp in those boxes had been caught last night or last week. They reused the decoys until they started to smell too bad.

"You got the numbers?" Cedric asked.

Taylor took out a piece of scrap paper and handed it over. "Name of the fishing boat's on there, too, if you need it."

"What's the weight?" Cedric asked, looking at the GPS coordinates and boat name on the paper, before stuffing it in his pocket.

"Right at five pounds," Taylor replied. "They said it's a lot better this time."

Two more men stepped off the boat and Taylor turned and started walking toward the rusting steel buildings, as they approached.

"The captain said it's better this time?" Cedric asked the older of the two men.

"This is a shit way to work," the bald man replied. "Yeah, it's better. But it's still crap, on account of the working conditions."

"How much better?"

"Almost seventy-six percent," the former pharmacist replied. "It should be eighty."

Raymond Black had been a moderately successful pharmacist for more than twenty years. Until the State of Florida came down on him. Toward the end of his career, he'd pocketed tens of thousands of dollars by unloading out-of-date prescription meds to a few less than scrupulous buyers. One turned out to be an undercover narcotics detective.

Cedric stepped aside as the two deckhands moved up the dock with hand trucks. "Seventy-six is still a lot better than any tweakers can do on their own."

"Hear anything more about the other crew?" Black asked as he and Cedric followed the deck hands.

Cedric opened the trunk of the Lexus and the two shrimpers removed the top three crates from one of the stacks. Black lifted the single crate that was on the bottom and put it into the trunk. Two more identical plastic crates were already there, pushed back under the rear windshield.

Cedric waited until the deck hands were out of earshot. "They all died in the explosion."

"The girl too?" Black asked. "How'd Ballinger take it?"

"He's hard to get a read on," Cedric replied. "You know about the history between them?"

"I introduced them," the ex-pharmacist said. "She had a ton of money she'd embezzled from her dad's business holdings and a really bad habit. The two of them probably went through half a pound of nose candy in a ten-day sex marathon."

"Yeah, well, he didn't seem too broke up about it. *Thank the gods for small favors.* His words."

"Such a waste," Black said, closing the trunk of Cedric's car and turning to leave. "She was hot. See ya next Wednesday."

"Yeah, later."

"See if you can get him to do something about the smell and contamination onboard," Black said, when he reached his own car. "I can bring it up to at least eighty percent. That'll bring a helluva lot better price on the street."

Cedric nodded and got in the car. The three containers in the trunk were worth half a million bucks, and Ballinger wanted to start ramping up production to ten pounds per run for each boat. Easy enough to do. It only meant the boats would go out for two nights instead of one.

Black had been right, though. If they could keep the labs inside the boats a little cleaner, with better ventilation, they could push the price up. The shit was already good, but if Black said he could do better, Cedric had to believe it. The guy was a brain.

He thought about the dead woman and Ballinger's reaction. Cedric had only met her a few times. Black was right on that count, too. One of the times he'd met her was on Ballinger's boat when Cedric had delivered some party supplies. She'd been wearing a black, long-sleeved, skin-tight dress that barely covered her hips. That, plus the shiny, raven-colored hair, made her skin look very pale, almost translucent. About the sexiest looking woman he'd ever laid eyes on. And Ballinger barely gave her death a second thought.

She'd gone out on the boat, pretending to be the skipper's girlfriend. Which wasn't hard for them to pull off, since he was screwing her, too. Ballinger thought the cooks were skimming him. The product they made didn't quite add up to the weight of the supplies and the methylamine and acetone weren't cheap.

Driving, Cedric thought about what might have caused the boat to blow up. He'd advised Ballinger against having more supplies on board than each boat needed for its daily cook, and the boss had decided to do just that, once they came back in. Besides giving the cooks the opportunity to overproduce and skim a few ounces, the shit was just too volatile. A cigarette or open flame near the exhaust port while they were cooking would be all it'd take.

Cedric pulled into the parking lot of Ballinger's warehouse. It was the weekend, so there weren't any cars in the lot. This time, he didn't park by the front door, but pulled around the side to the gate, which was controlled from inside the building. The heavy chain began pulling the gate open almost immediately.

Driving the car around to the back of the building, Cedric saw the large overhead door already going up, Ballinger himself was standing next to it, finger on the controller.

Cedric pulled in and stopped. He shut off the engine and popped the trunk before getting out.

"You're late," Ballinger said.

"Couldn't be helped, Mister B," Cedric said, lifting the first crate out of the trunk and placing it on a nearby cart. "Towing the wrecked boat took longer than anyone figured on. Had to wait on that pickup."

He fished into his pocket and handed Ballinger the scrap of paper the shrimp boat captain had given him. "The spot where he dropped the wreck."

Ballinger looked at the information on the paper. "He's sure about the GPS numbers?"

"Yeah," Cedric replied. "Said he dragged it two miles from where it went down."

"What's *El Cazador* mean?"

"Huh," Cedric said, lifting the second crate out and placing it beside the first. "Spanish for hunter, I think."

"But why's it written on here with the GPS coordinates?"

Cedric opened the containers. Inside each were five plastic bags, each marked with the weight that the bag contained in grams. All fifteen were close to four hundred and fifty-four grams, or one pound each. Inside the bags were hundreds of oddly shaped, milky white crystals. A total of roughly fifteen pounds.

Cedric turned around and looked at the slip of paper. "Oh, sorry," he said. "Taylor mentioned that a boat was hanging around close to them. That's why it took longer; he had to tow it farther out. He told me he wrote the name down. I guess *Cazador* must be the name of the boat."

CHAPTER TEN

Jimmy and Angie thanked me for the invitation to stay for supper, but said they needed to get back. Angie was working the evening shift at *Brass Monkey* and Jimmy had picked up a last-minute gig with Rusty, who suddenly needed all the help he could get.

"Carl and Charlie are going to move in just a couple of weeks," I told him, as they got into Angie's skiff. "Rather than move everything by boat, I offered to buy all the furniture in their house at cost. It's like new anyway."

"Makes good sense," Jimmy said.

"And it means you don't have to move much of anything in."

"I like that," Angie said. "Thanks, again, Jesse. Jimmy and I won't let you down."

"Drop by a few times before they move," I said. "Carl and I can go over what needs to be done."

Angie took her phone out of her pocket and tapped a few times on the screen. "I'm off all day Monday and Jimmy doesn't have a class, but he has to open the *Anchor* that morning. Rusty won't be back until about noon or so."

"Monday afternoon, then," I said, as Jimmy started the engine.

A minute later they turned east into Harbor Channel and Jimmy pushed the flats boat up onto plane. After a moment, he turned south, crossed the sand flats east of Howe Key, and disappeared.

I went up to the deck and looked out across the interior of the island. I thought about how different things were going to be. Carl and I got along exceedingly well and enjoyed a lot of the same things. We'd built a little wooden runabout together, enjoying the building process about as much as we did the finished product.

He should have Knot L-8, I thought, as I went down the back steps.

Kim walked toward me, a nervous look on her face. "Marty said you invited him to stay over if he wanted to."

I thought the conversation with *him* had been uncomfortable. Though she was my own flesh-and-blood daughter, Kim and I were more than a generation apart in our social views. That's all on me, though. I was raised from age eight by my grandparents.

"You're gonna be twenty years old next summer," I said, deciding that ripping the bandage off was the easier way. "I'm not gonna force my morals on you two. He's welcome to stay with you whenever you're here on the island."

"Did he come to you about this?" she asked, suddenly agitated. "I told him that I'd be the one to talk to you. When the time was right."

"No," I replied, a little confused. "I was the one who brought up the subject."

"*You did?*"

"Yeah," I said, throwing an arm around her shoulder, and guiding her toward the aquaculture system. "I was born in the sixties, but I was raised by a man and woman born at the turn of the last century."

"I know that," she said, picking up a basket and absently picking little cherry tomatoes from a bush. "You've told me all about grandma and grandpa dying and you being raised by Mam and Pap."

"Social norms change from generation to generation," I said, adding spinach leaves to her basket. "The attitude I have, I got from them. So I'm a little more old-fashioned than what most of your friends' dads might be."

"There's nothing wrong with old-fashioned ideals, Dad."

I turned my daughter toward me and looked deep into her bright, clear eyes. "You're a grown woman, Kim. That bunkhouse is your domain. You can decide for yourself when and with whom you want to share it. It's none of my business."

"It's also Chyrel's office."

"I doubt there will be much need of that anymore."

"I want the other half," she said. "I want to make it up the way I want. With its own bathroom and a little kitchen."

The other half of the western bunkhouse was barely seven hundred square feet. The whole thing was only a thousand. Same as the other bunkhouse and my house. I suddenly recalled the first house Sandy and I lived in when we got married. It was a sixty-foot, one-bedroom mobile home, which wasn't any bigger than the partial bunkhouse.

I smiled at Kim. "The first home me and your mom had was probably smaller. That'll be my and Jimmy's first project."

"And I want to help remodel it," she said. "I have sixteen days off for Christmas, starting in two weeks."

"Then we need a materials list," I said. "I'll have everything delivered before you come back down."

"Really?" she asked. "I can design it myself?"

"Yeah, just give me a list of what you want, and we'll make it happen."

Adding a few banana peppers to the basket, she lifted it. "I'll take this to Charlie. Then I'm going to start planning."

"I'll be back down in a minute," I called after her. "I gotta call Rusty."

I went up the steps and into my house. My phone was where I'd left it, on the table. I pulled up Rusty's number and called him.

"Will wonders never cease," my old friend said, instead of the usual hello. "Jesse McDermitt actually making a phone call."

I could hear music and a lot of people talking.

"Can it, assbite. What's got you in such a jolly mood?"

"You hear all that noise in the background?" Rusty said. "We're making money hand over fist, bro."

"You hear anything back about those shrimp boats?"

"Matter of fact, I just got off the phone. The guy who bought all three boats is a big-time manufacturer. Throws a lot of money around up there in your hometown. Fast boats, fast cars, and fast women. He likes to be seen with stars and big-name athletes. Name of Eugene Ballinger."

"What's he make?"

"Nothing out of the ordinary," Rusty replied, then he muffled the receiver and spoke to someone else, before removing his hand. "Makes air fresheners; ship's 'em all over the world."

"Air fresheners? And he makes enough for that lifestyle?"

"Must be a lot of smelly homes in the world," Rusty said. "Anything else?"

He didn't say anything for a few seconds. Then the closing of a door silenced the background noise. "There's a new boat over in Boot Key Harbor, a Grand Banks trawler called *Sea Biscuit*."

"Is that supposed to mean something?"

"Gorgeous boat," Rusty said. "About as big as the *Revenge*, but a stately old cruiser. Word on the coconut telegraph is that a single lady owns it, cruising the islands with her eight-year-old daughter."

Rusty was obviously telling me this for a reason, but damned if I knew what any of it meant.

"She involved with those shrimp trawlers somehow?" I asked.

"Yeah, you could say that. Her sister was killed in the one that blew up."

Savannah, I thought, my mind flashing back nine years like it was yesterday. Here already? On a slow-moving trawler, she would have needed to be close by. She'd probably only learned about Charlotte's death this morning. Could the Richmond sisters be involved in what I was beginning to suspect was going on?

"You still there?" Rusty asked.

"Yeah," I replied. "It's Savannah?"

"And her eight-year-old daughter."

What? "She didn't have any kids," I said.

"Not when *you* knew her," Rusty said. The numbers tripped in my head like a slot machine. We'd only been together for a couple of weeks when she left. I remember it was just before the Marine Corps birthday that year. It was just a little over nine years ago when I met Savannah. And now she had an eight-year-old daughter.

Rusty'd made the connection, too. I didn't see any sense in dodging the obvious. And Rusty wouldn't withhold anything, either.

"Did she tell anyone I might be the father?"

"Not that I know," he said. "I ain't talked to her, nor met the child. *Are* you the girl's daddy?"

No way, I thought, remembering the husband. I'd only met him once, and that was very briefly. He was a handsome enough guy, and quite successful, it seemed.

"She was still married," I reminded Rusty, while wondering when the girl's birthday might be.

"And that's supposed to mean the kid can't be yours?"

"Anything's possible," I replied, "but I seriously doubt it."

"Well, I thought you oughta have a heads-up, just the same."

Devon opened the door and came in. "Thanks for the intel, Rusty," I said, already feeling guilty. "If you hear anything more, let me know."

"What was that about?" Devon asked, when I ended the call.

I felt like it was all spelled out in big bold letters across my forehead.

"That was Rusty," I said. "He gave me the name of the new owner of that shrimp boat that went down."

"I did a little back-channel snooping of my own," she said. "Just a scroll through the coroner's records. No bodiless head has been brought in. Nor any headless bodies."

My eyes came up sharply, meeting hers. "But Marty turned it over early this morning."

"Doctor Fredrick is a notorious note taker," she said, as I opened the door. "He uses a speech-to-text computer program to record his findings, and those notes go straight into the file, unedited. Either the person Marty signed it over to hasn't turned it in, or Doc's working on it right at this moment."

I stopped in my tracks. "Marty said that his supervisor took it and would take care of it. He didn't mention having him sign for it."

"It's normal procedure," she said, leading me down the back steps. "I turn in or check out evidence every day. Many times. Signing for it is second nature, so I'm sure he did. Talking to a non-LEO, saying he signed it over might be awkward or require further explanation."

As we walked to the tables in silence, my mind drifted to Savannah again. In her letter, she'd said that her husband wanted to try again and that she wanted to as well. I felt certain that her child was the result of her attempt to start things anew with her husband. Her being single now meant the attempt had been a failure, nothing more.

But she was here. And apparently hadn't been far away.

Ancient history, I reminded myself. *Get your mind off it, McDermitt.* But part of my mind kept wondering how she and her sister were involved.

The others were sitting at the table. The hogfish I'd speared the night before, plus a few more from the freezer, had been grilled to perfection and everyone ate well.

"I want you to keep *Knot L-8*," Carl said when we'd finished.

"I was going to say you should have it," I said.

"Just one more thing to carry up to Louisiana. No, you should keep it. I had more fun building it than riding in it anyway."

"Okay," I agreed. "To buy out your half, let me pay for your move. How's that?"

Carl reached across the table and with the shake of a hand, the deal was made. After dinner, he led the kids into the house to get ready for bed, and Kim offered to help Charlie with the dishes.

"Jesse told me what you guys found on the shrimp trawler," Devon said to Marty, once the others were out of earshot.

"There was something in that boat's hold that shouldn't have been there," Marty said. "Some sort of huge, pressure-cooker thing."

"He didn't say anything about that," Devon said, looking at me.

"A round cylinder," I said, with a shrug. "About two feet in diameter with a lid that was pressure sealed and had a bunch of dogs or screw clamps around the top. There were gauges attached to it. The whole thing was mounted to the inside of the shrimp hold."

"Ah," she said. "That's what makes you think they were cooking meth out there." She looked back at Marty. "Was that part of the evidence you turned in?"

"No," he replied, looking from Devon to me, then back again. "We didn't have any tools to unbolt it from the bottom of the hold. We found a head that was impaled on a metal pipe with another pressure gauge on it. It was the head and the pipe that I turned in."

"Who signed for it? Your shift supervisor?"

Marty's eyes widened. "Signed? Oh, my gosh! I was so keyed up from the chewing out and being suspended, I forgot to have him sign the evidence log. Great! Now, I'll probably get fired."

"He didn't sign?" Devon said. "Who was it?"

"Sergeant Steve Brady," Marty said. "What should I do? Should I call him? Or the coroner maybe?"

"I checked the morgue records," Devon said. "It hasn't been logged in there, but it's Saturday. It could be sitting in a cooler at the morgue and Doctor Fredrick just hasn't gotten to it yet."

"You think I should call Sergeant Brady?"

Devon looked at me, and I could read the suspicion in her eyes.

"Maybe not just yet," I said.

Devon nodded. "Let's wait and see what Monday brings. I know Steve; he's a bit of a tight-ass, but he's a good cop. I can check the morgue records tomorrow; maybe Doc will come in. He's always fascinated by strange cases."

The others returned, and Carl said he and Charlie were going to turn in early. Kim was carrying a bowl of scraps for Finn, which she put on the ground for him. He wolfed it down quickly.

"Come with me," Kim said to Marty, taking him by the hand. "I want to show you what I have in mind for my new house."

She led Marty away, and I watched them leave with some misgivings.

"Your little girl is a woman now," Devon said, taking my hand and pulling me up.

The mention of her being a little girl made me think about Savannah and her daughter. She couldn't be mine. I think I'd somehow know if she was.

Hand in hand, we crossed the clearing toward the house. "I'm going to do a little more digging tomorrow," she said. "Marty's inexperienced and probably doesn't handle a lot of evidence. But Steve's been a deputy for more than ten years and handles evidence daily. He shouldn't have forgotten."

Looking back over my shoulder, I saw the lights come on in the larger side of Kim's house. That's what it was going to be called from now on, Kim's house.

"While you're snooping," I said, "can you find out if the Coast Guard has the new coordinates? Even from up there on the deck, the wreck would be beyond the horizon."

"How do you know that, without looking on a computer or something?"

"One of many things boaters should know, but most don't," I said. "The distance in nautical miles to the horizon is one-point-one-seven times the square root of your eye height in feet. The deck's fourteen feet above the water, and standing on it, my eyes are about twenty feet up. So the horizon is a little over five miles away."

Finn went up the steps ahead of us and I followed Devon, admiring the fit of her cutoff jeans below my work shirt. Finn stopped at the door, wagging his tail. Holding the door for them, I followed Devon inside. When I closed the door, she turned into my arms, pressing her body against me.

"I'm glad everyone wanted to turn in early," she whispered, standing on her toes, her lips brushing my neck. "I've wanted you since I got here."

She pushed me back against the door, kissing me passionately. We'd been together long enough to not be nervous about sex. From the moment she arrived, I knew we'd be making love tonight.

I returned her kiss, pulling her in closer. She reached over and turned off the single twelve-volt overhead light, pitching the room into almost total darkness for a moment.

When she pulled away and moved back slightly, the moonlight pouring in from the window illuminated one side of her body, throwing her curves into shadow. Slowly, she unbuttoned her shorts and wiggled them down over her hips, letting them fall around her ankles onto the rough-hewn deck. Stepping out of them, she walked slowly over to the small radio on the shelf and turned it on.

The monotone voice of NOAA weather blared out that the low would be sixty-two degrees, with light winds out of the northeast. Good weather for sleeping. Especially if you can share body heat.

She flipped the switch over to CD and turned the volume down slightly. The music was Mindi Abair and her sax, with a light bass accompaniment. The sound was smooth and sexy. Devon danced seductively back into the moonlight, unbuttoning my worn denim shirt.

She let it fall open and I could see that the tee shirt under it was only a half-tee, cut off just above her lower ribs. Her breasts held the bottom of it away from her flat belly.

Devon took my hand and led me to the bedroom.

CHAPTER ELEVEN

A sound woke me. My eyes opened, and I was fully awake. I listened intently. The only thing I could hear was the gentle movement of the water against the shore and the creaking of the boats' fenders against the docks below my house. Devon's breathing wasn't audible.

Judging by the angle of the moonlight through the open window, I knew that it was an hour still before the first light of dawn would replace the cool blue moonbeams.

Had I dreamed the noise? I didn't dream often.

Devon moved beside me, the warmth of her bare hip against my side felt good. That first feeling of arousal was suddenly replaced by guilt. More than once during last night's lovemaking, I'd thought of Savannah. Of how her tanned skin always felt warm to the touch and her hair always smelled like tropical flowers. We'd touched a lot during the few days we had together, and I'd inhaled her scent deeply.

Rising on one elbow, I looked over at Devon and forgot all about the sound I thought I'd heard. A shaft of moonlight from the partially open window fell across the side of her face. Her blond hair was all over the pillow and she still wore the half-tee she'd had on last night. How could any man think of another woman while making love with such a beauty?

A memory of Savannah in nearly the same pose popped into my head. But she'd been stretched out in the moonlight on the bow of the *Revenge*. We'd spent quite a few nights out on the water, making love under the stars.

I blinked my eyes, and Devon opened hers. She smiled at me looking down at her. Stretching and arching her back, the moonlight created a long shadow between the muscles of her middle abdomen as she sighed.

When she opened her eyes again, she reached out to me and pulled me down on top of her, wrapping those long legs around mine.

"I'm cold," she whispered with a deep sigh of contentment.

A slight scratching sound got my attention and I froze. Devon must have heard it, as I felt her body tense, as well.

A soft whimper came from the other side of the bedroom door.

"I think Finn needs to go outside," Devon said, sliding out from under me.

I rolled over onto my back. "I'll get him."

"You just lay there," she said. "Conserve your energy. I'm not finished with you yet."

Walking around the big bed, wearing nothing more than a cut-off tee-shirt, I admired her form. The woman moved with the grace of a mountain lion, her body flowing across the room.

She opened the door, and Finn looked up, his head cocked to one side. "You need to go outside?" she asked him.

He turned and trotted to the outside door.

"I really need to put in a doggy door," I said, flopping back on the pillows.

I heard the outer door open and then close again. A moment later, Devon appeared in the open doorway, silhouetted by the moonlight in the living room.

"I'm going to go ahead and set the coffee maker for an hour from now," she whispered. "The sun will be up about then, and an hour should give me enough time."

Grinning back at her, I silently vowed to give her my undivided attention. I closed my eyes, as she turned away from the door. I heard kitchen sounds, and a moment later, I could smell the coffee as she poured the fresh ground beans into the machine.

The door opened and closed again, and I heard the clicking of Finn's claws on the floorboards. Devon came into view, stopping and leaning against the doorjamb, her left hip cocked out.

"You better not have fallen back to sleep," she said.

"Who can sleep, knowing what's coming?"

"Me or the coffee?" she asked, pushing away from the door, and closing it behind her.

"Both," I replied honestly, as she crawled up onto the bed from the footboard.

Pulling the covers off, she drew them up over her hips and moved slowly on top of me. The anticipation began to build as her skin gently caressed mine.

Easing herself down on top of my body, straddling my thighs, she guided herself down onto me. We moved slowly at first, but her breathing soon grew labored. She began to moan softly, her movements becoming more intense. Arching her back, she pushed herself upward and back with her hands on my chest.

I could feel her body tensing, as she rocked back harder. Her soft moans became interspersed with quick inhalations as she tried to prolong the feeling. The intensity continued to build, and I held back for as long as I could, knowing that she was almost there. I gripped her thighs and forced her down onto me, harder and faster.

Waves of pleasure rolled through my body as Devon rocked back once more and froze in place, her whole body quivering. Moving only her hips, she squeezed me tightly for a moment before both our bodies convulsed, and she collapsed onto my chest.

We lay like that for several minutes, both totally spent and breathing heavy.

Finally, Devon rolled slightly off me, snuggling her face into the crook of my neck. "I think I'm done with you," she whispered. "For now, at least."

We both drifted into semi-sleep, gently stroking and caressing one another in that dream-like state of total satisfaction. Eventually, Devon stopped moving and her breathing slowed. She was asleep.

I must have drifted off too, but the smell of the coffee brewing soon woke me again. The programmable coffee-maker is better than any alarm clock.

Devon wasn't lying next to me. I usually sleep pretty light.

A sound from the kitchen gave me her location, but I recognized the sound as that of a skillet being placed on the stove. A very unusual sound for Devon to be making.

I got quickly to my feet, opened a drawer, and put on clean skivvies and shorts. Then I hurried into the other room. Devon was in the little corner kitchen, dressed in jeans and a loose-fitting gray sweater. Finn was sitting a few feet away, watching her.

"You're cooking?" I asked. Devon's not what you'd call a natural in the galley.

"I've been practicing," she said, as I hugged her from behind. "I can do bacon and scrambled eggs."

"Anything I can help with?"

"Coffee's almost ready," she replied, dropping half a slab of bacon into the heated skillet. "Pour me a cup?"

I filled two heavy porcelain mugs and carried mine to the recliner table in the living room. "I need to get dressed," I said, placing the mug on the side table between the two chairs.

In the bedroom, I dressed quickly for the cooler weather and returned to the recliner to watch. Devon had never taken any interest in cooking her own meals, preferring to eat out. She had a regular list of restaurants she alternated between for each meal.

"Why the sudden interest in cooking your own food?" I asked.

She turned and smiled. "I've never had anyone to cook for and you've made plenty of meals for us. So I've been practicing."

"On who?"

"Well, to be honest," she began. "I wasted a crap-ton of food, until I could eat it myself. But bacon and eggs are pretty easy."

Using a long fork, she pushed the bacon slices out of the skillet onto a plate that was covered with a paper towel. She then poured the bacon fat from the skillet over Finn's dogfood. Finn licked his chops in anticipation. Next, she poured what looked like half a dozen whipped eggs from a bowl into the skillet, causing it to sizzle.

A few minutes later, she spooned the eggs onto two plates. She added one slice of bacon to the smaller serving and piled the rest on the other. Though we've only been together a short time, she knew my weakness for bacon.

Rising, I strode across the room, and moved the plates over to the table. "Smells good."

She put Finn's bowl on the floor and I held her chair until she sat. The eggs were perfect and the bacon nice and crispy. Before we finished eating, a vibrating sound came from the small side table.

"That's mine," she said, standing, and moving quickly to retrieve her phone.

I continued eating while I listened to the one-sided conversation. She told whomever she was talking to that she'd be at their place as soon as she could, then ended the call.

"I have to go," she said. "Can you give me a ride? I don't want to ask Marty, since he's supposed to be suspended."

"Sure," I replied, eating quickly. She sat down and finished her meal, her brow furrowed in thought.

"Something at work?" I asked.

"A development in a case that Ben has me working on."

Lieutenant Ben Morgan was Devon's boss and sometime partner. A nice guy, he was pretty much counting the days until he retired. But he was still devoted enough to go out in the field with a younger detective. He'd been hoping he could reach retirement as a lieutenant. He told me that the idea of being promoted to Captain Morgan in a town where water is consumed almost as much as rum didn't much appeal to him.

"I'll get the boat ready," I said, taking the last piece of bacon and giving Finn half.

"Give me a minute to wash up and get my things," she said, stacking the dishes in the sink. "I'll be right down."

Outside, the sun was just above the eastern horizon. I saw Carl at work in the garden. I called down to him that I had to take Devon to Key West and would be gone most of the morning.

"I'll let Kim know," he called back.

The wind was still out of the northeast. It would be too rough in the Gulf for *Knot L-8* or the Grady. So, stepping through the door to the dock area beneath the house, I grabbed the keys for *El Cazador* from the hook just inside the door.

Stepping aboard, I switched on the batteries and tilted the console up. A quick check of the engine told me everything was well, and I closed it. At the helm, I raised the instrument panel and then started the engine. The gauges fell into the normal range as the engine settled into a low burbling idle. I clicked the key fob, remembering as the hinges squealed in protest to the saltwater environment, that they needed oil. With the engine warming up, I took a can of spray lube and hit the offending hinges liberally with it.

"We're not taking the big boat?" Devon asked, as she entered the dock area.

"*Cazador* will be faster," I replied. "We can take a few shortcuts."

"Remember where Ben's place is?" she asked, stepping aboard and stowing her things in the dry box under the forward port bench.

"He still in the houseboat?"

"Yeah. Just drop me there. I'll ride to the office with him."

Tossing the lines, I bumped the bow thruster to move the nose away from the pier before engaging the transmission. Navigating *El Cazador* was a cinch in tight quarters even with her single engine. At idle speed, you can use the bow thruster instead of the wheel and she responded more like a car, with the stern following the bow, instead of swinging out and pushing.

Fortunately, with a full moon just two days away, the tide was near its peak so the water was higher than normal. Instead of turning northeast in Harbor Channel, I pointed the bow due south and brought *Cazador* up on plane.

"I thought you had to go that way in the bigger boats," Devon said, pointing toward Harbor Key Bank.

"The tide's the highest it'll be for two weeks," I said, judging the distance to the turn between the Water Keys. "Hang on."

Turning the wheel sharply, *Cazador* heeled over and knifed through the shallows on her starboard chine. This raised the prop tunnel a little more. On plane, *Cazador* drew about twenty inches. Turning raised the keel a few inches more, providing plenty enough draft to clear the two-foot-deep sandbar.

"You're enjoying this too much," she said, as I navigated the unmarked shallows, keeping the boat in at least three feet of water.

"Anything Ben would call you in for on a Sunday has to be important, right?"

"It'd be nice to get there in one piece."

"This shaves a good six miles off the trip at this end. We can cut across the shallows at the other end and save another mile.

A moment later, I aimed the bow at the gap between Little Crane and Racoon Keys, seeing the white caps out on the Gulf. Clear of the two islands, I turned northwest and pushed the throttle down further.

The ride on the outside was rough, but *Cazador* took it in stride. Her big bow flares knocked the two-foot waves aside effortlessly and we stayed dry behind the three-sided windshield around the center console.

I *was* enjoying it. We could have taken the *Revenge* and traveled the longer route at a faster speed, and arrived at about the same time. But the smaller center console was just plain fun. My Maverick Mirage flats skiff was even more fun, ripping through the backcountry in water barely deep enough for a kayak. But going all the way to Key West in the open skiff would be a wet ride.

To a casual observer who knew the water, my route might seem foolhardy, but having lived out here for eight years, I've explored every inch of water for miles around, in boats and on foot. I knew where the dangers were.

Less than an hour later, I slowed and turned south toward Garrison Bight, crossing the flats off Dredgers Key. Bringing the boat down off plane, I navigated around the mooring field at an idle, heading to the narrow gap at Trumbo Point.

Devon called Ben and told him we'd be pulling up to the back of his floating house in just a minute.

Idling past Trumbo Point, I entered the shelter of the bight and steered toward Ben Morgan's houseboat. It was more than the typical factory-built houseboat. It was a boat, in that it floated on the water. But it was moored permanently at the dock, a floating barge with a little blue house built on it. From what I saw the one time I visited, the first floor was much like my combination living room, dining room, and kitchen. But his bedroom was a dormered loft over the kitchen and dining room, and it overlooked the living room, with its high vaulted ceiling.

Ben stepped out onto the little back porch, dressed as I suspected he always did, in a coat and tie. "Jesse, good to see you again. Sorry for spoiling your weekend."

"Always good to be seen again, Ben. It beats the alternative."

"Care to come in for coffee, or can I get you some water or something?"

I could tell by his body language that he was anxious to talk to Devon and get busy with whatever they were working on. Sometimes being involved with a police detective can be trying, but it is what it is.

"Thanks," I said, lifting my thermos. "I have enough for the return trip. You guys have important work; I'll just head back out."

Devon kissed me and gave me a quick hug before grabbing her things and stepping up onto Ben's porch. "Thanks for the lift, Jesse."

"Anytime, ma'am," I said, tipping my invisible cap.

I kicked the bow around with the thruster and shifted forward. Slowly, I idled away from the little houseboat community, toward Trumbo Point and open water.

Devon hadn't tried the coroner's website on the way there, and it was likely she'd forget. I passed Trumbo Point and the mooring field, then brought *Cazador* up on plane and turned east.

Maybe Doc would be at the morgue in the hospital. People rarely go in search of a morgue, but if you wanted to find Doc Fredrick, you went to where dead people gather.

I switched the VHF to the channel I knew Sunset Marina monitored. I asked for and received permission to fuel up and tie off for a couple of hours.

After fueling, I moved to the day dock and tied up. Lower Keys Medical Center was just half a mile down the road, and I knew the woman who worked as the morgue's gatekeeper. If Doc wasn't there, maybe I could get her to call him and I could ask him out for a coffee.

Walking in Key West is usually pretty safe. But on a Sunday, the hotels are emptying out, and the major roads get congested. But there were few cars on College Road and I managed to reach the hospital without becoming a hood ornament on a rental car.

Using a side entrance, I found the stairwell and went down to the basement floor. Basements in the Keys are rare, but in a hospital, it's vitally important. At the bottom of the stairs, I pushed open a steel door and entered the office area of the medical examiner.

"Jesse McDermitt," the red-headed receptionist said, looking up from her desk. "You finally decide to give in to my charms?"

Juli Wilkins had been with the sheriff's office for more than forty years. Always working in administrative jobs, she didn't carry a gun like sworn deputies. Which was a good thing, in my opinion. She'd never married, and was probably in her mid-sixties, if I were to guess. She never let her years get in the way of flirting with men half her age, though.

"I don't know how you've managed to stay single, Juli."

"On account of I don't want any full-time man around," she replied. "Once I use them up, what good are they? I'm thinking it'd take me quite a bit of using before I tossed you aside, though."

I smiled, though she made me uncomfortable. "Doc Fredrick's not around, is he?"

"You just missed him," she said. "He was here less than an hour ago. Wanted to look over some dive gear again."

"That tourist that had to go to the chamber last week?"

"Yeah," she said. "The guy's fine now and has only his own dumb self to blame, but he's suing the city."

"Doc say where he was going?"

She smiled brightly. "How important is it to you?"

My face flushed and she laughed.

"I can call him," she offered. "Let you talk to him."

"Would you?" I asked, hoping to get out with my dignity intact.

Juli picked up the phone and stabbed a single button on the dial pad with a very long, well-manicured claw.

"Hey, Leo, Juli here," she said into the receiver. "I got some boat bum here in the office wants to talk to you."

I couldn't hear his response, as Juli just handed the phone over. I took it and half-expected to hear the medical examiner declining to talk, but there was just laughter on the other end.

"Doc, it's Jesse McDermitt," I said.

"Captain McDermitt!" Doc said. "I thought that was you I saw in my mirror. I just left the detention facility. What in blazes are you doing in Key West?"

"I was just dropping my girlfriend off for work," I said, both as a reason for being here and to stack more bricks on the wall between me and Juli. "Got nothing else going on this morning, so I thought I might buy you a coffee and pick your brain a little."

"I'm just getting onto Overseas Highway, I'll turn around."

"Don't go out of your way, Doc," I said, hoping he would. "If you're working, we can do it another time."

I heard tires protesting the pavement and a horn blare.

"Nonsense, my boy. I'm already turned around."

"Thanks, Doc," I said, and handed the receiver back to Juli. "Gotta run; he's just a block away."

"Next time you have some time to kill," she said. "I know a great way to while away the hours."

I thanked her again and hurried to the door, yanking it open and taking the stairs two at a time. Outside, Doc pulled up to the curb just as I exited the hospital, and I got in the passenger side of his antique Peugeot. To call the old French sedan an antique only alluded to its age, not its desirability. Most locals drove cars like it—throwaways, or Keys cars. The salt environment, hot temperatures, and constant slow-speed, stop-and-go traffic would destroy a new car in a very short time.

"You're taking a risk," he said, putting the car in first and spinning the bald right rear tire slightly. "Miss Wilkins is probably responsible for half the missing men on this island."

"I'm glad you were close by," I joked. But not really.

"There's a Starbucks just around the corner," Doc said, turning right on US-1 and accelerating through the gears. Crossing the bridge over Cow Key Channel, he slowed before making the right turn onto Roosevelt. He hit second gear before the left-hand curve and moved across the left lane into the middle turn lane, known in Key West as the suicide lane. The little car's front air dam scraped as we bounced into the Starbucks parking lot.

"So, what's on your mind?" Doc asked, getting out and slamming the door.

Still shaking, I climbed out of the car. "What do you know about methamphetamine?"

We walked toward the door. "It's a stimulant," he replied. "It's been used successfully to treat ADHD, but having heard about your latest business endeavor, I think you're probably asking about its illegal use."

I held the door for the older man. "How did you hear about that?"

He smiled warmly. "There isn't much going on in these islands that I don't hear about."

"You're right," I said. "I'm specifically interested in how the stuff's made."

Doc ordered two large black coffees, smiled, and nodded to the girl at the counter when she served them, then carried his cup to a table. I reached for my wallet, but the girl waved me off. "No charge for Doctor Fredrick and his friends."

Sitting down across the table from him, Doc leaned in close. "Why exactly are you asking about this?"

"I'm not planning on going into the illegal drug business, if that's what you're asking."

"The thought never crossed my mind," he said. "I assume you're working on a case through your new detective agency?"

"I haven't brought it up at the board meeting yet," I replied with a grin. "I've just noticed some weird things are going on, and I think illegal drug manufacturing might be related."

"I see," he responded. "Methamphetamine can be made pretty easily using common products you can buy in a hardware or automotive store, along with certain over-the-counter cold medications."

"Something a user would make for themselves?"

"Yes, it's become quite widespread; you can easily find the ingredients and how to make it on the internet."

"What about something bigger?" I asked. "Like someone making it to sell in bulk?"

"The meth that users make is very impure and dangerous," he said. "Perhaps fifty percent purity. In a homemade lab, with the right equipment, one might be able to make a slightly better product, though not much purer. I've heard of more elaborate lab busts that were making nearly pure methamphetamine, upwards of ninety percent."

"How big would a lab like that have to be?"

"Most of the illegal methamphetamine used in this country comes from Mexico. Big super labs hidden in the desert or up in the mountains. Those are huge, probably thousands of square feet."

"What about something in between?" I asked. "Not for worldwide distribution but more on a regional scale?"

"A small storage building," he replied. "About the size of a one-car garage, but the odor would make it necessary to put the building in a remote area."

"Because of the acetone?"

"That, and other products. It creates a powerful odor, which law enforcement is all too familiar with. Like an overused cat litter box."

The hold in the trawler was about the size of a small garage, I thought.

"I guess it'd need some sort of specialized equipment, huh? Any idea what it'd cost to set up something like that? A one-car garage size?"

Doc sipped at his coffee, and looked at me over the rim. "Twenty to life here in Florida."

I chuckled. "Just want to keep my options open."

"Yeah, right," he said. "To set up a good lab, one that could produce about three or four pounds per cycle, in a highly pure state, you'd need that kind of room. And yes, the equipment can be very hard to come by. Most of the big stuff is tightly controlled and expensive. Probably a hundred thousand dollars to do it right."

"What's it look like? The drug, I mean."

Doc leaned forward. "You don't know what crystal meth looks like, but you suspect someone is making it near your home?"

"Just things I'm hearing, Doc. Nothing I can really go to the police with. Not yet, anyway."

Doc sat back in his chair. "It's a multi-faceted crystalline substance, usually clear to cloudy white in color. Depending on the quantity, it can vary in size from a small rock no bigger than a pea, to an oblong crystal as large as a man's thumb."

Now, all I had to do was find out if Doc knew anything about the head, without raising his suspicion.

"I appreciate the intel, Doc," I said, sitting back and casually sipping the coffee. "Any interesting cases come across your desk recently?"

He eyed me for a moment. I met his gaze and held it.

"You should never attempt a career as a poker player, Jesse. What is it you'd really like to know?"

"That obvious?"

He nodded. I didn't want to implicate Marty in something he'd get in trouble for. Maybe Doc wouldn't ask too many questions.

I leaned across the table and whispered. "Was a human head brought into the morgue?"

His eyes piqued with interest. "Just a head? No. Why do you ask?"

"A headless body, maybe? Besides the one you picked up at the wreck, I mean. Maybe a dark-skinned headless body?"

"Neither, Jesse," he replied. "The only body parts currently in the morgue were recovered from the wreck you reported on Friday. And of course, the body of the woman. If you know something about the explosion, another body part, or anything about a meth lab, you should report it."

This bothered me. Doc Fredrick is the chief medical examiner for all of Monroe County. He was brought in on investigations and consultations all over South Florida. If a head was ever turned in, he would have known about it.

"Just scuttlebutt I picked up. A rumor."

"A rumor about a decapitation?"

"There are extenuating circumstances, Doc."

He sipped his coffee as he studied my face. "I know more about you than most people around here," he said. "For instance, your connection to the dead woman."

There were only a handful of people in the whole world who knew about Savannah and me. "How do you know that?" I asked, genuinely curious.

Doc smiled, leaning back in his chair. "I told you—"

"Nothing happens in the Keys that you don't hear about."

"I trust that when there is something to report," he said, beginning to rise, "you will do the right thing."

"Thanks, Doc," I said, standing. "I will."

"Can I give you a lift back to your car at the hospital?"

"Thanks," I said, not wanting to put the man out any further, nor ride with him again, "but I came by boat. It's docked just across the bridge."

We walked back outside together, and I shook his hand, thanking him, once more. As he was getting into his car, curiosity got the best of me. "Doc, can I ask you something?"

"There's more?"

"The coffee?" I asked. "You have a regular bar tab with Starbucks or something?"

Doc Fredrick looked inside, and I followed his gaze. The young lady at the counter smiled and waved. Doc waved back.

"Her name's Connie," Doc said. "Sweet girl. She lives in my building. One day I heard a scream and looked outside to see a commotion at the pool. By the time I got down there, others had already pulled her lifeless son's body from the pool. I performed CPR and resuscitated the toddler. She's never let me pay for coffee since."

We said goodbye and I crossed the parking lot. Crossing Roosevelt on foot can be very dangerous on a Sunday, so I pushed the button at the crosswalk and waited. If Doc didn't know about the head, that could only mean one thing. Marty's shift supervisor hadn't turned it in. There were several reasons a conscientious police officer might delay that.

It was the weekend, for one thing. But would a good cop put a head in a cooler until Monday? I didn't think so. Perhaps he simply forgot, but within a few hours, the smell would be a constant reminder. And a man doesn't become a shift supervisor by forgetting something like a severed human head. Another possibility might be that he lost it, but a conscientious police officer would report the loss, even if it meant he'd get in trouble. Eventually, Marty was going to have to say something.

Could this Sergeant Brady have something personal against Marty? That would explain the suspension over what I would consider a minor infraction. If Marty hadn't dug up something, maybe. But whenever one of my troops failed to obey orders and did something that was good and right, I never considered punishing them for it. Initiative is a trait that needs to be cultivated, not cut. And it needs to be taught where the line really is. The line between initiative and dereliction.

Had Marty been derelict in his duty, by watching the wreck site after the Coast Guard had left it? Had we not found the head, nobody would have known he was out there. That changed things in my opinion. No, Marty hadn't been derelict. Why he'd chosen to go out there after being told to stay away from it by his superior, I didn't know. But he had. And we'd found evidence of criminal activity on the boat. At least I thought we had.

Walking slowly along Roosevelt, I wondered if the Coast Guard had found anything. If Brady hadn't turned in the head, it was likely he didn't relay the new location to the Coasties.

Passing the Marriot, I turned left toward the bridge. The walk was only two miles, and I wanted to think. Stopping on the bridge over the channel, I looked down into the clear, fast-moving water. Sea fans waved back at me and a few dark shapes moved here and there—fish hunting for a meal.

A boat passed under, heading south toward the reefs, rod holders at the stern bristling with tackle. I nodded at the two guys in the open center console just a few feet below me, and they nodded back. After a few seconds the disturbed water from their boat's outboard was whisked away by the current. The sea fans continued to wave, unfussed by the boat's passing.

A young woman pushing a stroller approached, and I stepped back against the roadside guardrail to give her room. She smiled, and I continued across the bridge, turning left onto College Road.

By the time I reached the marina, I'd ticked off every possibility I could think of but two. Either Marty's supervisor had a grudge against him and took advantage of his forgetfulness, or Brady was no good and didn't log the head and pipe as evidence for some unknown reason.

My phone vibrated in my pocket, startling me. It was Rusty. Pushing the *Accept* button, I said, "Find out anything more about that shrimp boat?"

"Not exactly," he said, "but there is a connection to something."

Another woman, walking hand in hand with a young girl, approached from the boardwalk that went around to the slips on the north side of the marina.

"What kind of connection?" I asked.

"That Grand Banks I told you about?" Rusty said, as I stared at the approaching woman. "She left Boot Key Harbor in the middle of the night."

"Yeah, I know," I said, absently watching Savannah walk toward me. "Gotta go, bro."

CHAPTER TWELVE

Savannah hadn't yet seen me. Ending the call, I shoved the phone in my pocket. I could easily take two steps to my left and be behind some trees, out of her sight, then just turn my back and walk away. Had I not stopped on the bridge, I'd already be tossing off the lines, anyway. My feet remained planted.

Her eyes came up and she saw me standing there.

My appearance has changed some over the years. When Savannah had been here before, I still wore my hair short, almost Marine Corps regulation, and I shaved at least every other day. Now, my hair was over my ears and past my collar, and the week's stubble on my chin was showing some gray.

The woman walking toward me hadn't changed at all. The same blue eyes that looked like two pools of deep, clear water were looking back at me. She had the same dark tan, and though her hair was slightly longer, it was the same sun-streaked blond I remembered. Even dressed in slacks and a light-blue, long-sleeved blouse, I could tell by the way she moved that she was still as agile and fit as any professional athlete. What stood out was that she was wearing shoes. The whole time we'd spent together, she'd worn flip-flops once and was barefoot the rest of the time. On her feet now were low, sensible, open-toed shoes.

She walked straight toward me, her eyes fixed on mine. She stopped five feet away and seemed to study my face. Up close, I could see the beginnings of fine lines at the corners of her eyes. She was only a few years younger than me, but looked a lot better than many women in their twenties.

"You've aged some, Jesse."

"And you haven't changed a bit," I replied.

"The new look becomes you."

"I guess this is where I should imitate Bogey," I said. "Talk about all the gin joints and all the towns."

"Except you already know why I'm here."

There was something else in those eyes. Some deep emotional scar that I couldn't get a read on. Something other than the grief of losing her sister.

"Yes," I said. "Word spreads in the islands. I'm sorry for your loss."

"She went off the deep end some time ago," Savannah said. "We tried to help her, but it was just a matter of time."

"Who is that man, Mommy," the little girl said, tugging Savannah's hand.

I looked down at her, realizing she was there for the first time. She was tall for an eight-year-old, but Savannah was tall, about five-ten. The girl had darker hair than her mother. But I had a feeling that if Savannah didn't spend so much time in the sun, her hair would be closer to that of her late sister, a rich brown. Their eyes were almost exactly the same.

"This is Captain McDermitt," Savannah told the girl. "Jesse, this is my daughter, Florence."

I smiled at the girl and extended my hand. "It's very nice to meet you, Miss Florence." She took my hand, and though she was just a little girl, her grip was firm and unafraid. Another trait she shared with her mother.

"I remember you thought that tradition was kind of hokey," I said to Savannah.

"People change," she said. "Circumstances change. What are you doing in Key West?"

For a moment, I completely forgot why I was there. I didn't want to tell her that I was probing around to find out why her sister was on a floating meth lab. Just looking in her eyes, I could tell she wasn't involved.

Easy, McDermitt, I reminded myself, *you've been fooled by a pretty face before. This same pretty face, actually.*

For some reason, I didn't want to share with her that I'd brought my cop girlfriend back to Key West from my island.

"I was supposed to meet a charter," I lied, "but they didn't show. So I walked over to Starbucks for—"

"Coffee, of course," she said, smiling. "Strong and hot, just like you like your women."

"Where are you staying?" I asked, noting the lack of even a tan line on her ring finger.

"We live on our boat, *Sea Biscuit.* I'm only in town to arrange for Charlotte's transport home."

To me, that sounded like a dismissal.

"I looked for your boat in Boot Key Harbor," she said. I caught her eyes flash briefly to my own left hand. "We stopped in yesterday. You're no longer docked there?"

Again, I'd read it wrong. I told myself that where women were concerned, maybe I should just start figuring whatever the opposite of what my gut told me.

"No," I said. "Different boat and different dock. Well, same boat, just a newer model. I developed my island up in the Contents and live there now."

"You built a house?"

"Several," I replied. "My house, my caretaker's place, and two bunkhouses for visiting fishermen."

Part of me wanted to make sure she knew I'd moved on, that she hadn't been all that big a deal. Another part was hoping she'd like the change, and still a third part was yelling and screaming at me that I had a girlfriend.

"It must be lovely," she said, "so why would you come all the way to Key West to pick up your clients?"

"Easier for them," I compounded the lie. "And they paid extra."

"We really must be going," she said. "After I take care of this, I want to catch the evening tide."

Now, I was being dismissed. Perhaps forever.

"It was nice to see you again," I said, thinking how stupid that sounded, given our history. Even as the words came out of my mouth, I grimaced.

She started to walk away, but stopped. "Maybe if you're around *Dockside* tomorrow, we'll bump into one another again."

I smiled. "That'd be nice." That third part of my brain went off the deep end, calling me all kinds of vile names.

"But *Dockside's* closed. Most of the Boot Key crowd hangs out at *Burdine's*."

"*Burdine's* then," she said, and turned away.

Taking Florence by the hand, they started up the sidewalk toward the hospital. I stood and watched them walk away. Ten yards, then twenty. Suddenly, Savannah tossed her hair, looked back over her shoulder, and smiled at me.

CHAPTER THIRTEEN

For someone who didn't like boats, Cedric felt he was spending way too much time on them, as the bouncing of the dive boat he was on jarred him awake.

He'd come to the Keys in the dead of winter nearly three years ago. Not because he was a boater or liked the water, but because Key West was as far as the road out of Detroit would take him; he didn't want to ever be cold again. It didn't take long to see that the Keys weren't a good fit for him. Too many unusual people and gaudy lifestyles. So he escaped slightly to the north, to the mainland and the lights of Miami. There, he could melt into the pavement, just another anonymous face on the streets. A lot like Chicago.

But in Miami, Cedric did whatever he needed to survive. He burglarized cars, picked unsuspecting tourists' pockets and purses, and made enough contacts on the streets to buy and sell a little weed and blow. He held no ambition to be famous, not even in his own apartment building. He stayed low, didn't have a bank account, no plastic, no car, and no driver's license. His Illinois license had expired long before he headed south. He was anonymous, a John Doe.

Mister Ballinger had wanted him on the dive boat, so that's where he was. Though they'd only known one another a few months, the man had accepted Cedric for who he was and appreciated his talent. In Detroit, Cedric was just another urban cretin living off the street. But unlike many around him, he just never developed the addiction for meth, using it only sparingly. He'd had a friend that made the stuff in small amounts and always tested it for chemical purity. The guy also bought and sold it, always testing purity. Subsequently, Cedric had developed a nose for purity, just by hanging around the guy. Just a pinch up one nostril and Cedric could tell within a couple of percentage points what the purity was. It was a talent Mister Ballinger had said would take him far in his new export company. At the time, Cedric thought he'd meant just buying drugs for him and his wealthy guests, and at first it was.

Then Ballinger got the notion that he could make better meth in his own lab. Cedric had told him about the problems with odor from cooking meth, but the idea never left Ballinger's mind. He asked Cedric more questions and he told Mister Ballinger everything he'd learned from his friend in Chicago.

It was about then that Mister Ballinger heard about Raymond Black. He'd contacted the ousted pharmacist and the three of them had discussed how much Black could make and what he'd need to do it. He'd been hesitant at first, but facing the idea of finding a job outside of the pharmaceutical business, and competing with twenty-something college grads for a Walmart greeter job didn't appeal to him.

After boarding the dive boat in the middle of the night, Cedric had slept most of the way to their present location. The boat was a regular charter boat, but everyone on board was part of Ballinger's crew, except the boat's captain. He was being paid enough to not ask questions, and knew how to not listen and look the other way.

The trip down from Fort Myers had taken over five hours; they'd arrived just after sunrise. The divers split up into two teams, planning at least two dives each, and maybe a third. The first two-man team in the water was only going to do a search, then tell the next two what needed to be recovered from where. After that, they'd worked out a regular interval of forty-minute dives, each team picking up where the other team left off.

Cedric had explained to the divers where everything should be, but cautioned them that because of the explosion, they'd have to search every square inch of the stricken boat. High on the list was locating and recovering the plastic box containing the product. More important though, was removing anything from the hold that pointed toward it being anything other than a shrimper. The boat had been on its way to its third anchorage, so it should have two packages in the box, a pound of meth in each package.

Just in case a situation like this were to come up, the hiding place wasn't just known, but had been assigned by Mister Ballinger himself. On this boat, the divers were to look under the captain's watch bunk in the wheelhouse. It had been fitted with a false bottom and covered with spare parts, ropes, and other boat junk.

Cedric looked at his watch. It was just past noon. The first two divers, now on their third dive of the day, should be coming up soon.

After their first dive, they'd reported that the aft deck and rear part of the pilothouse were severely damaged and there was little left in the hold. They'd spent most of the dive cutting and dragging away the nets that had tangled the whole boat. The second team had then worked on removing the reaction vessel, which had been bolted to the floor inside the boat's hold. Once they got it up, the first team went back down and spent forty minutes sifting through the sand that had been scraped up when the boat was dragged. They'd surfaced with the burner, which had been mounted under the reaction vessel. They'd also found one of the cooling trays, which had been mounted on gimbals to the sides of the hold. The gimbaled cooling trays allowed the product to slowly cool and crystalize, without being sloshed around.

After that, it was the second team's job to search the seafloor around the boat, especially the area in the direction that it had been dragged from. Anything that had been broken loose during the drag had been marked with a small surface float to pick up after the last dive. There were four floats stretched out behind the dive boat.

Sitting on the fly bridge, Cedric had a commanding view all around. As soon as they'd anchored, the boat's captain had been sent below to get some sleep for the return trip, so Cedric had the bridge to himself.

The other two divers were resting in the cockpit, waiting for the forty-minute timer to go off, alerting them to get ready. It would be their job to make one last sweep of the boat, retrieving the product from under the watch bunk and anything else they could find.

A low rumbling sound caught Cedric's attention. He scanned the horizon, but didn't see anything. The sound faded away. A moment later, he heard it again, but still couldn't tell which direction the sound was coming from.

The timer went off and Cedric watched as the two men in the cockpit began to get their gear together for their final dive. If the divers in the water now didn't find the box with the product, then these two men would make one more attempt. The product in the box was worth over seventy thousand dollars, so they had to at least try to retrieve it. But if they were unable to find it or couldn't get to it, they'd have a large demolition charge with them. Before surfacing, they'd place the explosives in the engine room for maximum destruction.

So far, Cedric thought they'd been pretty lucky. The Coast Guard either hadn't returned to dive on the original site, or they just weren't interested in looking for where it had been dragged to. Only one other boat had passed within sight, and it was a slow-moving private yacht headed south.

Over the sound of the men talking below, Cedric heard the rumbling noise again, louder this time. The sound was coming from the southwest. Looking around the bridge, Cedric opened several storage compartments and finally found a pair of binoculars. He scanned the horizon until he finally saw the source of the sound.

Though it was a couple of miles away, Cedric made out a fishing boat moving north at a slow speed. The big poles that kept the fishing lines from tangling each other were sticking out both sides of the boat.

"What is it?" one of the divers asked from below.

Cedric looked down at him. "Just a fishing boat."

That seemed to satisfy the man and he went back to work on his gear. Cedric looked through the binoculars at the boat again. It was now barely moving. He knew that this kind of fishing was called trolling, but had no idea what kind of fish the guy hoped to catch. He could barely make out the man on the boat, but it seemed as if he was alone. Occasionally, he'd turn and look forward, but mostly he just looked behind him, letting the boat drive itself.

There was a commotion at the back of the dive boat, and Cedric looked down to see the other two divers at the swim platform. The two men in the cockpit stepped down to help them with their dive gear. One of the men in the water handed up a large gray plastic box. Cedric put the binoculars back in the storage bin and went down the ladder.

"I'll take that," he said, as the box was handed up. "Go ahead and make one more sweep, then plant the charge."

Cedric had already found a good hiding spot on the dive boat while on their way out last night. He carried the box inside, raised the panel in the floor for the engine room, and took the box down into the cramped space below the floor. Toward the back was a metal tool chest that had to have been installed when the boat was built; he saw no way to move it into the tight area. He opened one of the larger drawers, and removed two large hand pumps. He had no idea what they were used for. He then opened the plastic container and removed the two packages, placing them deep inside the drawer and replacing the pumps.

Once he closed the floor panel, Cedric went forward to wake the captain, then went back to the bridge. As soon as the two divers returned, he wanted to get out of here and back to dry land.

The second crew stepped off the dive platform, and the other two divers handed down the explosive charge. It was set to go off thirty minutes after arming. That would give them more than enough time to get several miles away before the powerful explosives destroyed the wrecked boat.

Cedric looked through the binoculars at the fishing boat, now running parallel to the dive boat about a mile away. He could see the guy more clearly now. He looked like most of the other fishermen Cedric had seen down here, wearing long sleeves, a cap, and dark sunglasses. Every now and then, the man glanced over at the dive boat. He didn't seem to be interested, other than just making sure where it was.

Two splashes caused Cedric to look away. The divers that had just gotten out of the water had now dove back in with only masks and fins. They were swimming away from the boat toward the markers. After a moment, they reached the first two and started swimming back, looping the lines around their shoulders.

When they got back aboard, they pulled the parts up that the lines were attached to, and stacked the things with the other junk. Somewhere on the return trip, they'd dump everything in deep water.

The swimmers went back into the water and started out for the two farthest floats. Cedric watched until they reached the markers then looked west through the binoculars to see what the fishing boat was doing.

The guy on the boat didn't seem to be paying them any attention. He'd passed beyond the dive boat and seemed to be intently watching his fishing lines.

Just as Cedric started to lower the binoculars, he caught sight of the boat's name on the transom.

The captain was now sitting in the helm seat, his feet up on the dash, waiting to be told when to start the engines.

"Can you catch that boat?" Cedric asked the man.

"What boat?"

He handed the binoculars to the captain. "Over there," he said, pointing just a little north of due west. "That fishing boat."

The captain studied the other boat for a moment, then put the glasses down. "Nope," he said. "Probly not. I know I can outdistance him, but a boat like that'll run a good five or ten knots faster than my top speed."

As if to prove the point, Cedric heard the other boat's engine rev. When he looked again, the guy had pulled in his lines and was heading straight away from them. In seconds, it was up on plane, plowing through the light chop effortlessly.

The swimmers and the two divers arrived at the transom at about the same time. While the divers got out of their gear, the other two men hauled the last of the recovered items aboard.

"Let's get out of here," Cedric ordered.

"Hey!" the captain yelled down to the men in the cockpit. "One of you guys wanna get the anchor?"

Minutes later, the dive boat started moving toward the north, gathering speed and rising out of the water. Cedric looked at the instruments. They were going twenty-five miles per hour, or knots; he wasn't sure what the difference was. They'd be at least five miles away when the explosives went off.

They'd covered a good two or three miles, when one of the divers climbed up to the fly bridge. "That other boat's heading back," he said.

Cedric retrieved the binoculars and looked back, trying to steady himself. The guy was right. Though only the top of the fishing boat was visible, it was moving directly toward where the wreck was.

"He'll soon wish he hadn't," Cedric said with a malicious grin. With any luck, he might be able to tell Ballinger that he'd killed two birds with one stone.

"Slow down," Cedric told the captain, trying to steady himself. "Is this the most powerful binoculars you got?"

CHAPTER FOURTEEN

My feet felt light as I walked out onto the board-walk. I kept telling myself that it was stupid and wrong, but Savannah's smile lit something inside me. A long-dead dream of slipping away to some island paradise, a beautiful woman at my side. One who appreciated a quiet anchorage and deserted beaches.

I was comfortable with Devon and she was fun to be with. Her only flaw, at least in my mind, was that she just wasn't all that crazy about boating. Living on an island, a boat is kind of necessary.

Savannah's boat was pretty easy to recognize. Rusty had told me it was a big Grand Banks trawler. *Sea Biscuit* was a regal-looking yacht, a good forty feet in length, with a large salon amidships and lower houses extending fore and aft, which I assumed were the staterooms. The large fly bridge was completely covered from the sun by a blue Bimini top, with roll down plastic windows to protect the occupants from wind or spray. They were all rolled up. The aft house had a small dinghy on the roof, with a mast and hoist next to the steps to the fly bridge, for lowering and retrieving it. The dinghy was covered with the same blue canvas as the Bimini. The decks were teak and looked immaculate.

The rails were polished wood, with a netting below it. That didn't make sense, as Savannah's daughter was easily tall enough to climb over the rails. Maybe she'd put them on when the girl was a toddler, and just neglected to remove them.

A low rumble told me I wasn't alone. Looking toward the bow, I saw a large black and brown dog with a bobbed tail walking along the side deck. A Rottweiler. The dog stopped at the steps to the roof of the aft cabin, its lips curled back just enough to display large canine teeth.

I continued down the dock, walking backward.

Aboard *Cazador*, I started the engine and looked back at Savannah's boat. A large dog for protection wasn't unusual for a woman with a child, living alone in a house in the suburbs, but a woman and child living alone on a boat was a little unusual. I don't know why it struck me as odd that they'd have a guard dog aboard.

I tossed off the lines and used the bow thruster to turn the boat away from the dock. Minutes later, I pushed the throttle forward as I left the confines of the marina. Once on plane, I followed the channel west about halfway to Dredgers Key, then turned northwest, crossing the three-foot deep flats toward Bluefish Channel and the open waters of the Gulf, just beyond.

Once I was through the channel, I turned northeast, headed for home. The sun was high overhead, and Kim would need to get back to the *Anchor* soon, so she could make the long drive back to Gainesville.

For the next hour, I kept the northern most islands of the backcountry a mile off the starboard side, running in twenty feet of water. It was a beautiful day, with a cloudless sky overhead, and the temperature was barely in the seventies. Not cold, but I'd worn a long-sleeved work shirt against the wind. The low rumble of the diesel engine under the console numbed my brain.

My mind kept drifting to Savannah. She'd dressed up to go see her sister one last time and arrange for her body to be shipped home. I felt bad for her that she had to do that alone, and cursed the ex for apparently not following through with his desire to work through their problems. She needed someone right now.

Forcing my mind back to the problem at hand, I thought again of any reason Brady would have for not turning over the head to the morgue. Marty wasn't the kind of kid that rubbed people the wrong way. He was an honest and forthright young man, who sometimes wore his heart on his sleeve. I couldn't think of how someone might hold a grudge against him, especially one of his superiors.

The wreck's not far out of the way, I thought. I could just swing a little farther to the north once I reached Snipe Keys and I'd be able to see the spot, and certainly see the Coast Guard boats. Snipe Keys were easy to spot, being much larger and sitting farther north than the surrounding islands. It would only add thirty minutes to my route back to my island.

I turned slightly north as I neared Snipe Point, plotting a rough course in my head. I turned on the radar and it took a moment for the unit to warm up. When the image appeared, it swept the area around *Cazador*, showing the islands of the backcountry falling away to the south. Two green echoes marked two boats.

One was closer and headed south. Scanning the horizon to the north, I spotted the motor yacht headed in my general direction at trawler speed.

The second echo was farther away. I zoomed the radar out and could tell from the echo's relationship to islands I knew that it was pretty close to where Marty and I dove the wreck.

The Coast Guard had found it. With any luck, they'd find more evidence and maybe have the tools to get that boiler thing unbolted from inside the hold.

I was about to turn and make a beeline for home, but changed my mind. In for a dime, in for a dollar. The wreck site was six miles away and I'd be able to see the Coast Guard boat in just a few minutes.

At three miles, I could see the upper half of the boat. But it didn't have the usual diagonal red mark of Coast Guard vessels. It looked like a dive boat. I slowed to about ten knots, bringing *Cazador* down off plane, and got my binoculars out.

It was a dive boat. An old Silverton express that had been neglected for years, perhaps decades. There seemed to be one man on the bridge and two in the cockpit. All three looked as though they were waiting on something. I needed to get closer. The old boat looked vaguely familiar, but beat-up express cruisers lay all over the boatyards and anchorages of the Keys, victims of the tourist business and hundreds of thousands of anglers. Those boats are the reason I charter so little. I'd hate for the *Revenge* to look like them. The eye becomes numb to them.

I brought up the saved waypoint on the GPS. Both it and the radar showed exactly the same distance and heading to the boat I was looking at. They were on the new wreck site.

Going up to the bow, I retrieved my go-bag. Some weeks ago, I'd seen an ad on TV while celebrating the Marine Corps birthday with Rusty at the *Anchor*. The commercial was for a pair of magnifying eyeglasses. They were only two-power magnification, but when stalking bonefish on the flats, any advantage in eyesight was good. They looked goofy as hell, but bonefish don't care what a fisherman looks like.

I took them out and placed them on the console. Just in case, I put two teaser lines in the water, attached the lines to the clips on the outriggers and moved them out. If anyone looked, I'd just be a guy trolling for dinner.

Moving back to the helm, I set a course that would take me past the dive boat, within a mile of it. I put on the magnifying glasses and looked at the other boat. Though I was still three miles away, I could just make out the man on the bridge. He was scanning the horizon.

Slowing *Cazador*, the engine quieted. I didn't want to alert the men on the boat to my presence any sooner than necessary. It was a calm, clear day, and if they had radar on and looked at it, there was no way I could hide. *Cazador* was smaller, with a top that matched the color of the water. I doubted they'd be able to see me until I was closer.

I set the autopilot and went behind the console, watching aft like a solo fisherman would do. Every now and then, I'd turn and look forward, stealing a glance at the other boat.

Nearly abreast of the boat, I glanced over and saw the man on the bridge watching me through binoculars. Just from the way he stood, I sensed that he wasn't very much at home on the water. He was a smallish man, with shaggy brown hair and a sparse stubble on his face. Two divers surfaced, and the captain looked down at them from the bridge.

Once I was slightly past the other boat, I could chance a longer look as they fell astern. One of the guys in the water was handing a gray box up to another man on the swim platform. The captain climbed down and took the box, disappearing into the boat's cabin. A few minutes later, he returned with another man that I hadn't seen. There were six onboard.

The captain and the new man climbed up to the bridge and the first man watched me again, then pointed in my direction, handing the binoculars to the other man, now sitting at the helm. The man at the helm looked at me and I quickly looked away. He looked much more at home on the bridge than the other guy. And I could swear I'd seen him before.

The jig was up. They'd taken way more interest in my presence than a typical dive operator would. I put the glasses on the seat, then brought in the lines and outriggers.

I turned due west and mashed the throttle. The engine roared and *El Cazador* climbed on top of the water, speeding away and quickly reaching thirty knots.

The radar showed the other boat beginning to move, so I slowed to see which way they'd go. I wasn't worried about them chasing after me. Most dive boats can barely reach planing speed, some maybe twenty-five or thirty knots, unlike the *Revenge*, which could reach fifty. But the *Revenge* was primarily a fishing boat, and charter customers liked a boat with enough speed that their time isn't wasted on getting out to the Gulf Stream. This dive boat wasn't a newer model, nor had it looked like it was as well cared for as it should have been.

The dive boat moved away to the north. I slowed and then brought *El Cazador* to a dead stop. The dive boat's echo on my radar showed it moving almost due north at probably twenty knots.

Turning around, I headed straight for the wreck site at low speed. The other boat continued to speed away. I set the autopilot and quickly got a tank from the rack and my gear from the forward dry storage. Carrying it all to the stern, I put my dive gear together. If they continued north, I wanted to drop down and see what they'd been doing.

My tank wasn't full. Nor were any of the others onboard. They hadn't been refilled since Friday night. I inwardly slapped myself. I always fill tanks when I get back, or on the way back, if I'm on the *Revenge*. But it had been nearly dawn when we'd returned home from the Friday night dive, and we were all exhausted.

The tank I grabbed had a little over fifteen hundred pounds of air. I could manage my breathing and allow about fifteen minutes at forty feet, but that would leave the tank almost empty.

Laying the rig on its side by the transom with my fins, I pulled my mask over my head and let it hang below my chin. One less thing to do once I dropped anchor. I went back to the helm and throttled up slightly, still a mile from the waypoint on the GPS. The other boat was nearly out of sight; the radar showed it was three miles away. If they turned back, I'd have only six or seven minutes.

But I wanted to see what those men were doing.

The waypoint was coming up, so I slowed. Checking the radar, I saw that the other boat had also slowed, but was still headed north nearly four miles away. That was better. Even if they started to turn around at the very moment I hit the water, I would still be able to stay down till I'd sucked the tank dry, leaving me about a minute to get aboard and get out of there. I'd hear them if they turned around, so I wasn't too worried about that.

When I reached the spot, I saw the wreck on the depth finder. I turned into the current, waited until I was more than a hundred feet past the wreck, then killed the engine. I went quickly to the bow and dropped the hook, letting out a hundred and twenty feet of rode.

I took one last look at the radar. The other boat had slowed to a crawl, just shy of five miles due north of me. I picked up the tank and lifted it over my head, letting it slide down my back, as my arms moved through the shoulder straps of the BC. I quickly secured it, put my fins on, and swung my feet over the transom, adjusting my mask. I purged the second stage, put it in my mouth, took a breath, and stepped into the sea.

Below the surface, I started kicking for the bottom, the wreck clearly visible below and just forward of *Cazador*. Immediately, I could tell that the divers had at least untangled the nets from the boat. I swam straight to the starboard side of the work deck.

Coming down next to where I knew the gaping hole was in the side, I peered into the gloom. The cylinder was missing. I breathed slow, listening to the sound of the other boat. It was barely audible, which told me they were still a good distance away. The sand that had accumulated in the bottom of the hold had been pushed around, as if the divers had searched through it for something.

I went up and over the starboard rail, or what was left of it. Fish had already staked claim to the boat, hiding among the wreckage. I stuck my head inside the pilothouse. It was a mess, but the mess was wrong. An explosion will knock stuff off shelves, and the cabin had been partially destroyed, but there was more boating detritus than there should be. Dock lines, fishing reels, small fenders, and other junk floated, or lay on the deck. These were things usually stored in a closet or under a bench.

The watch bunk's mattress was lying on the deck, under some of the gear, and the storage bin below the berth was open. I looked inside and saw that it had been fitted with a false bottom, which was lying off to the side. I tilted the panel out of the way to look inside.

All boats have hiding places, some better than others. This one was done well. The handle to lift the false bottom out looked like melted plastic attached to the bottom of the storage bin under the bunk. Finding junk there would be normal, so anyone searching randomly probably wouldn't attempt to pry the melted thing off after digging through apparent years of junk.

The hiding place was empty, but whoever had lifted out the false bottom had just dropped it to the side, without turning it over. That told me they knew exactly where to look and had taken whatever was there. My elbow bumped the false bottom and it slid off the berth, turning over slowly. There was a small package duct taped to the underside of the panel. Yanking it free, I stuck it in the cargo pocket of my shorts and went to the aft part of the pilothouse where a deck hatch lay open.

I didn't have a dive light, but enough light spilled into the engine room when I moved the hatch, that I felt comfortable probing further. It was a dogged hatch and the dogs were loose. That doesn't happen in an explosion. I paused for a moment, listening. The sound of the other boat was gone. It had continued north.

Arching my body, I kicked down into the engine room. The overhead was only about five feet above the cluttered lower deck. On the surface, that'd be a head-knocker for me at six-three, but diving, there was plenty of horizontal room.

Noticing a large canvas pouch stuffed into the bilge behind the engine and transmission, I swam toward it to investigate. It looked like the same kind of heavy green canvas that my sea bag was made of. And it was totally out of place, stuffed in the bilge. The satchel was square, about a foot each way. I felt a tingle on the back of my neck.

There was a clasp on the top of the bag, so I opened it. I instantly knew what I was looking at, and I knew that I was way up the creek and no paddle in sight. The timer on the display of the explosive charge said I was going to be blown to bits in fifty-four seconds. No time to disarm it, and I didn't have any tools, anyway. I was going to need most of that time to get to the surface.

The concussive effects from an underwater explosion are compounded immensely compared to the same blast on land. Air compresses, water doesn't. I grabbed the satchel and swam hard for the hatch. If I was underwater when this thing blew, the concussive effect would at the very least knock me unconscious and I would drown when the air in my tank ran out. At worst, the concussion would stop my heart. Not that drowning is any better.

Exiting the pilothouse, I swam with the current until I was well clear of the wreck. There I dropped the satchel, part of my mind noting that I had twenty seconds.

When I released it, I started kicking toward the surface. In the excitement of finding the IED, I'd neglected to manage my breathing and when I took another breath, it was with a lot of effort. Experience told me I had one, maybe two more breaths at this depth. Three if I exhaled slowly on the way up. The clock in my head told me I had ten seconds.

I could see *Cazador* above me, the sun reflecting off the surface like sparkling diamonds. Though it risked an embolism, I kicked as hard as I could to get to the surface in time.

I felt the shock wave at the instant I heard the blast. I was only two more kicks from the surface. The concussion of the blast pushed my upper body out of the water. I hit the surface ten feet from the swim platform and slowly sank back down, stunned, and unable to move, ears ringing.

As I slowly descended back toward the bottom, I thought it ironic that a bunch of bloated fish were now rising slowly toward the sunlight. My last conscious thought was that their swim bladders had been ruptured.

CHAPTER FIFTEEN

By the time Cedric got back to Fort Myers on the dive boat, the sun was gone from the sky. Red and pink clouds took its place, but the colors were quickly fading.

Cedric carried the box to his car, nervous at the number of people still milling around the marina. He opened the trunk and placed it inside before taking his phone out of his pocket. Scrolling through his short contact list, Cedric stabbed a listing.

"Mission accomplished," he said, when Ballinger answered.

"Did you get everything?"

"Everything we could find, including the box and a bonus."

Ballinger paused for a second. "Bonus?"

"Remember that hunter boat?" Cedric asked.

"We'll take care of that in the morning."

"No need," Cedric said. "The same boat was out there just before we left. The guy dove on the wreck, after we left."

"Was the last package delivered?" Ballinger asked.

Cedric hadn't seen it, but he did see the geyser shoot up behind the guy's fishing boat. They'd been too far away to see anything more than the roof of the boat. But he knew from the size of the explosive that it would have killed anything close to the wreck.

"He was still in the water when it was delivered," Cedric said. "I saw the aftermath and the boat was still there. It didn't leave. We waited fifteen minutes."

"You should have gone back and taken care of the boat."

"Couldn't," Cedric said. "A private yacht must have seen it too; they were headed toward the guy's boat, so we got the hell away."

There was a pause, so Cedric got in the car and closed the door. He knew a little about explosives and felt pretty certain that if the man on the fishing boat had still been in the water, he wouldn't have survived.

"Couldn't be helped," Ballinger said. "Another accident at sea. How soon can you pick up some party favors? I'm having out of town guests aboard tonight."

"Three hours for me to get back to the city," Cedric replied. "Then an hour. I can be there before eleven."

"See that you do," Ballinger replied. "That's when things will get into full swing. And plan to stay this time. I have someone I want you to meet."

Cedric ended the call and started the car. Before leaving Fort Myers, he filled up with gas at the ramp to I-75. The drive across the state was without incident, and Cedric stopped at his apartment in Opa-Locka to get cleaned up.

After showering and dressing, Cedric went to his closet and kneeled to open the small safe he'd mounted to the floor with heavy anchor screws. Cedric kept Ballinger's stash in his apartment; one of the many risks he took for the man. Removing several small bags, he stuck them in his coat pocket, locked the safe, and left.

The drive to the gated island community of Sunset Islands in Miami Beach took nearly as long as crossing the whole state, but Cedric arrived well before the appointed time.

He parked in front of one of the garages, far from the other cars, and got out. Knowing better than to waste time ringing the bell, Cedric walked around the side of the house, following a stone path to a gate. Crossing the backyard, Cedric heard party sounds—talking, music, and women laughing—as he walked toward the short pier and the big boat docked there.

"He's waiting," a big bald man said, as Cedric approached the foot of the pier.

"Everything okay?" Cedric asked Christian, Ballinger's sometimes-overzealous head of security.

"Peachy," the big man sneered. "Cowboys are only up by six."

Cedric noticed the wire going up from the man's collar to his ear and nodded. "The spread's thirteen. Not playing well?"

"Defensive struggle on both sides," Christian said, pushing the gate open. "Giants just kicked a field goal and the Cowboys have the ball with just five minutes left on the clock. Giants' defense is killing Romo; sacked his ass for a safety a few minutes ago."

"They'll cover the spread," Cedric said, walking past the man.

He continued out onto the short pier, then along the dock to the back of Ballinger's yacht. Another security man stood at the steps.

"The Cowboys ain't gonna pull it out," Phil said. "Hope you got the cash, man. 'Cause Christian don't take IOUs."

Cedric nodded at the man. Phil was even bigger than Christian. "I ain't worried. They'll score."

Mounting the steps, Cedric stepped lightly down into the finely appointed cockpit. Though there was ample seating, it seemed all the guests were inside. He slid the glass door open and stepped in.

Ballinger was at the far end of the big room, talking to two men. He pointed to five women who sat tightly together on the long couch, clustered around a glass-topped table. Any one of them could have jumped from the pages of Playboy. Cedric liked that Mister Ballinger always had a higher ratio of women at his little parties.

Cedric smiled at the women as they all looked up in unison, like little baby birds waiting to be fed. They took one look at him and dismissed him completely. Until he reached into his pocket and dropped one of the little bags of coke on the table, along with a little pill bottle, containing ecstasy.

"The candy man's here, bitches," Cedric said, leaning over the table with a twisted grin. "Time to party."

CHAPTER SIXTEEN

Rising from his bed, Rusty showered and dressed quickly. Fifteen minutes into his workday, he was crossing the yard, ready to start another day at his little hole-in-the-wall bar and grill. It'd been a long time since he'd had three back-to-back days like the past weekend. The bar and restaurant did okay through the week with the local clientele, and there were a handful more people on the weekends, but not much more. Over the years, he'd been able to renovate and expand, but the *Rusty Anchor* held firmly to its Conch roots. The closing of *Dockside* brought in quite a few more locals, those who split their time in more than one joint. It also brought a heavy dose of tourist dollars.

He and Eric had settled on an open-ended agreement, where Eric would play four nights a week, Thursday through Sunday. They'd learned more about the closing, and it didn't look like *Dockside* would be reopening anytime soon. And definitely not without a big outlay of cash.

Even with the recent success and the possibility that it might continue for some months, he felt a little melancholy lately. Julie had been gone for a while and Rusty was lonely, though he'd never admit it to anyone. He had the bar, and his friends were always around, but he missed having someone to look after.

The wind shifted slightly, and he heard subdued voices from out back. As he unlocked the front door to the bar area, the breeze brought the scent of Rufus's cooking to his nostrils. Rufus opened the kitchen early. The fishing guides would be heading out as soon as the sun was up, and their clients arrived. Then a few liveaboards staying at his dock would replace the guides at the outdoor grill, plus a few folks who stopped by on their way to work. Rufus's antics and conversation were a big reason for the breakfast bunch.

Walking inside, Rusty turned on the lights. He went behind the bar and switched on the VHF and NOAA weather radios. A speaker out on the deck was connected to the weather broadcast and the monotone mechanical voice, who Rusty called Noah, began informing the guides what they were in for, up and down the island chain. Noah was a comforting sound to folks who worked or lived on the water.

He went out the back door, onto the deck, and took a seat at the first stool, nodding at Dink and The Other Jack, two guides who kept their skiffs at the *Anchor*.

Rufus put a large mug in front of him and filled it with dark-brewed coffee. Rusty thanked him with a nod and took a sip.

"When yuh gwon get yuh a woman?" the old Jamaican asked.

"Why?" Rusty asked. "You know someone dumb and blind enough?"

"Don sell yuhself short, Mistuh Rusty. Yuh a good man and dem are hard to find. You want di usual?"

Rusty nodded and Rufus turned back to his grill.

"Sounds like it's gonna be a pretty good day out there," The Other Jack said. His real name was Jack Clark, but since there used to be another guide in Marathon named Jack, everyone took to calling him The Other Jack. The first Jack was long gone, back to the mainland, but the name hung on.

"Permit still running?" Rusty asked.

"Probably a few good weeks left," Dink replied. "After Christmas things'll slow down."

The popping sound that preceded a broadcast on the VHF cut in on Noah. "*M/V Sea Biscuit* hailing *Rusty Anchor*."

"Bring it in for me, Rufus?" Rusty asked, as he got up from the stool. Rufus waved a hand in the air and Rusty went inside.

He knew the boat, and he knew the woman calling. What he didn't know was why she'd be contacting him.

"*Sea Biscuit* to *Rusty Anchor*," she hailed again. "Are you still monitoring seventy-two?"

Rusty picked up the microphone and answered. "*Rusty Anchor* to *Sea Biscuit*. This who I think it is?"

"Yes, it is, Rusty," Savannah replied. "All the mooring balls are full in the harbor. I heard you might have some room."

Rusty looked out the window toward the docks. There was only one spot available on the inboard side of the canal. It was just in front of Eric's and Kim's boat, *Rainbow Connection*. Going by the dock cleats he'd had installed at ten-foot intervals along the concrete dock, he knew there was only fifty feet of room.

"I have fifty feet clear on the inboard side, *Sea Biscuit*," he said into the mic. "The other side is wide open. What's your overall length?"

"Forty-two feet," Savannah replied. "Can I have the inboard slip for a day, maybe two?"

"If you can get it in there," he said. "I'll come down to the dock and give you a hand."

"Take your time," Savannah said. "I'm just leaving Sister Creek."

"I'll keep an eye out for you," he said. "*Rusty Anchor* out."

Rufus brought his breakfast in, placing it on the bar. "I recognize dat voice," he said.

"Yeah, me too," Rusty said, sliding the plate of eggs and Jamaican sausage toward him. "No idea what she's wanting here."

Rufus grinned and turned away. "Only di gods know what be in di hearts of women."

"Ain't that the truth," Rusty said, digging in.

"Sometimes, dey tell me things."

Rusty looked at his chef. Rufus was an odd one, that was for sure. From things he'd said, and stories he'd told, Rusty knew he had to be in his early seventies, but you'd never know it to look at him. He kept mostly to himself when he wasn't working, spending most of his time sitting in his little shack on the back of the property, looking out over the ocean, or reading.

"They tell you anything about her?" Rusty asked.

"Only dat I will know when I see."

Rusty shook his head, as Rufus started toward the back door.

"Hey," he called after him, "I got an email this morning. Your new oven has shipped and should arrive by Thursday."

"I will tell di gas mon to bring me anuduh bottle and hose for it."

After eating, Rusty deposited his plate in the big bin. Jimmy would be coming in after breakfast to wash dishes for a few hours. If the weather was bad, there'd be a line of guides who would take the job for a few extra dollars. Rusty never had trouble finding people things to do when their regular jobs got slow.

He strolled down to the docks, again thinking of his daughter. She and Deuce only lived about forty miles up island, but with both their schedules, they hadn't seen each other in over a month.

Looking down the long canal, Rusty saw the big trawler idling toward him. He could tell by the sound that it was a single screw. Not much of a problem, if she was good at the controls.

To his surprise, Rusty saw the young girl sitting at the helm on the boat's fly bridge. Then he noticed that the side hatch was open, and Savannah was standing at the lower helm. She brought the boat to a stop next to the vacant spot where Rusty was standing. Everyone had different methods of docking, depending on engines and hull design, so Rusty just waited to see how he could help her.

She went forward and picked up a coiled bow line and tossed it to him, telling him it was a spring line. Rusty caught it and moved to his left, looping it twice over a cleat and holding the bitter end.

"Okay, Flo," Savannah called to the girl. "Idle speed forward, left full rudder."

Amazed, Rusty watched the little girl as she followed her mother's instructions. With the spring line looped on the cleat at about the right length and near the stern of the boat, Rusty held it firmly, as the boat's prop wash pushed the stern sideways toward him. He allowed a couple of feet of slack, seeing the stern coming too close to the *Rainbow Connection* and the big trawler moved forward to clear it.

"Bring the wheel amidships," Savannah called up, readying another dock line.

The girl did as she was instructed, and the bow started to slowly move toward the dock. Seeing that it was positioned properly, Rusty tied the spring line off, and then seeing another dock line on the gunwale, coiled and ready, he tied it off, as well.

Catching a third line from Savannah, Rusty moved to his right and helped pull the bow in to the dock. He quickly secured the line and moved a small set of fiberglass steps into place by the rail.

Without being told, the girl at the helm shifted to neutral and then shut off the engine.

"Been a while," Rusty said, as Savannah handed him a heavy electrical cable. He plugged it into the pedestal, not even bothering to ask if she had all the breakers turned off. After seeing their docking maneuver, he didn't need to.

"I guess it has," Savannah said, stepping down beside him and giving him a quick hug.

The little girl climbed down from the fly bridge and came over to the rail followed by a Rottweiler that very nearly outweighed the both of them. Savannah helped the girl down, but the dog stayed put.

"This is my daughter, Flo," Savannah said. "Flo, this is the man I told you about, Mister Thurman."

Rusty knelt in front of the girl. "You're quite the boat pilot."

"Thank you," Flo said. "You're the man who helped my mom in a hurricane?"

Rusty laughed. "She'd likely have been fine on her own. But yeah, we rode out the storm together."

"Is that real?" she asked, pointing at Rusty's thick red beard.

"Give it a tug," he said, thrusting his chin out and pointing a finger at his beard. "See for yourself."

When she did, Rusty winced. "I'm sorry if I hurt you," she said.

Rusty laughed and stood up. "I was just fooling with you, Flo."

The girl smiled.

"She parked that big ole Grand Banks better than I've seen a few seasoned skippers do in much smaller boats."

"She grew up on it," Savannah said. "She's only spent a little over twenty nights ashore her whole life. Have you talked to Jesse this morning?"

Rusty eyed her suspiciously. His friend valued his privacy, and Rusty valued Jesse's friendship above just about anything else. He knew what had happened between the two of them so many years ago. He knew that Jesse shouldn't see her, but he also knew that the man would do whatever he wanted.

In this case, Rusty didn't have to lie. "Talked to him on the phone yesterday, about noon."

"That was about the time Flo and I ran into him at Sunset Marina."

"I see," Rusty said, now understanding why Jesse had acted so strangely on the phone. "I bet y'all are hungry;

come on in and I'll have Rufus fix you up with some hot food."

"Can I have pancakes, Mommy?" the girl asked.

"You'll have to ask Mister Rufus," Savannah replied, taking Flo's hand. "Do you remember me telling you about him?"

"Uh huh," Flo replied, as they walked around the side of the bar.

"I really need to reach Jesse," Savannah said. "I was in Key West yesterday to arrange transportation for my sister's body."

"I heard," Rusty said. "Really sorry for your loss. It must be hard."

Leading the way inside, Rusty pulled two chairs out for them at a table by the window. From there, Savannah could easily see her boat.

"Thanks," she said, sitting down with her daughter. "The coroner won't release her yet. And he wouldn't tell me anything that happened, saying it was an ongoing investigation."

"Let me take your order out to Rufus," Rusty said. "Then we can talk about it. Is your dog okay on the boat?"

"Woden?" she said, looking out to her boat. "Yes, he'll come ashore if he has to, but he's been trained to stay on the boat."

Rusty looked out the window. The dog was sitting on the side deck, right at the boarding steps, head up and vigilant. There wasn't any chance that someone would attempt to board that yacht.

"Woden, huh? The old German god of war?"

"It fits his temperament," Savannah said.

"Okay, so pancakes for the pilot," Rusty said. "What can I get for you, Captain?"

"Just a couple of breakfast burritos and coffee."

"Gimme just a second," Rusty said, and went out the door to give Rufus their order.

Before going back in, Rusty looked through the window at Savannah and her daughter. Both were looking out toward open water, the same tranquil, far-away expression on their faces. He'd seen that look before.

"Food'll be up in a minute," he said, turning the third chair around and straddling it. He smiled at Flo. "Rufus said he's gonna bring you a special treat."

"Can you call Jesse?" Savannah asked.

He could, and after yesterday's phone call, he did. A few times. Kim's car was still parked outside, and he'd been worried. But the calls all went to voicemail. This wasn't unusual where Jesse was concerned.

"I don't wanna seem insensitive," Rusty said, "but Jesse kinda likes—"

"His privacy," Savannah interrupted. "Yes, I know. But while I was with the coroner yesterday, I saw Jesse's name on one of the forms in the file the doctor had for Sharlee."

Rusty looked down at the table. Dink was right outside, and he'd been right there with Jesse and Carl, and had seen everything they saw. But if Savannah was to be told all the details, it'd have to come from Jesse. Even though their affair had been short and a long time ago, they had history that Dink didn't.

Rufus came through the door carrying a tray. He smiled at Savannah, and then looked at Flo. He stopped short for a second, then his smile broadened, as he placed the tray on an adjacent table.

"Yuh must be di little one dat drove dat big boat in here," he said. "Work like dat must make yuh hungry. Do yuh like coconut and papaya, Cap'n Flo?"

The corners of the girl's mouth practically met at the back of her head, she smiled so brightly. "My favorites! Are you Mister Rufus?"

"Yes, Miss," the old Jamaican said, serving the plates of food, then squatting to be at eye level with the girl. "I come from a beanie island a long boat ride from here."

"We've been to Jamaica," Flo said, digging into the pancakes.

"You have?" Rufus asked, rising from his squatting position effortlessly. "Den yuh and I should sit down some time and talk about dat." He turned to Savannah and smiled. "If yuh need anything at all, Cap'n Savannah, yuh just ask Rufus."

She smiled and thanked him.

After Rufus left, Savannah said, "We left Key West at sunset and ran on the outside for most of the night to get here. I really need to get some answers, Rusty. When I ran into Jesse there, we arranged to meet in Boot Key Harbor later today, but I can't wait. That's why I left there to come over here."

"Go ahead and eat," Rusty said, rising from the chair. "I'll try to call him again."

Going behind the bar, Rusty went into his office. There was a phone under the bar, but he didn't want Savannah or the girl to overhear. Her daughter was a dead ringer for Jesse, but aside from hair color, she looked a lot like her mom, too.

He tried the number twice, but both times it went to voicemail. Nothing new, but it was troublesome.

"No answer," he said, returning to the dining area, "but that's normal for him. I left him a message to call me, PDQ. I've heard bits and pieces about what happened. Is there anything I can tell you?"

Savannah looked at her daughter. "Why don't you go get Woden and take him for a walk down by the water."

The girl left and ran across the yard toward the dock. Halfway, she called to the dog. It immediately sprang to the dock and went running toward her. Together, they took off in the direction of the boat ramp, the dog bounding beside her like a pup.

"Guess you don't need to worry much with a dog like that on board," Rusty said.

"Woden is devoted to us," Savannah said. "What can you tell me about how Sharlee died?"

"A boat accident," Rusty lied. "Least that's what everyone's guessing. She was on a shrimp boat out of the Fort Myers area, when it exploded and sank."

"On a shrimp boat?" Savannah asked, genuinely perplexed. "I'm sorry, I haven't talked to Sharlee in a long time. She'd, um, distanced herself some years ago. But a working shrimp boat is way out of character for her."

Rusty looked out toward the boat ramp. Flo was picking up broken shells and throwing them in the water. The dog sat nearby, head up and constantly looking around.

"She's a beautiful girl," Rusty said. "Reminds me a lot of my own daughter when she was little. You and her daddy must be proud."

He looked back toward Savannah and was met with an honest, level gaze. "I wouldn't really know about how my ex feels. I haven't seen or talked to him since before Florence was born."

Her eyes changed, a dull look covering them. It quickly disappeared, but not before Rusty saw pain there.

"You mean he doesn't know?" he asked, and immediately back pedaled. "Sorry, none of my business."

"When I went back," Savannah said, "I thought he was going to change. I wanted him to change. It lasted a week, then he got worse, became verbally abusive. So I kicked his ass to the curb. He went crawling back to his family in Jersey."

A week? Rusty thought. That wasn't a lot of time.

"When is Flo's birthday, Savannah?"

She looked at Rusty for a moment, then sighed. "She turned eight last July."

"July, huh?"

"I never told Derrick I was pregnant," she said. "We were already legally separated, even before I came down here. And I'd already kicked him out by the time I learned I was pregnant. When he left, my dad hired a lawyer, a good one. We had a pre-nup, so he knew he wasn't getting anything and signed the divorce papers. It included language where he gave up custody of anything he left behind. Dad gave me *Sea Biscuit* and told me if I stayed away from Derrick for a year, he'd do a complete refit, pulpit to transom. So I did. I moved onto the boat and went to Charleston. That's where Flo was born."

"And he still has no idea?"

Savannah looked deep into Rusty's eyes, as if searching for something. "He hit me, Rusty. And forced himself on me. Flo doesn't have a father."

Rusty wrung his hands, not wanting to ask the obvious question.

"You're wondering if Jesse might be Flo's father," she said.

"I'm just a dumb ole Conch," he replied, "but I can do math."

"I don't know, Rusty. And I really don't want to know."

"You don't?" he asked.

Savannah fidgeted in her seat, then looked out at Flo playing with the dog. "Derrick wasn't daddy material. Never was and never would have been. I don't acknowledge him as Flo's father, nor do I need him as the father. I just don't want to know."

"And Jesse?"

Savannah looked at him, again searching his eyes. "I'd never want to put the burden of that possibility on him."

"There are ways you can find out."

"I know," she said, sighing once more. "But I couldn't ask him to do that. Besides, what kind of dad would he be?"

Rusty grinned, noticing Marty's pickup pulling into the lot and parking next to Kim's car. That was one of the reasons he'd tried to call Jesse; to find out why Kim hadn't left that afternoon.

"Well," he said, "you could ask one of his daughters."

CHAPTER SEVENTEEN

"A quick bite," Kim said, as she and Marty got out of his truck, "but I need to get back early. I don't have any classes today, but I have a lot of studying to do before tomorrow."

Together, they walked into the *Rusty Anchor*. It was nearly empty, except for Rusty, who was sitting at a window table with a blond woman. He waved them over and stood.

"Hey, Kim," he said. "Shouldn't you be back in Gainesville already?"

"No class today, Uncle Rusty" she said. "Dad was gone most of the day yesterday, so I had Marty bring me back to my car."

"I'd like y'all to meet an old friend," he said. "This is Savannah Richmond. Savannah, meet Kim McDermitt and Marty Phillips."

Savannah stood and shook hands with them. Kim felt some strange connection when she took the woman's hand.

"We were trying to get ahold of your dad," Rusty said, waving a hand at the next table. "Have a seat. I'll let Rufus know you're here."

The two sat down, adjusting their chairs to include Savannah.

"You're Jesse's daughter?" she asked. "I knew him a long time ago. I remember he'd mentioned that he had two daughters, but hadn't seen them in a long time."

"It's a long story," Kim said, deciding she liked the woman, "but I came down here looking for him a few years ago and met him basically for the first time."

"So you live here with your dad?"

"Every other weekend," Kim replied. "I go to college up in Gainesville, but I spent nearly a year living on his island and loved it."

"And you're also in college, Marty?"

"No, ma'am," he replied. "I'm a sheriff's deputy right here in the Middle Keys."

Rusty came back in and straddled the seat he'd left. "Your burritos will be up in just a minute, Kim. Savannah here knew your dad back when he first came down here after he retired."

"Richmond?" Marty said, recognition showing in his eyes. "From up in South Carolina?"

"Marty's a deputy," Rusty said. "He might be able to tell you more."

Kim caught the cautionary look Rusty gave Marty.

"You're investigating my sister's death?" Savannah asked.

"No, ma'am, not exactly. That is, it happened in international waters. We're a small department down here, so we help out the Coast Guard when we can and vice versa."

"So you wouldn't have any idea why my sister was on that boat?"

"No, ma'am, I surely wouldn't," Marty replied, earnestly. "But if I did, I wouldn't be able to talk about it while the investigation is still going on."

Savannah looked down at her hands for a moment. When she looked up, Kim could see the hurt. "Do you know how long the investigation might take?"

"Could be days, or months," he replied. "I'm guessing you're asking about how long before the ME releases the body?"

"Doctor Frederic said to check back with him on Wednesday."

"That sounds about right," Marty said. "I meant that the whole investigation might take months."

A little girl followed Rufus in, who carried another platter. He smiled at Kim. "Where yuh puttin' all dis food, Miss Kim?"

"Your cooking is hardly fattening," she replied, picking up one of the burritos and taking a bite. "Mmm—I don't know how you do it."

The girl stood next to Savannah, who introduced her to Kim and Marty. Rufus stepped back, crossed his arms, and seemed to be admiring the girls.

"What're you grinning about?" Rusty asked the old man.

"Di gods, dey like to play games sometimes," Rufus said, his wide, gap-toothed grin giving his ebony skin a darker hue. "I just admiring something I don see very much of. Dese three girls all have di same aura; pink and purple, but with a lot of di orange of passion."

"You're a mystic?" Savannah asked him.

"Nah," Rufus replied. "I just a cooker. But sometimes di gods whisper things to me. Most times I don know what it means they tell me." His grin grew wider. "Yuh have come a long way, Cap'n Savannah. But yuh have arrived at di place where di mother and child should be."

Taking the tray, Rufus turned and went back out to the kitchen. Rusty stared after him, wondering just what he'd been getting at, if he could actually *see* the connection that Rusty had always thought was there.

"Is he always like that?" Savannah asked.

Kim wiped her mouth. "It's hard to understand what Rufus is talking about, sometimes. You have to kinda think beyond the words."

"Where does your sister live?" Savannah asked.

"Just up in Miami," Kim replied. "She's married, with a little boy, so she doesn't get down here very often."

Savannah's eyes went wide. "Jesse's a grandfather?"

"Pappy," Kim corrected her. "That's what Fred calls dad."

"Fred is your nephew?"

"Alfredo Jesiah Maggio," Kim replied. "Named after both his grandfathers."

Savannah smiled. Kim thought she had a nice smile; the little lines at the corners of her eyes told her the woman smiled a lot.

"Jesse's real name is Jesiah?"

Kim laughed. "Don't tell him I told you. My great-grandparents on Dad's mother's side were Jewish and my grandparents wanted to honor the ancestry of both their parents in naming Dad. His middle name's Smedley. Guess where that came from."

"Hey now," Rusty said, as Savannah covered her mouth to hide a grin. "Smedley Butler is one of the Corps' greatest heroes and your great-grandpa served with him."

"I really have to run," Kim said. "Final exams start tomorrow, and I need to study."

Rusty stood as Kim rose and he gave her a hug. "Yeah, God forbid you get just a regular A in one of your classes."

CHAPTER EIGHTEEN

Waking slowly, I felt pain all over, and my ears were still ringing. By the angle of the sun through the window, I surmised that I'd slept for about eight hours. I slowly sat up in my bed, wincing from the effort and remembering the events of the day before.

After the explosion, I'd blacked out for a moment, but managed to reach the surface with the tank sucked dry.

I'd somehow managed to climb back aboard *El Cazador*, but the near brush had sapped me. I'd simply collapsed on the deck for quite a while, lucky to be alive. When I'd finally gotten to the helm, the radar showed the dive boat was a good ten miles away. I'd calculated that it'd take me an hour to catch them. And if I had, it would have been six against one. That wouldn't have been the first time I'd gone up against high odds, though. A glance at the fuel gauge had told me I could probably catch them, but wouldn't have had enough fuel to return. I'd kicked the tank with a bare foot out of frustration. That had only added to the pain I felt in every joint.

As I'd started to pull the anchor, I saw another boat approaching. I'd gotten the ground tackle up quick and motored toward them and away from the wreck site. I doubted they'd believed me, but I'd told them that my engine had backfired, before I pushed the throttle down and left them behind.

I didn't want to come straight home; Kim would have asked too many questions. So I'd gone to the only person I knew who had any experience with concussion injuries. He wasn't hard to find, but every ripple on the water jarred my body.

The whole Key West shrimp fleet worked together and anchored up together just a little over an hour west of the wreck site. Bob Talbot used to be a Navy Corpsman and had served with Marines in Afghanistan. I woke Doc up and he'd checked me out. Nothing broken and no rupture to either ear drum. It was nearly dark before I'd managed to get back to the island.

I dressed slowly, then walked out onto the deck surrounding three sides of my house. It was mid-morning. It was quiet. Finn was laying on the fixed pier in front of my house.

"Charlie took the kids to school," I heard Carl call out. I looked toward the island's interior. He was on the far side of the garden, cutting suckers off the tomato plants. "She said she was going to go into town to the Kmart to get some packing crates."

He started up the steps. "Damn, you look awful. What happened?"

I probably felt worse than I looked. My body felt like it had been used as a heavy bag in a boxing gym.

"Had a run in with those shrimpers yesterday," I replied, slowly sitting down at the table. "At least I think it was them."

"Are they still alive?"

The chuckle hurt, and I winced. "Coming back from dropping Devon off, I decided to head out and see what the Coasties were doing with the wreck. When I got close enough to see, divers were working the wreck, but they weren't Coast Guard."

Carl sat down, a concerned look on his face. "What'd they do? Wreck your boat?"

"They left as I got closer, so I waited until they were a good distance away and dove down to see what they'd been up to. They planted an explosive on the boat."

"Were you still in the water when it blew?"

"Right at the surface," I replied. "I had Doc Talbot check me out. He said I was just dinged up, nothing broken, and the ringing would probably go away in a day or two."

"Man, you could have been killed. Why didn't you go to the ER? I mean, I like Bob, hell he was my first mate, but he's not a real doctor."

"He was a Corpsman with a Marine combat infantry unit in Afghanistan, Carl. He's probably treated more blast injuries than every doctor in the Keys combined. I'll take his word. And I know he won't say anything."

"Which leads to my next question," he said. "You didn't contact the Coast Guard."

"That wasn't a question."

"No, I guess it wasn't. Here's a question; why the hell not?"

Carl rarely gets angry and I wasn't in any mood for it. "I don't like drug dealers in my backyard, Carl. Damned cops are more concerned about not hurting some panty-waisted drug addict's feelings and getting them help for their disease than they are about protecting innocent people from their filth."

He stood up, looking out over the deck to the south. "Someone's coming. Probably Jimmy and Angie."

Damn, I thought. I'd told them to come out today to get an idea of the day-to-day running of things.

"Sorry," I said, standing next to him. "I shouldn't've lashed out at you over what happened."

"Don't worry about it. I'd be pissed if someone blew me up, too."

"Can you handle this with them?" I asked, nodding toward the buzz of Angie's outboard to the south. "I have to go somewhere."

"Where?" he asked. "Never mind. I probably don't want to know."

"I just have to meet an old friend," I said.

I went down the steps quickly. Finn came bounding up to me, as I reached the door to the dock area.

"No, you stay here," I told him.

Finn cocked his head, arching his ears. He usually rode with me anywhere I went, so he was confused. I didn't need the distraction.

Within minutes, I had the big doors open and idling *El Cazador* out as Jimmy and Angie approached the channel from the south. They waited for me to come out.

"Where ya headed?" Jimmy asked.

"Got a last-minute charter," I lied. "An old friend, paying top dollar. Carl's gonna show you around."

I didn't wait for a reply. Pushing the throttle halfway, I turned northeast to go around Spanish Banks to Rocky Channel. The boat skimmed across the skinny water and I turned south in the channel, accelerating to thirty knots. It would have been better to take the Grady, but *El Cazador* needed fuel anyway.

Half an hour later, I was tied up to the fuel dock at *Burdines Waterfront*. It's a small marina at the west entrance to Boot Key Harbor. Once I'd paid for the fuel, I moved the boat to the day dock. Above it was a restaurant on stilts, with an outdoor dining deck. I took a table at the end, where I had a good view of the harbor.

When the waitress came out, I asked if it was too late for breakfast and she said that it wasn't. I gave her a large order. I wasn't all that hungry, but I knew I needed it.

Savannah didn't say she would *definitely* stop here, but I thought there was a good chance that she would. Wherever she was going from Key West, Marathon is a good jumping off point and nearly a full day in a slow trawler.

I ate slowly while I thought it out. I didn't go to the Coast Guard because I'd wanted to find these guys and crack their heads together myself. Going up to Fort Myers and just walking in blind wasn't something I'd normally do, but the thought had occurred to me. I tempered that notion with reason.

Savannah would have information. She might not know what it was, but there was a reason her sister had been on that shrimp boat. At least that's what I kept telling myself. When she'd looked back at me yesterday in Key West, it was just like the day we'd met.

From the vantage point of the deck, I could see a good portion of the harbor, and the approach to Sister Creek. I moved my eyes across the lines of boats tied to mooring balls in a highly regimented fashion. It looked as if every ball had a boat swinging from it. Savannah's trawler wasn't one of them.

She could be in one of the other marinas, tied up in a slip, but she'd said she wanted to leave on the evening tide. My instinct told me it was because she didn't like crowded places, so she probably planned to spend the night in a secluded anchorage near Key West. Moving at night when you don't have to is best avoided.

Running on the Atlantic side from there to here at trawler speed would take a good five or six hours. If she left before sunrise, she'd be here before noon.

While I waited, I took my phone out and scrolled through my contact list. Chyrel answered almost immediately.

"You want me to snoop the Coast Guard computers?" she said, instead of the usual *hello*.

"Are you practicing your mind reading?" I asked.

"It doesn't take a mind reader, Jesse. A boat blew up near your house. It was only a matter of time before you got curious. You're pretty see-thru about a lot of things."

Predictability can be a good thing. In nature, it's a great deterrent. I don't need a warning sign telling me that if I encounter a grizzly bear in the woods that I shouldn't poke it with a stick. The bear's reaction to such a provocation would be a lot like my own. Very predictable.

"Yeah," I replied. "I'm calling about the Coast Guard. Can you do some searches for me?"

"What do you wanna know?"

I thought about it a moment. All I had was suspicion and conjecture, but if anyone could connect Savannah's sister to the new shrimp fleet owner, it would be the ex-CIA computer analyst on the other end of my call.

"The guy who used to own the boat, sold it recently, as well as the rest of his fleet. The guy who bought them is a man named Eugene Ballinger. The boat's home port was Cape Coral, Florida." I paused for just a second, envisioning Chyrel grinning on the other end. "But your curiosity about my curiosity tells me you already know all that, though."

"Oooh, Now *I'm* getting predictable."

"Predictability isn't always a bad thing," I said. "It can save time."

"Ballinger is squeaky clean," she said. "He's a successful businessman with warehouses in Fort Myers, Tampa, and Cocoa. They manufacture and market a variety of industrial, commercial, and residential air fresheners, distributed world-wide."

"Do you know how long ago he bought those warehouses?"

"He's owned all three for five to eight years."

"What about any warehouses or facilities that he sold recently?"

"Sold?" she asked.

"The three that he has are on the coasts. But none are deep-water ports for worldwide shipping. A good business man would at least want a big warehouse near his shipping hubs."

"I'll check on that," Chyrel said. I could envision her grin fading. But only slightly and not for long.

"The dead woman on the boat was Charlotte Richmond, of Beaufort, South Carolina. I used to date her sister, a long time ago."

"Knew the first," she said. "Didn't know the last part, though. My condolences."

"I want to see if you can come up with any connection between Charlotte and this Ballinger guy. She was the daughter of Jackson Richmond, who owns a fleet of commercial fishing boats up in South Carolina."

"I'll see what I can find out," she replied. "It's a slow day. I was just about to run down to the café for coffee and donuts. I'll call you back when I find something. Um, one thing."

"Right now, it's pro bono," I said, anticipating the question. "There might be a payday at the end of it, there might not."

"I wonder if we're thinking the same kinda payday. You having history with the dead woman's sister and what all."

"The family is wealthy," I said. "If we can find out why she died, the parents might be generous."

"Uh huh."

I thanked her, put my phone on the table, and continued eating. The eggs were good and the bacon crunchy, but the sound it made echoed inside my head as I chewed.

When the food was gone, I asked the waitress to bring me more coffee. A moment later, she refilled my cup and presented me with the check. "Whenever you're ready," she said, and started to turn away.

"Wait," I said, digging into my wallet. The breakfast bill was just under twenty dollars. I handed her two twenties and said, "Keep the change. And can you leave the pot?"

She smiled and folded the bills, along with the cash register receipt into the pocket of her apron. "It'll get cold. But I have a thermos under the counter. I'll fill it for you."

Though there weren't any other people on the deck, I like to pay rent if I'm going to occupy a table for a while. It's only fair. And in my experience, people will usually respond in a favorable way when you treat them fair.

My phone vibrated on the table. I picked it up and saw that it was Rusty. I was about to answer it, but thought better of the idea. Rusty and I go way back. He probably knows me better than anyone, and he'd know I was up to something.

So I ignored the call. A moment later, he called again. I ignored that one, too. If it was important, he'd leave a message.

What am *I up to*, I thought. If Savannah came here, was I just going to motor out to her boat, thinking we could just pick up where we'd left off nine years ago? Was my only reason for being here out of curiosity over her sister's death and drug dealers being in my backyard?

Devon and I had a good thing. We didn't pretend to be anything we weren't. But was what we had everything there was?

My late wife Alex had been everything I wanted. Devon wasn't Alex. Nor was Savannah.

Did we only get one single shot at the so-called everything?

Another moment went by and my phone pinged the alert tone for a voicemail. I played the message. *Bro, call me when you get this. Savannah is here at the Anchor.*

Minutes later, I steered *El Cazador* past the remnants of the old bridge to Boot Key and turned south, bringing her up on top of the water. I rounded Sister Rock, then slowed as I neared the entrance to Rusty's channel. I could see Savannah's Grand Banks trawler docked just ahead.

After tying off, I was momentarily distracted when I saw Kim's car parked outside, Marty's pickup next to it. My heart skipped a beat. She should be back in Gainesville by now.

When I opened the door, I almost ran into Kim coming out. "I thought you left yesterday."

"Hey, Dad," she said, giving me a hug. I winced slightly. "Are you okay?"

"Just a little stiff in the joints," I said. "It sucks getting old. Why aren't you in Gainesville?"

"It's finals week, no class today. I was just about to leave, so I could study for tomorrow's exam."

I stepped back away from the door and she and Marty came outside. "Did you come back to the island last night?"

Marty stepped slightly away, looking off toward his pickup in the parking lot.

"No, Dad," Kim said. "I didn't stay on the island last night."

The realization hit me. The years that I'd missed as she and her sister were growing up were unrecoverable. Her sister, Eve had turned six, just a few days after my first wife left me, taking the girls with her. I'd been deployed to Panama. Kim had been just five months old. She was her own woman now and could make decisions on her own.

"Well, be careful, okay?" I said. "And kill it on the exams."

She kissed my cheek and Marty walked her over to her car. I turned and went inside. Rusty was sitting at a table in the corner with Savannah and her daughter.

As I approached, Rusty got to his feet. "Would it be okay if Flo showed me your boat?"

Savannah smiled up at him and nodded. After they left, I straddled the chair he'd vacated and watched them walk across the yard. The big Rottweiler trotted along between him and Florence.

"Your dog won't eat my friend, will it?"

"Woden wouldn't hurt anyone," Savannah replied. "Unless Flo or I told him to."

"I was over in Boot Key Harbor for the last hour," I said.

She smiled. "No place to moor there and the bottom gets my anchor locker all muddy. So I came here. Drove straight through the night." Her smile faded. "Do you know something about my sister's death? Because I saw your name on a report in the coroner's office."

"What happened with Charlotte?" I asked.

Savannah looked off toward the docks. "She had trouble, Jesse. I haven't seen her in a couple of years. She didn't even come to Dad's funeral."

"I didn't know he'd passed," I said. "I'm sorry."

When she looked at me again, I saw the same pain in her eyes that I'd seen yesterday.

"No way you could have known," she said. "It happened last year and it's not like we've been pen pals since Hurricane Irene." Her words were like a knife in the chest and it must have registered on my face. "I'm sorry," she said. "I shouldn't have said that."

"It's okay," I lied. "You're under a lot of stress."

Her eyes found mine. "I'm also sorry for the way I treated you, for lying about Derrick, and for sneaking off in the middle of the night."

"No apology needed," I said, "but thanks."

"Sharlee had started doing drugs the year before Dad died, mostly weed and coke."

Drugs, I thought. *Could that be the connection?*

"Why would she be on a shrimp boat?" I asked.

"I have no idea. But like I said, I haven't talked to her in some time. The last straw was three months ago. She withdrew a large sum of money from Mom's account without permission."

"Who's running your dad's business," I asked.

"Mom tried, but she was in over her head. I went home and together we made a pretty good go of it, but neither of us really wanted to do it. It wasn't the same without Dad. So we sold everything."

"Have you ever heard the name Eugene Ballinger?"

"No," she replied. "Did he have something to do with it?"

"He was the registered owner of the shrimp boat."

"How did she die?" Savannah asked. "Do you know? Did she suffer?"

Telling relatives about the horrible details of their loved ones' deaths has never been easy. Most don't ask and don't want to know. It was hard to tell with siblings; they wanted to know that their brother or sister had died valiantly. I decided that Savannah should be spared the truth. Call me a coward.

"She was killed in the explosion," I lied. "It happened near my island and I was one of the first ones there. Charlotte was already gone when I found her, but I don't think she suffered."

"I just met your daughter," she said, glancing toward the door Kim had exited through.

"She turned out pretty good," I said, thanking her in my mind for accepting my statement and changing the subject. "I didn't see her much when she was growing up. Time flew by and now she's a woman."

"She's doing well in college?"

I grinned. "You could say that. Four-point-oh average and planning to graduate a year early."

"She looks a lot like you," Savannah said. "Does your other daughter look like you, too?"

"Eve looks more like her mother."

"There's a whole side of you that I never imagined."

"You were barely here two weeks," I said, and immediately regretted it.

"I deserved that," she said. "What I did was wrong."

The front door opened and when I glanced over, I saw Devon standing there. She motioned for me to follow, then stepped back outside.

"Excuse me for just a minute," I said, starting to rise.

"Girlfriend?"

"Sheriff's detective," I replied. Why I didn't answer yes, I don't know. But I didn't.

Stepping out the door, Devon was waiting off to the side. "I tried to call you a couple of times yesterday," she said.

A black Crown Vic sat idling in the parking lot. Devon's usual partner, Joe Clark sat behind the wheel.

"I headed offshore after dropping you off," I said. "No signal. Is something wrong?"

"The Coast Guard never got an updated GPS location on the wreck. I reluctantly had to tell Lieutenant Morgan about Marty's report and the head."

"What'd Ben say?"

"It'll have to go to Internal Affairs," she replied. "I shouldn't be saying anything at all about it, least of all to you. Ben ordered me and Joe to conduct the initial investigation. Before IA gets it, he wants to know whether the missing evidence was Marty's dereliction for not getting

Sergeant Brady to sign for the evidence, or if Brady's involvement points toward something else that we don't know about."

"I'd start digging into Brady's background first."

"Of course you would. But you're biased; I can't be. Who's the blond woman?"

I've been stretching the bounds of truth a lot lately, and didn't like the taste it left in my mouth. "Her name's Savannah Richmond," I replied. "She and I had a short affair about nine years ago. The dead woman on the shrimp trawler was her sister and she came here to make arrangements to have her sister's body transported home to South Carolina. She and her daughter live on their trawler, docked out back."

"An old girlfriend?" Devon's eyes didn't look accusatory, but it was a charged question. She was in cop mode.

"I wouldn't go that far," I said. "She was a tourist in town. It lasted less than two weeks."

Devon looked inside, and I followed her gaze. Rusty and Florence had returned.

"And the eight-year-old-looking girl?"

"Her daughter."

"I see," Devon said. "Do you know where Marty is?"

"He was here about thirty minutes ago," I replied. Then I remembered something. I dug into the cargo pocket of my shorts and took out the package I'd found under the false bottom.

"I'm no expert," I said, "but I bet this is meth."

Devon took the package from my hand and looked at the crystals inside the plastic bag. "Sure looks like it. Where'd you get this?"

"I dove the shrimper again yesterday. I can give you the GPS numbers, or should I give that package and the numbers to the Coast Guard?"

"We'll still need to talk to Marty," she said, ignoring my question, and looking inside once more. "He has to make an official statement. Did you find anything else?"

"An explosive charge," I replied. "Another boat was diving it before I got there. They removed other things that Marty and I saw, then rigged the boat to blow."

"What happened? Is there anything left of it?"

"It's intact. Or as intact as it was after blowing up and being dragged two miles. I didn't have time to defuse it, but I managed to carry it away from the boat."

Devon hefted the bag in her hand. "You're going to have to stop by the sub-station on Cudjoe Key to file a report on this. It was turned in by a civilian to county law enforcement; out of the Coast Guard's hands. About fifteen hundred?"

"Is that really necessary?" I asked. "Can't I just sign something right here?"

"That's not the way the law works, Jesse. The Coast Guard will probably want to talk to you, as well. About disturbing their crime scene and the explosives."

"The Coasties wouldn't even know where to look if Marty and I hadn't found and dived it. And if I hadn't been there yesterday, there wouldn't be much left for them to look for."

"True," she said. "And they may or may not be appreciative. You know how they can be."

"Yeah, I sure do."

"We have another stop on Big Pine before we go over to Marty's," she said. "If we miss him and you see him, tell him to call me. He's not answering his cell."

She started to turn away, but I stopped her with a hand on her shoulder. "What's that stuff worth?"

"This is distribution weight," she said, hefting the package again. "Almost half a pound. Depending on its purity, anywhere from fifteen to twenty-five thousand."

"Dollars?" I asked, very surprised. "I thought it was the *poor man's cocaine.*"

"It was," she replied, walking toward the car. "It's a lot more addictive, though. Supply and demand. This much meth is worth about twice what the same amount of coke would be."

I went back inside. Savannah waited at the table. I didn't really know what else to say to her.

"I liked your daughter," she said, as I approached. "In another time, under different circumstances, we'd probably be friends."

She nodded toward the parking lot. "Did that have anything to do with Sharlee's death?"

"Indirectly," I replied, straddling the chair again. "Where was Charlotte living the last time you heard from her?"

"I didn't exactly hear from her, but the transfer of funds she took from Mom went to a bank in Fort Myers."

"Was she into methamphetamine?"

"I don't know anything about that part of her life, but I guess it's possible."

Without thinking it through, I said, "If you and Florence aren't in a hurry to go somewhere, I'd like to show you my island."

She just stared at me for a moment, her eyes becoming distant and unreadable. "Right now?" she asked, gathering her things.

Before I could reconsider my offered tour, we were walking out to her boat. Rusty gave me an odd look, when I told him we were going up to the island for a little while.

"You're not bringing your dog?" I asked, as we walked down the dock.

"Woden protects the boat while we're ashore."

"So his job's not to protect you and Florence?"

"Sometimes," Savannah replied. "But I can take care of us just fine."

I helped Savannah and Florence aboard and they went straight to the fore and aft dock lines, waiting for me to start the engine. It took Florence only a couple of seconds longer than her mother to untie the dock line and coil it.

Using the bow thruster, I spun *El Cazador* around and we idled slowly past the boats toward open water.

Florence sat on the console seat between Savannah and me. "Do you know who owns that?" she asked, pointing at my plane.

"I do," I replied.

She looked up at me. "You know, or you own it?"

"That's my plane, *Island Hopper*."

"Really?" Savannah asked. "I didn't even know you could fly."

"Flew helicopters a little in the Corps," I said. "Took some lessons a few years ago and got a license. A friend was moving and didn't want the plane anymore. I use it sometimes to take clients to places a boat would have a hard time getting to, or are just too far away."

"Like where?"

"Fresh water lakes in the Everglades," I said. "Cape Sable and The Ten Thousand Islands, sometimes. The Bahama Banks, Cay Sal Bank, places like that. I can mount two kayaks or canoes to the pontoons."

Florence showed no fear when I pushed the throttle forward as we left the canal. *Cazador's* bow came up, and the boat climbed up on top of the water. Florence seemed delighted at the speed.

"You live alone on this island of yours, Jesiah?"

I looked over Florence's head at Savannah, surprised at the mention of my given name.

"Your daughter told me," Savannah said, grinning broadly. She slapped her knee, laughing heartily. "Jesiah Smedley McDermitt."

I grinned at her. "Another couple lives there and helps me run the place." She had a nice laugh.

CHAPTER NINETEEN

The world outside of the Keys was strange. Or at least it seemed so to Steve Brady, after living and working in the islands for ten years, the first seven of which were on the water. He didn't like to go to the mainland anymore. But these days, it seemed that every time he did, he came back with a good-sized wad of cash. That's why he was on his way up US-1 on his only day off. The lure of easy money.

Steve's wife had left him the previous year. Not unusual for people in law enforcement; the stress on the spouse is high every time a cop goes to work. But Steve was tied to a desk for the most part. Patti didn't like the island life and wanted all the things that went with a lieutenant's or a captain's job. And she wanted regular hours and weekends. She claimed that he had no chance for advancement in his job, unless someone died or retired. It was her leaving that eventually led him to first meet the man he was on his way to see now.

When alcohol no longer killed the pain, he'd started using prescription medications. It wasn't long before he couldn't function without them. His doctor would only prescribe so much for the pain he sometimes felt from an injury to his shoulder.

But that wasn't the pain he was self-medicating to find relief from. It was the emotional pain of knowing that his wife had been right. He was in a dead-end, nowhere job, and unless he moved to a different department, he'd remain at the desk he currently occupied until he retired as a sergeant. But Steve really liked living in the Keys. Lately, being single again had taken a fun turn. He knew it was because of the extra money, but he was having the time of his life. The notion that information he gave Ballinger might get one of his co-workers injured or killed never occurred to him.

The previous summer, he'd found a guy in Miami who could get him anything he wanted. But when Cedric Harper had found out that Steve was a cop, he'd vanished from the streets. Steve tracked him down and became a regular customer, making the trip to Miami at least once a week.

Cedric had introduced him to Ballinger, who didn't give his name at first. The man was in the information-buying business. Steve knew that if this man was involved with Cedric, the information he'd give him would be used to break the law. But the amount the man was offering was substantial. Eventually, Ballinger let him into his inner circle.

Gene Ballinger had invited Steve to a party on his yacht. There were a couple of minor celebrities aboard, along with a few of Ballinger's closest business friends. There were also half a dozen women dressed in very skimpy swimsuits. Liquor, sex, and drugs flowed freely.

At the height of the party, Ballinger had sat down next to him. Steve had a cute blue-eyed, barely-legal blonde bouncing on his lap and laughing at everything he said. She was excited and amorous, the result of a snoot full of coke and a hit of ecstasy.

"I need you to do something for me, Steve," Ballinger had said.

He offered Steve more money than he'd make in a month, just for a few scraps of information. The money was tempting. Ballinger continued to ply him with the dulling influence of good tequila. The supple twenty-two-year-old spent the rest of the night on his lap or between his knees, and that took care of the rest. The blonde turned out to be a call girl, but Steve didn't care. They now had a standing date every Sunday night. Today, if Ballinger told him to jump, he jumped.

Cedric had called the night before, as Steve was watching a football game. Ballinger wanted to see him, and it was important. Steve told him he could be in Miami by nine o'clock.

Cedric said no, that Mister Ballinger would meet him halfway, in Islamorada. Cedric had given him the address of a strip mall and told him that Ballinger used it as a small retail distribution hub for his legitimate business. Steve had agreed to meet the man there at eight.

The GPS on his phone warned him that the address was just ahead, and he slowed the car. He was right on time. The parking lot of the strip mall was nearly empty. Eight o'clock on a Monday morning, that was to be expected. It looked like most of the stores were retail shops catering to tourists and probably didn't open until noon. The business on the end had three cars parked in front of it, a big black Suburban, a yellow Jeep, and a large, boxy SUV.

Recognizing Cedric's Toyota parked in front of a small store in the middle, Steve pulled in next to it and got out. There was only one other car in the whole lot. An old Honda with a flat tire was parked at the far side of the lot, backed up to the sidewalk that ran alongside the highway.

As Steve approached the store, he caught movement out of the corner of his eye. He glanced over and saw a woman getting in the driver's side of the ungainly truck at the far end of the mall.

The door in front of him opened, and Cedric stepped out. "He's just a coupla minutes away," he said, lighting a cigarette and extending the pack.

Steve stepped up on the curb and accepted the cigarette Cedric shook loose. Lighting it with his own lighter, he drew the smoke deeply into his lungs. His car was department issued, and they took the no-smoking policy to the extreme.

"What's he want?" Steve asked, as the blonde drove by in what he could now see was a very old Land Cruiser.

"Dunno," Cedric replied. "He just told me to meet him here, and to tell you to come, too."

A car coming from the north slowed and turned into the parking lot, stopping in front of them. It was a newer model Cadillac with tinted windows and a deep burgundy shine. Cedric turned and locked the door as the passenger's side window of the car buzzed down.

"Get in," Ballinger ordered.

Cedric got in the backseat. That left Steve the option of walking around the car and getting in behind Ballinger, or getting in the front seat and having Cedric behind him. Ballinger seemed impatient, so Steve got in the front seat beside the man.

The window went up and the car turned around. Ballinger turned back onto the highway, continuing south. Just ahead, Steve saw the Land Cruiser turn into a small café, just off the highway.

"There's a problem," Ballinger said. "And I need you to make it go away."

CHAPTER TWENTY

When we arrived at my island and turned into the little channel, I could tell by the look on her face that Savannah was impressed with the simplicity. On the ride out, I'd told her a little about how I'd built the structures and developed the island, keeping things simple and functional. She'd asked a few questions, seeming honestly interested.

"Where's your charter boat?" she asked, as I gently nudged *El Cazador* up to the long dock behind Angie's boat.

Pushing the button on the key fob, I heard the click of the release latch. The doors started to slowly swing outward on their spring-loaded hinges. Under the left side of the house lay the *Revenge*, taking up most of that berth. The smaller boats were all tied up under the right half.

"Wow!" Florence exclaimed. "That boat's bigger than ours."

"A little longer," I said, as Savannah and I tied the dock lines to cleats on the pier, "but I bet yours is a lot sturdier."

I stepped up onto the pier and offered Savannah my hand. She took it and stepped up beside me. "Welcome to my island."

"Does your island have a name?"

"No, it doesn't," I replied. "It didn't have one when I bought it, and I guess I just haven't come up with a reason to change that."

We went up the steps leading up to the deck, where we met Charlie coming up the other side. "I thought I heard a young voice."

"Charlie, meet Savannah and Florence. We knew each other some years back." I turned to Savannah. "This is Charlie. She and her husband Carl take care of things around here."

The two women shook hands and exchanged pleasantries, then Charlie knelt in front of Florence. "My kids are a little younger than you, but they're at school," she said. "Finn's around somewhere. He's Jesse's dog."

"Flo is home-schooled," Savannah said. "We're never in the same place long enough for her to attend classes."

Charlie rose and faced me. "Angie went with Carl to pull the lobster traps and Jimmy's wading in the garden. I never realized that boy knew so much about plants."

He's probably grown his share of marijuana, I thought.

It suddenly occurred to me that Carl and Charlie might not even know about Jimmy's pot smoking. It's not exactly something a woman would reveal to her dad and stepmom about her boyfriend.

"Jimmy's a smart guy," I said. "No telling all the stuff he's picked up along the way."

"I have one more box to get from the boat," Charlie said, heading toward the front steps.

"Need any help?"

Charlie waved me off. "Nah, it's just one little old box."

"Garden?" Savannah asked.

Leading her over to the rail, I pointed to where Jimmy was standing in calf-deep water among the vegetable plants. "We raise our own food in one tank, and grow freshwater fish and crawfish in the other tank, mostly to sell to restaurants."

"It's beautiful," she said, looking out across the island's interior. "Which house is yours? This one?"

"Yeah," I said, then pointed to the Trents' house. "That's where Carl and Charlie live. But they're moving next week, and it will be Jimmy and Angie's house then. Angie is Carl's oldest daughter from a previous marriage, and Jimmy works for me from time to time. The other two buildings are just bunkhouses, but Kim is going to remodel the one on the left for her own use."

Finn came loping across the yard and up the steps. He stopped at the top and sat. He doesn't meet new people very often, especially out here, but I've at least trained him to remain calm around visitors.

"This is my buddy, Finn," I said, touching Florence's shoulder. "He loves to chase sticks out in the water."

Florence looked up at Savannah. "Is it okay, Mom?"

Savannah looked at me and I nodded. "Sure," she said to the girl. "And introduce yourself to Mister Jimmy when you get down there."

"You'll keep an eye on her, Finn?" I asked.

He barked once by way of reply, turned, and started down the steps, the girl following behind him.

Florence and Finn ran across the yard in halting gaits, neither very sure about the other. She stopped near the garden and said something to Jimmy, who smiled and waved at her.

"Is it safe out here?" Savannah asked.

"Sure, Finn wouldn't hurt anyone. Or did you mean something else?"

Savannah turned and faced me. "She won't come across any guns or bombs, will she?"

"Guns? Bombs? I don't know what you're—"

"I'm not naïve, Jesse. I heard about Earl Hailey's escape. It's one of the reasons Flo and I started moving around when she was little. I also heard that he disappeared into the Everglades. I seem to remember you grew up in that area, right?"

Savannah wasn't without means. From what I'd gathered in the short time we were together, her family had money. Could she have hired a private detective? Would he have spoken to Peter Dietrich, the Lee County detective that was working the case? It bothered me that she'd felt the need to run and hide from the man.

"Earl Hailey is ancient history," I said. "He's long gone and will never go after anyone."

She stared into my eyes for a moment. "A part of me would like to believe that," she said. "Another part is afraid of the why."

Looking into her eyes, I could see no subterfuge. "Earl's dead, Savannah. Of that I'm certain. But I didn't kill him."

Turning, she looked over to where Florence and Finn were on the little beach in front of the Trents' house.

"Why did you bring me out here?" she asked. "Though you barely made any contact with that female detective, I could tell you and she are together."

I pointed out over the bunkhouses. "It happened about four miles out there," I said.

Her eyes moistened, as she gazed out over the Gulf. "Can you take me there? The exact spot?"

"Yes, but you have to know something first."

She turned and looked at me, the same hurt showing in her eyes. The pain of loss. "What?"

"I think the boat she was on was a floating meth lab. A big one."

There, I'd said it aloud. Having looked at pictures and diagrams on the internet, I was certain that's what the equipment was that Marty and I had seen bolted inside the shrimp hold.

"You think Sharlee was involved in making it?"

"I don't know," I replied. "Can I ask you something? You don't have to answer if it's none of my business."

"What is it?"

"How much money did Charlotte take from your mom?"

Savannah hesitated a moment, before answering.

"Three hundred thousand dollars."

Exactly the number Doc Fredrick had given me. Multiplied by three boats.

"To a bank in Fort Myers?" I asked. She nodded. "Did you report it? Family or not, it's stealing."

"No," she said, as we walked down the steps. "Mom wouldn't, and I couldn't. She was my sister. My only sibling."

Jimmy stepped out of the garden pool, as we approached. "You and Carl are raising some primo veggies, man."

I introduced Savannah to him, then we walked out to the north pier. She was quiet as we walked. At the end of the pier, she looked out over the water for a moment.

"What makes you think they were making meth?" she finally asked.

"Carl and I were sitting right here," I said, then pointed toward Content Passage. "We noticed the shrimp boat out there, headed east. Carl owns one. Shrimpers need flat grassy bottoms to drag their nets across. We thought it strange that a shrimp boat was going that way, because there's no good place to trawl out there."

Pointing toward where the boat had gone down, I said, "We were talking, and the flash of the explosion caught our eye a second before we heard the blast. I've seen an explosion or two. Carl, also. There was something unusual about it. It was a lot bigger than exploding diesel tanks should be."

"So that means they were making meth?"

"Later that evening, Kim, Carl, and I were diving a sinkhole I'd found last week. After the first dive, we noticed a slow-moving boat out near where the wreck went down. Marty showed up out of nowhere to check us out; he'd been watching the wreck site on his radar from over in the Contents. Since the wreck was beyond the three-mile limit and he was actually off duty, he joined us on my boat and we approached the wreck site. Another shrimp trawler was using its nets to drag the wreck away. We followed, and then waited for them to clear out. They'd dragged the wreck two miles north."

"Why would they do that? To hide any evidence?"

"That was what we thought," I said. Marty and I dove on it and found equipment that could be used to manufacture the drugs. Everything was hidden in the boat's shrimp hold."

"Could it have been something else?" Savannah asked.

"In the hold of a fishing boat? You grew up around them, used to skipper one. What was in your hold?"

"Fish and ice," she replied. "And I kept it sparkling clean."

"Yesterday, after we ran into each other in Key West, I went back out there. A dive boat was on the wreck, with divers in the water. I again waited for them to clear out and dove down to have a look."

"What'd you find?"

"The equipment in the hold was gone," I replied. "And they'd left a bomb to blow up any other evidence."

She turned suddenly toward me. "Jesse, you could've been hurt."

"I was," I said, matter-of-factly. "Damned near got myself killed, but I managed to drag the charge away from the boat before it blew. Everything's still as intact as it was before those guys dove on it and took the evidence. But I did find half a pound of meth."

"The package I saw you hand to your girlfriend?"

"Yes, on both counts," I replied. "Devon and I have been seeing each other for a few months. She's a detective sergeant with the Monroe County Sheriff's Office."

"So the sheriff's office is investigating Charlotte's death as it relates to the manufacture of illegal drugs? Is that why the coroner won't release her body?"

Taking her by the shoulders, I looked into her eyes. "There are a lot of moving parts, Savannah. The explosion happened outside of territorial waters, so it's the Coast Guard that's investigating. It was probably them that ordered Doc Fredrick not to release the body."

"So, what is it that your girlfriend is investigating?"

"Devon's exploring something related and involves Marty. I can't say anything more than that."

She moved into my arms. It felt natural and comfortable. Her body convulsed in small spasms as she cried on my shoulder. I had a feeling that she'd been holding it all together for her daughter's sake. I held her and gave her the time she needed. Finally, she stepped away, turning, and wiping at her eyes with the back of her hand

"I don't have a hankie," I said, opening the small cabinet Carl built on the floating dock. I handed her a beach towel. Savannah burst out laughing, drying the tears from her cheeks.

"Thanks," she said. "Leave it to you to use a ten-pound sledge where a tack hammer would do."

My phone vibrated in my pocket. Taking it out, I saw that it was Chyrel calling. "I hope you don't mind," I said, holding up the phone, "but I asked someone to look into a few things about Charlotte's death. This is her."

Answering the phone, I put it on speaker. "Hey, Chyrel. I'm with Savannah Richmond. You're on speaker."

Chyrel knew me well enough that she understood that I was conveying to her that I trusted Savannah.

"I did some digging into Ballinger's background," Chyrel said, her voice sounding tinny over the small speaker. "He's solvent, but just barely. His business is all legit, but it's failing, and he won't let go of the lifestyle it provided through the eighties and nineties. And you were right about the warehouses he sold."

"In port cities?" I asked.

"One city," Chyrel replied. "Two warehouses on the Miami River. He sold them four months ago. They were small and run-down, but he got just enough for them to buy three shrimp boats."

"Good work," I said. "Anything else?" There was always something else with Chyrel.

"Maybe you'd better take me off the speaker," she replied.

Pushing the button, I held the phone to my ear. "Okay, what is it?"

"I followed the money," Chyrel said. "That's where they usually screw up. After buying the boats, Ballinger's business was down to nothing, flat broke, and in debt to his eyeballs. But the very next day, a single large deposit was made into the operating account of his business in Fort Myers. It was almost immediately transferred to Ballinger's main bank in Miami, and within hours, every cent was spent ordering new industrial equipment from several manufacturers. And that ain't all."

"Let me guess," I said, looking at Savannah. "You dug deeper and found where Ballinger's money came from. It was a three-hundred-thousand-dollar bank transfer from the Richmond family's business account."

"Oh, you're gettin' good at this," Chyrel said. "I take it the other Miss Richmond knows that her sis was mixed up in drugs?"

"She does," I said. "Thanks, Chyrel."

Ending the call, I looked at Savannah. "So, it's true?" she asked. "She was involved? And that involvement cost Sharlee her life?"

"That's not proof," I said, hearing Carl's Grady start up out on Harbor Channel, "but it does appear that way. A friend who knows more about this than I do told me that the equipment to set up a meth lab would run about a hundred thousand bucks. The man your sister gave the money to had just bought three shrimp boats. I'm sorry, Savannah."

"Who was that on the phone?" she asked. "How are you able to find these things out even before the police or the Coast Guard?"

While we watched Florence and Finn on the little beach, I told her about Deuce and his team, and how I'd become part of it after the death of my wife. I told her about Chyrel and her hacking skills. I told her about the mission to Cuba, about chasing Smith all over the Caribbean, I told her about Elbow Cay, the Russians down in the Bahamas, and finally the mission in her own hometown.

"That was you that got that rat-bastard?" she asked. "Daddy never trusted that beady-eyed SOB. I was in town when Cross was arrested at Waterfront Park. It happened just before my dad died."

"Do you still want to go out there?" I asked.

"No," she said, with a sigh. "I guess not. I loved my sister, but she'd brought everything on herself. Daddy paid for her to go to rehab several times. And each time she'd get out, she'd fall right back into it."

"Y'all are welcome to stay here tonight," I said, again unable to control my mouth. "There's plenty of room."

She smiled and for a moment, we were back on the deck of her boat, rafted together with my boat and another cruising family's trawler who we'd met on the way to my hurricane hole.

"I don't think that's a good idea," she said. "Besides, I have my boat and Woden to think about."

She was right, it wasn't a good idea. But I knew that she was only mentioning her boat and dog to avoid the bigger obstacle. That I was in a relationship with another woman.

"But if there's food involved," she said with a smile, "we could stay for a little longer."

"Mom, look!" Florence shouted, as she ran toward us on the pier.

Savannah turned to her daughter. "What is it?"

"Clams!" Florence exclaimed, holding about a half dozen in her shirt. "Finn gave them to me. I thought you said there weren't any clams around here."

"He must really like you," I said, as the phone in my pocket vibrated intermittently, telling me I had a text message. "He doesn't usually share his food with just anyone."

CHAPTER TWENTY-ONE

Reaching the landing of the townhouse, Joe and Devon noticed the door was slightly ajar. When there was no response to the doorbell, both detectives drew their weapons and moved to opposite sides of the door frame.

The apartment was part of a group of duplex townhouses built on stilts, located on the Gulf side of Little Torch Key. The two detectives were standing on the landing of the main floor, ten feet above the parking area.

Joe shouted, "Sheriff's detectives! Open the door!"

Ten slow seconds passed. "No answer, and the door's open," Devon whispered, pulling a latex glove from her pocket.

"Textbook entry," Joe said.

Devon didn't have to be reminded. Whether serving a warrant or making an entry for probable cause, when it was the home of a person you were absolutely certain had a gun and knew how to use it, the entry had to be made very carefully.

Joe nodded his readiness. Devon used the glove to push the door open. Joe moved in first, fast and low, with his pistol up in front of him. Devon followed, crossing behind him, sweeping the left side of the living room with her Kimber. Joe moved to the right as Devon crossed the room. She crouched by the breakfast bar and covered him as he checked the door to the porch overlooking Big Pine Channel. He shook his head, then pointed toward the kitchen.

Devon waited until Joe was against the far wall in the dining room. Then she rose quickly and looked over the counter, aiming her sidearm down at the floor in the kitchen, sweeping left to right.

Joe moved to his left, checking behind the breakfast bar where Devon couldn't see. He pointed to his left, then up. Devon nodded, then moved past him to the other side of the kitchen. There was a half-bath there, the door facing the stairway to the bedrooms on the second floor.

The door to the bathroom was partly open, but one of them would have to check inside, exposing themselves to the stairwell. Devon pointed two fingers at her eyes, then pointed up the steps. Joe nodded, and they moved at the same time, Devon stepping into the gap and aiming her Kimber up the steps, while Joe entered the small bathroom covering her six.

Joe came back out and shook his head. Slowly, the two detectives made their way up the steps. They stayed close to both sides to avoid creaking steps.

On the landing at the top of the stairs, there was a closed door and a long hall to another door, which was open, barbells visible on the floor. With Joe covering her from the landing, Devon went down the hall, her back to the wall.

Finding nothing but an orderly exercise room, she looked back and shook her head. Joe moved across the hall, weapon pointed at the closed door. Devon quickly moved to the other side of the door, which was at an angle to the hallway.

Joe turned the knob and went through the door with Devon crossing behind him, fanning out as they entered the master bedroom. A man lay on the floor beside the bed, blood pooling under his prone body.

Both detectives recognized the young man immediately, and holstered their weapons. Devon went to the stricken man's side, slowly rolling him onto his back.

Joe took his hand-held radio from his belt, keyed the mic, and spoke urgently. "Officer down! Officer down! This is Detective Clark. We need EMT and an ambulance at Little Torch Apartments, number twelve."

Holstering the radio, Joe knelt next to Devon. "Is he alive?"

"Yeah," she replied, "but he's lost a lot of blood."

The sliding-glass door was open, and Joe went over to check the porch. Across the channel on Big Pine Key, they could hear the sirens from the fire station. Within minutes, emergency personnel and several other deputies arrived.

"Stay here," Devon said to Joe, as the EMTs loaded the stretcher into the ambulance. "Start processing the scene. I'm going with him to the hospital and I'll be back as soon as I can."

She climbed in the back of the ambulance and one of the other deputies closed the door, slapping the side of the van. The EMTs worked quickly, cutting away the bloody tee shirt. He'd been shot high in the right side of the chest.

Devon moved past them and sat on a small jump seat next to the younger deputy's head and buckled her seatbelt. He somehow looked smaller, more vulnerable. His eyes fluttered open as she put her hand on his shoulder. They locked on Devon's.

She leaned closer to him. "We're taking you to the hospital, Marty. You're gonna be okay."

"We'll have to take him to Fishermen's," one of the EMTs told her. "They have a better trauma center."

Devon nodded and took Marty's hand, continuing to reassure him, though his eyes were now closed and he was unresponsive.

Crossing Big Pine Key and the Seven Mile Bridge, the ambulance arrived at Fishermen's Hospital, and Marty was rushed into emergency surgery. Devon waited in the ER lobby. She went into the restroom to wash the blood from her hands. There was a stain on the front of her white shirt that wasn't going to come out, so she buttoned her suit coat to hide it, then went back and paced the lobby.

Her first instinct was to call Jesse. She took her phone out and instead called Joe. "Find anything yet?"

"No sign of forced entry," Joe replied.

In Devon's mind that meant it was probably somebody who Marty knew. "Fingerprints?"

"Still waiting for forensics to get here," Joe replied. "Maybe the door was unlocked when the killer arrived. There's blood on the bed. It looks like Marty was shot while he was napping. There was a book on the bed, also. It had a little bit of blood on it and what looks like a bullet hole through half of it. Happened maybe two or three hours ago."

Devon knew that Joe had worked in the forensics lab for some time before becoming a sworn officer up in Palm Bay. He was well versed in blood and spatter analysis. In his mind, Joe could read a crime scene in a matter of minutes, just by observing where the blood was, the shapes of the drops, and how it had congealed over time.

"So if there's no forced entry," Devon said, "his being asleep means it could be anybody. Not just someone he might have let in."

"I'm leaning toward someone he knows," Joe said. "I mean, it was late morning; in broad daylight. There are quite a few onlookers here, so I'm sure someone saw or heard something. I have deputies taking statements and canvassing the other apartments."

Devon knew something she hadn't told Joe yet. She believed Marty when he'd told her about turning over the evidence to Steve Brady. And now Marty was shot. And Jesse also knew about the head.

"Has Marty's shift supervisor arrived yet?" she asked.

"Phillips was off duty," Joe replied.

"If it had been you who got shot while taking a nap, where would Ben be right now?"

"Point taken. I'll find out who Phillips's shift supervisor is and give them a call, find out what cases Phillips is working, if anything."

"His name's Brady," Devon said. "Sergeant Steve Brady. Let me know what he says, and if forensics finds anything interesting."

"Got it. Any word on his condition?"

"Nothing," Devon replied, staring out the window at the ambulance driveway. "They took him into emergency surgery."

"Hope he makes it," Joe said. "I only met him once or twice; struck me as a sharp guy. Anything else?"

"Yeah, Joe. What was Marty reading?"

"College textbook, of all things. Oceanography."

The door they'd taken Marty through to the treatment area opened and a woman in scrubs came out, looking around.

"Thanks, Joe," she said, ending the call as she approached the woman.

"I'm Detective Evans," she said. "Deputy Martin Phillips was brought in with a gunshot wound to the chest."

"He's being moved to recovery in the Intensive Care Unit," the woman said, extending her hand. "I'm Doctor Trumble."

"Will he be okay?"

"Probably," Doctor Trumble replied. "It was a heavy-caliber bullet, probably shot from long range. The bullet was lodged in his upper chest, barely penetrating his right lung. Had the shooter been closer, the deputy might not have survived."

"Long range?" Devon asked. "What if it was close range and something shielded him?"

"Like through a wall or something?"

"A college textbook was lying beside him, with what appears to be a bullet hole in it."

"And they say college learning no longer helps young people," the doctor said. "Yes, the shooter may have been just feet away in that case. A thick book would slow the bullet enough to cause the type of injuries he sustained."

"Will he be awake anytime soon?"

"Not for a while. He's probably out of the woods, but it will be at least nightfall before the anesthesia wears off."

"Thanks, Doctor," Devon said, checking her watch. It was after two, so she wouldn't be able to talk to Marty for at least three hours.

Her phone chirped, still in her hand. It was Joe.

"He's out of the ER," she said without preamble. "He's in ICU recovery."

"That's a relief. I'll let the guys here know. I spoke to his supervisor. Brady said that Phillips wasn't working on much of anything recently. A couple of boat thefts and an ongoing poaching investigation. That's about it."

"Okay, thanks," Devon said, her mind racing. "I still haven't called his family."

"I'll do it," Joe offered. "I know his dad."

"Thanks, again. Keep me posted on anything else you find. I'm going to call Ben and see about posting security here at the hospital."

There was a pause before Joe said, "I found something else."

"What?"

"A used condom in the trash can."

"Okay," Devon said. "Have forensics bag it, along with any prints they can lift."

The call to Ben took all of one minute. He said he would be at the hospital in less than an hour and would arrange twenty-four-hour security. Marty wasn't even part of his section, that's just the kind of guy Ben was.

Knowing that she needed to let Jesse know, Devon pulled up his number on her contact list. Marty and Jesse's daughter were dating, and Kim would want to be here. The last time she'd seen Jesse, just a few hours before, he'd been with the sister of one of the explosion victims. A woman with whom he had once had an affair. It hurt to remember the sight of the little girl and how much she resembled Jesse. She somehow knew there was more of a connection there than just a long-ago fling with a tourist woman.

She opened her phone's text app and sent him a message to call her as soon as possible.

Devon continued her pacing, waiting for Jesse to call. While she waited, she thought about who would know Brady's whereabouts from mid-morning on. There was a clerk at the Cudjoe substation Marty worked out of. She'd met the woman once earlier in the summer.

What was her name? Devon thought. *Beverly something?*

Devon called the switchboard and had them connect her to the Cudjoe substation. A woman's voice answered, identifying herself as Deputy Saint.

"Hi, Beverly," Devon said. "This is Detective Devon Evans. We met last July at a cookout."

"Yes, I remember," the woman said. "What can I do for you?"

"My partner and I are the ones who found Deputy Phillips."

"I just heard. Is Marty okay?"

Devon needed to keep the conversation short, in case Jesse called. "I just spoke to the doctor. He's in ICU, but they think he'll live. I was wondering if you could help me with something."

"Anything I can do," Beverly replied.

"My partner already talked to Sergeant Brady, but I thought that you would probably have a better idea of what Marty might have been working on, more than what's in the official reports."

"I file the reports for all of them," she said. "A lot of times, the deputies would talk about their cases. How can I help?"

"Sergeant Brady said that Marty was working a couple of boat thefts and a poaching case. Is that about it?"

The woman recited a few details about the cases Marty was working. Nothing jumped out.

"Maybe something recent?" Devon asked. "Something that came up before Sergeant Brady came on duty this morning or while he was at lunch?"

Over the phone, Devon heard her typing on a keyboard. "Hmm," Beverly sighed. "I don't see any updates. Sergeant Brady and I came in at the same time this morning, and he always eats lunch at his desk. I don't see where he updated anything on Marty's cases on the computer. We record all radio traffic and the audio files are linked in the daily reports. I don't see where Marty called anything in at all today."

Her phone buzzed. It was Jesse. "Thanks, Beverly. I have another call coming in."

Tapping the screen to end the call and accept Jesse's, she held the phone to her ear. "Jesse, Marty's been shot."

CHAPTER TWENTY-TWO

Ignoring the vibrating phone, I walked with Savannah and Florence back to the tables in front of the bunkhouses.

"How does he know where to dig for them?" Florence asked.

I smiled at her inquisitive nature. "That's the big mystery," I replied, as we sat at the table. "He wasn't quite a year old when I got him and the lady I got him from said he just started doing it on his own."

Jimmy came over and sat with us. "I never realized you guys had all this going on out here."

"I never thought it'd get this big," I said, taking my phone out. I had a text from Devon asking me to call her. Why she hadn't just called instead of texting, I didn't know.

"Excuse me a minute," I said. "I need to make a call."

Walking over to the fire pit, I called Devon. Her statement hit me like a ton of bricks.

"Is he okay?" I asked, my mind reeling. "How'd it happen?"

"Yes, he's going to be okay," Devon said. "He's at Fishermen's now and I just talked to the doctor. He's in intensive care."

Sitting on the fallen palm trunk, I absently stirred the ashes in the fire ring. "Where did it happen?"

"In his home," she said. "Was Kim there last night?"

"Whoa! Back the hell up. She didn't have anything to do with it."

"I doubt that she did, Jesse, but I need to know if she was there. If she was, we need to get her fingerprints, so we can rule hers out of all the fingerprints collected."

Standing, I slung the stick sideways into the underbrush. "Yeah, she was there, but there's no way in hell she had anything to do with his getting shot."

"Where is she now?"

"Probably halfway back to Gainesville; she left from the *Anchor* about nine this morning. Marty dropped her off."

"She's ruled out as a suspect, Jesse, but I do need to talk to her. And you. Either of you might know something you don't even know you know. First things first, though. Do you know if your name was on the report that Marty gave to Sergeant Brady?"

"Report?" I asked. Then I made the connection. The missing head.

"The report Marty turned in along with the evidence you and he collected on the wrecked boat."

"Yeah," I said, my mind already leaping ahead. "But only my name. He told me he left Kim's and Carl's names out of it. Have you found out anything, Devon?"

"Jesse, you need to stay out of this. Let us do our jobs."

I could feel the anger building inside me. I glanced over at the tables. Jimmy was joking with Florence. Savannah looked at me, concerned. She'd sought me out for a reason. She at least suspected that I had something to do with Earl Hailey's disappearance and she wanted to find the person responsible for her sister's death. So she'd come to the only person she knew of who might have a vigilante mentality. Me.

"I told you to look at Brady first."

"There's nothing pointing to him," she said. "And we've already checked. Brady came on duty at zero nine hundred and never left the office. Marty was shot around noon."

"I'll be there in thirty minutes," I said. I didn't wait for Devon to reply, and ended the call. *And I'll have my own damned security.*

Pulling up Kim's number, I hit *Send* and waited. After the third ring, I was about to hang up when she answered.

"Where are you?" I asked, a bit too urgently.

"Just past Fort Myers," Kim replied. "I stopped to get gas. What's wrong?"

At least she's not driving, I thought.

"You need to come back," I told her, as Savannah walked toward me. "Marty's been hurt. He's in the hospital."

I gave Kim directions to the little airport in Labelle and told her that a friend of mine would meet her there shortly. I told her what I knew about Marty and told her that he was going to be okay, though I had no way of knowing that. Then I called Billy Rainwater, who lived in Labelle.

"Billy," I said. "It's me. I need help."

"Just name it," Billy said. He and I had grown up together, hunting and fishing all around southwest Florida.

"My daughter's boyfriend's been shot."

"Who did it?" Billy asked. "I'll take care of it myself."

"Nothing like that, brother. Kim's on her way up to Gainesville. She's near Fort Myers now. You know a good pilot I can hire?"

"I'll make a call," Billy said. "We'll have the engines spooled up and waiting when she gets here."

Calling Kim back, I told her to look for Billy when she got to the airport and he'd make sure she got here quickly.

"What's going on?" Savannah asked, concern in her voice and in her expressive eyes.

"There's been a shooting and Marty's hurt," I said.

"Is there anything I can do to help?"

"I need to go to the hospital on Marathon," I told her. "But I need to get you to the *Anchor*."

"Don't worry about us," Savannah said. "We can get a ride from the hospital back to the boat."

Within minutes, we'd said our goodbyes to the others and cast off. I made some other phone calls on the way. If Marty's boss had anything to do with it, he'd be in danger from the inside. I wanted people I knew I could trust at the hospital, just in case.

We arrived at Marathon City Marina twenty minutes and two more phone calls later. I explained what was going on to the dockmaster, a guy I'd met a few times.

"Y'all go ahead on over," Gregg said. "I'll put your boat in a slip."

Thanking him, I led Savannah and Florence through a few parking lots, reaching the hospital entrance on Overseas Highway just a few minutes later.

We made our way through a maze of corridors and found the emergency-room lobby. Ben Morgan was there, but Devon wasn't. Morgan and a doctor were talking to Marty's dad, Ben Phillips. We shook hands and the doctor introduced herself as Melissa Trumble. She continued talking to Phillips. Apparently, he'd only just arrived himself.

"He should be waking up soon," Doctor Trumble said. "I'll take you both back to see him in just a moment." Then she turned to Morgan. "But please limit your questions and if I say leave, you leave. Do you understand, Detective?"

"Yes, Ma'am," Morgan replied.

I grabbed Morgan's arm as he started to leave. "Where's Devon?"

"I sent her back over to Marty's house," he told me. "She and Joe are good. And they work well with the tech guys."

"What do you know, Ben?"

Morgan held a finger up to the doctor. "Give us just a minute," he said and led Phillips and I over to a group of chairs. We sat, and he explained all that he said he knew—but he didn't mention Brady. The rage inside me seethed, but I kept it under control. Ben Phillips took it all in. He seemed in shock or something. When Morgan finished, he and Phillips joined the doctor and disappeared through the door.

We waited. Rusty was the first to arrive. I paced. Deuce got there an hour later, along with Julie, Chyrel, Tony, and Andrew. Deuce told me that Paul Bender and Tom Broderick were both out of town, but would be returning tomorrow.

Tony and Andrew both carried bags. I knew what was in them. Enough food, clothes, and anything else they might need to last them two days. I knew these guys well. I was one of them, and that made Kim and Marty one of them by default. They'd be close by for as long as it took.

Though Marty was still in intensive care, there was now zero chance that he'd be hurt again.

Kim called; she was in a twin-engine Beechcraft and would be landing in ten minutes. Julie volunteered to pick her up, but Kim said that Billy and his friend had a car waiting at the airport. We waited some more. I paced some more.

Finally, Kim arrived along with Billy and another man. When she came through the door, she looked around until she saw me, and came running into my arms. I held her. Rusty came over and put an arm around her, then Julie and Deuce, followed by Tony and Andrew. The whole time I held her I whispered repeatedly, "He's okay, he's okay."

Morgan came out, putting his note pad in the inside pocket of his coat. "Miss McDermitt," he said. "Marty's awake. He's asking for you."

Morgan pushed the call button and a nurse opened the door. "Take Miss McDermitt to see Deputy Phillips, please."

Kim ran past him and disappeared through the door. I took Billy's extended arm and pulled him in close. "Thanks, brother."

"I know you, my friend," he whispered softly. It was a greeting he and I used, and we'd only shared it with one or two others. Growing up, Billy and I had shared a lot and we knew each other as well as any two brothers. Releasing my old Indian friend, I turned to his pilot.

His face was familiar, but I couldn't place him until Billy reminded me of the time I'd flown up to Labelle last hurricane season. Steve Carter had put my plane in his hangar for a few days.

"Thanks for bringing my daughter down," I said to Steve and Billy, as I pulled them aside and reached for my wallet.

Billy stopped me. "I took care of it."

"Another favor?"

"Poker debt," Steve said, with a grin. "Any excuse to get in the air, right?"

Knowing Billy as well as I did, I had serious doubts that it was a poker loss. Gambling requires risk, and Billy's about the most cautious person I know. I thanked Steve and told him that if he wanted to stay over, I'd cover his hotel and meals.

My oldest daughter Eve arrived a few minutes later, along with her husband and father-in-law. The elder Maggio eyed me warily and finally got me off to one side.

"If there's anything me or my firm can do to help," he said.

Several years ago, the Maggio law firm was involved in something that quickly got them in over their heads; a plot to not only steal a fortune in treasure that Doc Talbot had found a clue to, but also to kill anyone who got in the way. I was one of those who was in the way, along with many of my friends. The East-European thugs that were hired weren't quite up to the job. The fact that his son was married to my daughter is the only thing that kept them alive. They quickly learned the error of their ways, turned over a new leaf, and no surprise, became more successful than in the past.

"Thanks," I said. "My guys will handle it."

"I still know people," Maggio said, then grinned. "Haven't talked to any of them in a long while, but I still know them."

"Our guys are more than up to the task," I replied.

One by one as they'd arrived, I'd introduced Savannah to my extended family. She and Florence stayed. The little girl busied herself with a coloring book, while Savannah sat down with Julie, and Eve in the corner. I joined them, sitting next to Savannah. We talked in low whispers.

The sun's rays were angling into the lobby area through the door. It was nearly sunset. The automatic doors opened, and a uniformed deputy strode in. He wore sergeant's chevrons. He moved toward the counter, then spotted Morgan and angled toward him. Seeing the man's nametag, I started to rise. Savannah grabbed my hand and pulled me back down between her and Florence.

She leaned close and whispered softly into my ear. "This isn't a good place. Is that the man you suspect?"

"Marty's boss," I said quietly, so only Savannah could hear. "The guy he turned crucial evidence over to, which somehow never went any farther."

Savannah put a hand on my bare knee. "Evidence about the wreck my sister died in?" Her hand on my knee distracted me. The warmth radiating from her touch sent chills up my spine.

The idea hit me like a ton of bricks. There wasn't any grudge or misunderstanding between Brady and Marty. There was a lot more to this. Brady was involved in something, and it had to do with the shrimp boats and meth. The missing head and the attempt on Marty were parts of a cover-up. I could almost smell the guilt on him.

I stood up slowly, not taking my eyes off Brady. Out of the corner of my eye, I saw Tony rise from another small couch where he and Chyrel had been sitting, working at her computer. On the other side of the lobby, Andrew was leaning against a wall talking to Deuce. Both men turned, when they saw me moving toward Brady and Ben.

"Because major crimes is my bailiwick," Ben said to Brady, as I got close enough to hear.

Devon hadn't informed me just what she'd told Ben about the missing head. From his body language as I approached, I assumed she'd told him everything. He stiffened and stepped back slightly.

"Have you learned something?" I asked both men, extending my hand to Brady.

Savannah was suddenly at my side, holding my left arm with one hand and clutching Florence close to her with the other.

Brady took my hand without thinking. "And you are?"

"Jesse McDermitt," I replied, squeezing his hand much harder than necessary. Deuce, Tony, and Andrew formed up around us.

His grip had been firm until I said my name. Hearing it, he flinched as if he were certain that he'd never be meeting anyone by that name, ever again. It was almost like he thought I'd been blown up on a wrecked shrimp boat, outside territorial waters. The rage simmering inside me cranked up another notch.

I've met my share of bad people; they're all over the world. The worst ones are those who pretend to be on the side of good, and all the while, their moral compass doesn't show true north.

I felt Andrew's presence behind me. He's an imposing man. Not quite as tall as me, but every bit as heavy. He was built like a fireplug, with broad shoulders and a barrel chest.

The change in Brady's eyes was more than enough to tell me that he had something to do with both the explosion on the wreck, and with Marty lying in a bed somewhere here in the hospital.

"Jesse," Ben said, as my eyes bored holes through the back of Brady's skull. "Can I talk to you?"

Releasing his hand, I slowly moved toward Ben, while keeping my eyes on Brady. My friends were right, I don't have much of a poker face. My thoughts are easily transmitted in my expression, and right now, I was wondering just how long it might take me to strangle the son of a bitch. Probably less than a minute and a half, at most. I'm also pretty good at reading other's expressions. His reaction to my presence told me that he had it coming.

I followed Ben outside.

When the doors whisked closed behind us, Morgan turned toward me. "I didn't like the look in your eyes, just then."

"What do you know?" I asked him bluntly.

"I know you were with Deputy Phillips when a human head was found, along with parts of what might or might not have come from a meth lab. I know you're a very dangerous man, and I know that look I saw in your eyes. I know Sergeant Brady has been having financial and marital problems. What I don't know is what connection he might have to any—"

The door made a swooshing sound as it slid open. Chyrel and Deuce came out to join us.

"I followed the money," Chyrel said.

Deuce eyed Morgan. "And your Sergeant Brady just left by the main entrance," he added.

Morgan's head jerked around suddenly, looking inside. "Okay," he said, turning to Deuce. "You guys have resources unavailable to us. Or more precisely, unusable in court. I know this, and I know how it works. Tell me what you know."

"You first," I said. "What did Marty say?"

"He saw the guy," Morgan said. "It wasn't Brady, and Brady has an alibi. He was at his desk from nine this morning, until he left to come here."

"That doesn't mean he's not part of it somehow," I said.

Morgan looked over at Chyrel, who was thumbing through her tablet. "No, it doesn't. But it certainly lessens the likelihood."

"Not necessarily," Chyrel said.

Morgan grinned. "Go ahead. But I'm doubting that anything you tell me will be admissible in court."

"It won't be," she said, with a disarming smile, "but once you get probable cause, you can subpoena his financials. You'll definitely find something of interest there."

"And what's that?" Morgan asked.

"The average Monroe County deputy, at a sergeant's pay rate with Brady's time with the department, earns about sixty thousand a year, or five thousand a month, before deductions, right?"

"I haven't checked lately, but knowing you folks, I'd say that's probably a true-enough assessment."

"Do you know if Sergeant Brady has another job, moonlighting as security at the mall or something?"

"Nothing," Morgan replied. "A lot of the younger deputies do, but County employees are required to divulge anything like that, and Brady hasn't. I already checked."

Chyrel smiled. "Then how's he depositing an extra five thousand a month, besides what the county pays him through direct deposit, every month since July?"

CHAPTER TWENTY-THREE

The forensics team spent two hours bagging and tagging a bunch of evidence. The inside door knob had a good thumb print that at first glance didn't match any of the dozens that were lifted from the barbells in the spare bedroom. All the prints lifted would be run through the computer for a more positive identification or elimination.

"I'm betting that the print on the door knob is our shooter," Joe said. "He or she let themselves in, they knew where to find Deputy Phillips, and shot him in his sleep. Considering the used condom, maybe a jealous lover?"

"I know the girl he's dating," Devon said, standing at the foot of the bed where Marty had been shot. "That'd be so out of character, my mind can't reach around it."

"Happens all the time. Guy has another girl on the side, wife or girlfriend catches them, and the wife just snaps."

"We don't have anything to go on yet," Devon said. "You go sit on the lab rats and let me know when they come up with anything useful."

"You're going back to the hospital?"

"Yeah," Devon replied. "Marty should be waking up soon."

They left the room and went down the stairs to the main floor. Devon's mind kept straying. The truth was that she felt haunted by the sight of Jesse with Savannah Richmond and her daughter. It hurt her a little, that the child might be his. If so, he'd want to make things right by the woman, maybe even be an active participant in raising the child. It's the kind of man Jesse was. Besides, she knew that their relationship probably wouldn't be a lasting one. They had different lifestyles, and eventually it would come down to him moving to Key West or her moving to his island, neither of which had any chance of happening. The Richmond woman was more suited for Jesse; she lived on a boat.

"Call me if you learn anything," Joe said, as they both went down the outside stairs to the parking area.

Outside, Devon looked around. Marty's patrol boat was tied to the dock just fifty yards away. "Did anyone check Marty's boat?"

"I don't think so," Joe replied. "Think the killer might have been on it or something?"

"No idea," she said, walking toward the patrol boat.

Stepping down onto the boat, it rocked slightly, causing Devon to nearly lose her balance. The boat was immaculate, fiberglass polished to a bright shine and all the chrome glittering in the last rays of the sun.

She went forward, noticing a few flies on one of the forward fish boxes. The smell hit her, as she neared the bow. Opening the box, she wretched as the stench escaped.

"Call the forensics team," she said up to Joe on the dock. "Tell them to turn around. And call the coroner."

"That what I think it is?"

"Nothing to lose your head about," Devon said, stepping back up beside him on the dock.

"You're a sick bitch, you know that?"

"I try," Devon said, as she turned and started toward the parking lot. "Tell Doc Fredrick to see if he can get a blood and DNA match to one of the other body parts he has."

"Does he really need to come out here?" Joe asked. "I mean, it's just the head. Even I can tell the guy's dead."

"Procedures, Joe, procedures."

Devon got in her county-issued sedan and drove while she thought about the events of the day. The drive from Little Torch Key to Marathon wasn't a long one, but the Seven Mile Bridge allowed her time to put things together in her mind before she arrived at the hospital.

When she turned from Overseas Highway into the parking lot at Fishermen's Hospital, the sun was almost to the horizon in her rearview mirror. In front of the main entrance, Devon saw two sedans, similar to her own, parked in the emergency vehicle parking area and was about to continue and park next to Ben's car, when she saw Steve Brady getting out of the other sedan.

She quickly turned into an empty spot in the general parking area, close to the ER and watched Brady. He stopped outside the door and lit a cigarette. This struck Devon as odd. If he was concerned enough to come to check on Marty's condition, why would he stop for a smoke break. It was another tick in her *check this guy out* column.

Devon reached into a bag on the passenger-side floor and took out a pair of binoculars. She focused on Brady standing by the door. She wasn't worried that he'd see her, it was growing dark quickly, and the sunset was behind her car. He casually stood beside a column, smoking.

Through the glass windows behind Brady, she could see several people she recognized. She scanned the lobby and found Jesse. He was sitting on a couch, talking to his oldest daughter, Eve, and Rusty's daughter, Julie. The Richmond woman was sitting on one side of him and her daughter on the other. The girl was busy writing or drawing something. Devon couldn't help but think that they looked like a family.

Jesse started to rise, but the woman took his hand and held him in place, as Brady walked through the door. The woman put a hand on his bare knee, leaning close to his ear and saying something. The touch of her hand seemed to steady Jesse slightly.

As she watched, Brady went straight over to where Ben was standing and the two began talking. Jesse rose and walked toward the two men. Ben stepped back slightly as he approached. The look on Jesse's face was one of murderous rage; he looked like he was barely holding it together.

Devon watched anxiously as the three men exchanged words. The rising fury that Jesse was barely holding in check was clearly evident in his body language. She was worried that Jesse might do something rash.

Jesse's friends moved and formed a semi-circle around him, as if anticipating trouble. The Richmond woman came alongside Jesse, holding onto his arm and pulling her daughter close in front of them, as if their presence might calm him. She seemed to have some influence over Jesse. Devon watched, somewhat detached, realizing that this woman, whom he hadn't seen in a long time, held more sway over him than she did. She somehow felt certain that the child was his.

Ben motioned toward the door and Jesse slowly followed him outside. Brady watched them leave, and then he turned and disappeared down a corridor she knew led to the main entrance of the hospital.

A moment later, Jesse's friends, Deuce and Chyrel, came outside. The four of them talked for a minute, Chyrel reading something from a small tablet computer.

Turning the binoculars toward the hospital's main entrance, Devon watched for a moment. Just as she was about to move the glasses back to Jesse and Ben, Brady came out of the building. He moved in the direction of his car quickly, looking toward the corner of the building that shielded the ER entrance.

Devon dropped down low in her seat, as Brady drove past her. She waited until he reached the exit, then started her car and backed out. Brady turned north on the highway and she followed him, staying back far enough to not be obvious, allowing two cars to get between them on the four-lane highway.

Brady kept going north on US-1, passing Key Colony Beach where she knew he lived. It was at his house that Devon had met Beverly Saint, the admin clerk at the sub-station on Ramrod. Brady had still been married then, but Devon could see the writing on the wall with them and knew they were headed for a breakup.

Continuing north, she followed Brady as he passed the Dolphin Research Center on Grassy Key and started out onto the series of longer bridges to Long Key. On one of the bridges, Brady crossed the center line slightly, over corrected, and nearly scraped the retaining wall. Devon doubted he'd been drinking since he just came off duty. Probably texting or making a phone call.

Traffic thinned out and Devon had to lay back even more, so Brady wouldn't think he was being followed. Long Key fell behind them, and Devon became worried that he might be running. With only one road into the Keys and one road out, getting a head start when things go south was probably the prudent thing to do, if one was so inclined. She checked her gas gauge, pleased to see that she had more than half a tank. Eventually, she'd have to call it in to Ben and let him make the decision to bring in more deputies to make a traffic stop.

She thought about Jesse as she drove. She thought about the Richmond woman and her child. Her eyes misted, and a lump caught in her throat. Devon knew that Jesse wasn't the right man for her; too wild and adventurous. And she wasn't right for him, either. The whole island and boat thing just wasn't for her. She knew he'd never be happy living in Key West, or any other town for that matter. He loved his solitary lifestyle, sharing it with only a select few people. A single tear streaked down her cheek.

Finally, the brake lights on Brady's car came on and he turned into a strip mall on the ocean side of Islamorada. Devon slowed as she approached the entrance, noticing that most of the stores were closed and there were only ten or fifteen cars in the lot.

Turning left on a side street on the bay side of the highway, Devon parked on the side of the road and quickly doused her headlights. She grabbed the binos from the passenger seat, got out, and trotted back to the intersection, staying close to the foliage bordering the entrance to the subdivision.

Watching through the binoculars, she saw Brady approach the door to one of the stores. The door opened, and a man came out. He was young, about twenty-five or thirty, average height and slight build, with shoulder-length brown hair and a scruffy growth on his chin.

The two men didn't shake hands, but both lit cigarettes and smoked as they talked. Devon wished she could get close enough to hear. A moment later, a burgundy Cadillac CTS turned in off the road and parked next to Brady's Crown Victoria.

Digging her phone from her back pocket, Devon opened the camera app and zoomed in on the men across the street. The lighting wasn't very good and even zoomed in all the way, their faces weren't very distinguishable, but she snapped several dozen pictures as the three men talked for a minute before going inside.

Devon went back to her car and drove a few houses down before turning into a driveway and backing out again. She pulled the car close under a large gumbo limbo tree and waited. She thumbed through the pictures, enlarging each one, and either deleting it because it didn't show the other two men's faces well enough, or saving it if it did.

When she had it down to five pictures that seemed decent enough to maybe get an ID from, she attached them to an email and sent them to the forensics lab and to Ben. She'd give him a few minutes, then call him to report what she'd seen.

CHAPTER TWENTY-FOUR

Returning to the ER lobby, we continued to wait. Ben Phillips had been back with Marty for nearly half an hour, along with Kim, when Ben finally came out.

"The doctor said my boy's gonna be fine," Ben said to Morgan. "You find out who did this, you give me ten minutes alone with him."

"You know I can't, Mister Phillips," Morgan said. "No matter how much I'd like to do just that."

"They're moving him to a room," Ben said to me. "Kim's going with him." Then he turned to Morgan again. "The doctor also said you can talk to him again once they get him settled. Room forty-nine."

"How's he feeling?" Morgan said, genuinely concerned.

"Said it hurts like all hell," Ben replied, "but they got him on meds and put blood back into him. He said he was hungry, and that's a good sign. I was gonna go to Dion's for some chicken. The doc said if it wasn't fried it'd be okay."

I knew how Ben was feeling. When someone you care for is hurt or injured, you want to be doing something, anything, to help them.

After Ben left, Deuce and Julie walked over. Julie was going to go get food for everyone. I asked Morgan if he'd like anything and he started to reach for his wallet.

"I got it, Detective," Deuce said.

Morgan put his wallet back and pulled his phone out. I could hear it vibrating in his hand. He tapped the screen several times, then looked up at me and Deuce.

"A text from Devon," Morgan said. "She followed Brady when he left here. He's in Islamorada, talking to two men. Recognize either of these guys?"

He turned the phone, so we could see it. The picture was grainy and not well lit. The man was looking at a slight angle away from the camera. He appeared to be mid-forties or so, fit, with dark blond hair.

"Never seen him before," I lied.

Deuce's eyes flitted up to mine for a moment, but he followed my lead. "Me neither."

"How about this guy?" Morgan asked, swiping the image aside, replacing it with another.

The second man was the guy I'd seen on the fly bridge of the dive boat out on the wreck site. No doubt about it.

"Haven't seen him before, either," I said.

The security door whisked open and Doctor Trumble came out into the lobby. "Detective Morgan," she said. "You and Mister Phillips can go up now."

"His dad went to get some food," Deuce said. "Would it be all right if Detective Morgan and I visit Marty for a moment? I'll leave as soon as his dad gets back."

"Sure, the more friends the better," the doctor said, with a smile. "But no more than three at a time."

"Give us a second?" Deuce asked Morgan, taking my arm and leading me away.

"That was Ballinger in the picture," Deuce said in a low voice. "The guy you said bought the shrimp boats."

"Yeah," I replied. "The younger guy was on a dive boat I saw diving the wreck this morning."

"The storefront in the pictures where they were talking?" Deuce said. "It's four doors down from our office. What do you want to do?"

"Are Paul and Tom near Islamorada?" I asked.

Deuce nodded. "Tom just texted me that he would be leaving the office in a few minutes. Paul's already on his way here."

"Find out from Morgan where Devon is and maybe Tom can help her out somehow. I'm going to go up to Fort Myers aboard the *Revenge*. I want to know more about these floating meth labs. Can you see that Savannah gets back to the *Anchor*?"

"I'll take them," Rusty said, walking toward us. "If the boy's out of the woods, I got a business to run. You be careful, bro."

Rusty followed me to where Savannah was talking in whispers with Eve and Nick. Florence lay beside her with her head on Savannah's lap, asleep.

"Marty's gonna be fine," I said. "I have to run an errand, Savannah. Is it okay if Rusty gives you a lift back to your boat?"

She agreed, and I gave her and Eve a hug, then turned to leave. Billy caught me at the exterior door, following me outside. "I'm going with you," he said.

"Going where?"

"Steve won't be flying back until morning. You're going to Fort Myers tonight. Thought I might ride along."

"What makes you think I'm going to Fort Myers?" I asked as Billy fell in beside me. We turned toward the parking lot next to the hospital.

"Because that's where *Eliminator* and *Alligator* are."

Billy had a knack for understanding more than he hears. That or he was just clairvoyant. As a kid, he was always telling me how the spirits of his dead Seminole and Calusa ancestors talked to him. I decided it was a waste of time to try to figure out how he knew about the meth labs.

Stopping, I looked Billy in the eye. "It might be dangerous."

"Living is dangerous, Kemosabe. It's the dying part that's easy."

Though it was late, the moon was bright, and we made it to the island in just thirty minutes. Billy and I didn't exchange more than a few words the whole way. I knew what I was about to do, and Billy has known me long enough to know it, too.

It wasn't long after meeting Savannah for the first time that I'd made a similar run up to Fort Myers. Billy and I had gone up into Okaloacoochee Slough, near where he and I grew up. We'd hunted and fished the area many times, but this time we'd been hunting a man. We knew that area well from our childhood. We'd found Earl Hailey, deep in the swamp, and disarmed him. A woman whom he'd been holding captive had grabbed Hailey's gun and shot him. She'd kept pulling the trigger until the gun was empty. Billy saw to it that the woman made it home safely, and I disposed of Earl's body and belongings, making sure his campsite looked like nobody had been there. Billy didn't need to be cautioned on what we were about to do.

Arriving at my island, we wasted little time. I swung both doors open as we approached, and backed *El Cazador* in quickly. While Billy tied her up, I climbed up to the fly bridge on the *Revenge* and started the engines.

The side door opened, and Carl entered the boathouse. "I'm not even gonna ask where you're going at this hour."

I looked down at him. He was wearing only his shorts, obviously roused from sleep by our approach. I climbed down to the cockpit to join him. "I wouldn't tell you if you did."

"Be careful," he said, and turned away, leaving through the side door.

"You need to get anything?" Billy asked, standing at the bow line.

"No, everything we'll need is aboard. Go ahead and cast off."

I climbed back up to the bridge while Billy loosed the lines from the cleats. He stepped aboard and quickly coiled the lines, as I nudged the big boat out from under my house. When we were clear, I pushed the button on the key fob to close the doors.

Billy climbed up to join me and sat in the second seat, studying the array of electronics. "You have a plan?"

"Not really," I replied, feeling the phone in my pocket vibrate. I looked at the screen. It was a text message from Deuce. I'd lose the signal soon after leaving the island. "Do me a favor," I said to Billy. "Go down to my cabin. There's a satellite phone in the charger on the port bookshelf. Grab it for me?"

He went down the ladder, and I turned *Gaspar's Revenge* into Harbor Channel and slowly pushed the throttles about halfway. Once up on the step and with the bow pointed toward the light on Harbor Key Bank, I opened and read the message from Deuce.

I don't know what you hope to find up there, but good luck. Marty positively identified the younger man in the pictures Ben showed him as the guy who shot him. Morgan is trying to get a warrant.

I typed a quick response, telling him I was turning off the cellphone and would be on the sat-phone. I also told him to send the pictures if he could get them from Morgan and anything else he finds out to the sat-phone. After sending the message, I powered the unit off and dropped it into a drink holder.

When Billy returned to the bridge, I turned on the sat-phone. We cleared the bank and found the deep waters of the Gulf of Mexico. I pushed the throttles up to not-quite-full speed, adjusting to maintain forty knots, then set the autopilot. The GPS showed three hours to Sanibel Causeway.

The water was flat calm, and visibility was excellent. The only light on the bridge was the red overhead light, to retain our night vision. It provided enough light to make out the helm and instruments with their backlights off. I adjusted course to go a little further to the west to avoid all the lobster trap floats between Marathon and Cape Sable.

A soft chirp from the sat-phone alerted me to a message. I opened the app and saw the same pictures Morgan had shown us earlier.

I handed the phone to Billy. "Recognize either of these guys?"

Billy flipped through the pictures, then flipped back. "The older guy is Gene Ballinger. Flies in high circles, actors, sports figures, even politicians."

"Recently, he bought some shrimp boats and converted them to meth labs," I said. "At least that's the way it looks. There's a dirty cop involved, too. That's how Marty got shot, because he found evidence of the drug making equipment. Know anything else about Ballinger?"

"Not really," Billy replied. "Send me those pictures and I'll ask around."

"You won't get a signal out here."

"What?" Billy said, grinning, and pulling a phone from his pocket. "You think only whites have satellite phones?"

"You do it," I said, and handed him my phone. "The younger guy works for Ballinger, I think. He was diving the wreck of one of the floating meth labs this morning. And he's the one who shot Marty."

Billy worked with my phone for a few seconds, then handed it back. "I'll send his picture to a few people I know. How sure are you that Ballinger's making meth? He's got a pretty good rep in the business community."

"After that younger guy left the wreck, I dove it myself. They'd removed some things from the hold. Equipment that was bolted to the interior bulkheads. I found half a pound of meth in a watertight package."

"And this guy just let you dive the wreck?"

"They had a scuttling charge planted on it," I replied. "I found it and dragged it off the boat before it detonated. They thought I was killed in the blast."

"Dammit, boy!" Billy exclaimed. "You're lucky to be alive."

"A few times over," I said. "Ballinger's dirty. I don't care what kind of reputation he has in the business world. In my world, he's a turd fondler and needs to face justice or be put down."

My phone chirped. Another text from Deuce.

Tom is with Devon. No warrant yet. Me, Tony, and Andrew are riding with Morgan to Islamorada.

CHAPTER TWENTY-FIVE

Devon continued to watch Brady and the two men inside the store. They seemed to be having a disagreement, and the older man was doing most of the talking. The parking lot and sidewalk in front of the store were well lit.

Suddenly, a shadow moved next to her car and a man was at her window, seeming to appear out of nowhere.

"Detective Evans, I'm a friend of Jesse's."

Her hand was going for her sidearm, before his words registered.

"Easy, Detective," the bald, black man said, stepping back and raising both hands. "My name's Tom Broderick. Jesse and I served together in the Marines, and now I work for him and Deuce."

The man had his face turned slightly, as if watching the store across the highway.

"Jesse sent you?" she asked. "What for?"

"Actually, Deuce sent me," he replied. "Um, would you mind if we continue this with me inside the car? I'm sort of out in the open here."

"Go around the front of the car," Devon replied.

As Broderick went around the hood, keeping both hands in plain sight, Devon pulled her weapon from the holster and turned in her seat, so that her back was against the door. She wasn't taking any chances. Broderick gently opened the door. Leading with his hands, he slowly slid into the seat.

"I promise I'm not here to hurt you," he said. "May I close the door?"

"Use your left hand," she ordered, noticing the hideous burn scar covering the side of his head, and the missing left ear. "Keep your right hand on the dash."

He did as she instructed, and an uneasy silence enveloped the two of them. Broderick turned his head toward her. "I'm deaf," he said, "but I read lips. If you want to tell me something, get my attention first."

"Why did Jesse send you?"

Broderick looked anything but harmless, though that was the vibe she got from him. He was a muscular six-foot, and seemed to carry himself very well. She kept the gun pointed at him.

"Deuce thought I might be able to help you."

Suddenly it dawned on her. "Use the binoculars," she said. "Tell me what they're saying."

Broderick picked up the glasses from the dash and trained them on the store. "There's three guys. One's older, one's younger, and one's a cop."

"Can you tell what they're saying?" she asked, holstering her gun.

Broderick continued watching through the binoculars. She reached over and touched his arm. When he looked at her, she repeated the question.

Broderick looked through the binoculars again. "Write this down," he said. "I'll call them Old, Young, and Cop. Old is pissed. He seems to be calming down, though. Like it's the end of an argument. He says he can't believe how amateurish the other two were."

Devon took a notepad from her jacket pocket and began writing down what Broderick told her.

Broderick continued, as if giving a play-by-play announcement of a football game. "Young is saying he did what he was told."

"Now Old is saying that the two of them need to work together and finish the job."

Devon continued writing furiously, trying to keep up, and falling into a rhythm, using abbreviations.

"Cop says if he's getting any deeper, he wants more money."

Broderick paused. "They're having a stare down. Old just put a briefcase on the counter and opened it. Cop and Young are both looking in it. Cop asks how much. Old is facing away, I can't see his answer."

Devon's phone beeped. She looked and saw that it was from Ben telling her that he was twenty minutes away, but the judge still hadn't signed off on the warrant.

"Cop agreed," Broderick continued. "Old says he wants the fisherman dead, too."

"You're sure about that?" Devon asked. Then she touched his arm and repeated the question when he looked at her.

"Yeah, the older man just told the other two that he wants the deputy and the fisherman dead before the sun comes up."

"Okay," Devon said. "Keep watching. This gives us probable cause." When Tom resumed watching, she added, "I doubt it'll hold up in court, though."

"They're going into the back room of the store," Broderick said, putting the binos on the dash and turning to face her. "You and Jesse are seeing each other."

"Is that a question?" Devon asked, thumbing the little keypad on her phone. She quickly conveyed the threat Broderick had seen said in a message to Ben, and sent it. Knowing even as she did it, that there wasn't a snowball's chance in hell that anything the deaf man said could be used in court.

"I've known him for more than thirty years, Detective. Knew his wife and was there the day his second daughter was born."

"You said you and he served together?"

"I was fresh out of OCS," Tom said. "That's Officer—"

"Officer Candidate School," Devon finished. "I'm a Marine, too."

"Ooh rah," Tom grunted. "No wonder you and Jesse get along. I was a second lieutenant when I met him. I was assigned to command his platoon. Jesse was a sergeant then. He helped me evolve as an officer."

"You were an officer?" Devon asked.

"Colonel Tom Broderick, medically retired. Call me Tom."

"Then you call me Devon, Tom."

"Pleased to meet you, Devon."

"What was his first wife like?" she asked.

"Sandy?" Tom said. "Nothing like Jesse. She was pretty, and they made a handsome couple, but they were like oil and water."

"Let me guess. Sandy didn't like boats."

"Did you say boats?" Tom said, confused. "Sorry. Sometimes I miss words."

"Yes, I said boats. Was that their falling out? Because she didn't like the water?"

"No, I don't think that had anything to do with it," Tom said. "At least not that I know of. They had differing ideologies. She hated him going on deployments, and he was attracted to the action. She left him when we deployed to Panama. That was nineteen years ago, almost to the day. At the time, we were both with the Fleet Antiterrorism Security Team's First Platoon. None of us were even given the chance to call our families when we were ordered to Panama. My wife told me that Sandy had movers at their house the next day. Took the girls and every stick of furniture in the place. Jesse slept on the floor in a sleeping bag for two weeks, hoping she'd return."

"Did he love her?"

"Yeah," Tom replied. "In his own way. I think Jesse was more in love with the idea of being the stalwart Marine husband and father, though."

"What was he like with his daughters?" Devon asked.

"Kim was just born; couldn't have been more than six months old when they split up. Jesse doted on those girls. He'd sit and drink imaginary tea with Eve and her dolls. I'd say he was a devoted father. Why the interest in ancient history?"

Devon was about to answer when her phone chirped. She picked it up and saw that it was Ben calling. She held the phone up to Tom, to signal her intent, before answering it. She did make sure to hold the phone to her right ear. Marine officer or not, police communication had to remain confidential.

"I'm here with Tom Broderick, Ben."

"Good, we're almost there," Ben Morgan replied. "Uniformed deputies are in route and should be there any minute. Where are you?"

Devon gave him the name of the cross street and told him to go a few houses down the street to turn around and then he could park right behind her. Moments later, Ben's brown sedan drove past them. She watched in her mirror as the car's lights turned off and it turned into a driveway.

A moment later, Ben pulled in behind Devon's car and parked. Both front doors opened, and Ben moved quickly to the driver's side and got in the backseat as another man got in behind Tom. It was Jesse's friend, Deuce.

"What's going on?" Ben asked, not bothering to introduce himself to the man sitting in front of him.

Devon turned in her seat. "Brady and the other two men went to the back of the store about twenty minutes ago."

"The store's owned by Eugene Ballinger," Ben said, consulting his notebook. "Has homes and yachts in both Miami and Fort Myers. He owns a manufacturing company that makes deodorizers for commercial and industrial air conditioning systems. The older guy you photographed with Brady is Ballinger. No warrants and no record to speak of, just a few traffic infractions and a possession charge eight years ago."

"Possession?" she asked. "Meth?"

"Cocaine," Ben replied, looking over his reading glasses. "An eight-ball. Paid a fine and did community service."

"You get the warrant, yet?" she asked.

"Just came through," he replied, patting his jacket pocket. "We'll move on the store as soon as backup arrives."

"I know we're civilians," Deuce said, "but my men and I are armed if you need us."

"Thanks, Deuce," Ben said, "but I can't involve you. You know that." Then he grinned over at Jesse's friend. "However, when we go in, if the bad guys shoot us all, feel free to take them out when they come back outside. Just don't be around afterward."

Deuce winked at Devon. "I kinda doubt that's gonna happen, but we're here, just in case."

A sheriff's patrol car turned onto the side street and rolled slowly past Devon's cruiser. A moment later, a second and third one arrived. Each turned around and parked behind the two unmarked cars, blocking the driveway of the first home.

Four deputies got out of the three cars. Devon and Ben got out, and Tom and Deuce joined them. The four of them met the uniformed deputies as two more of Jesse's friends got out of Ben's car.

"Four uniforms and six detectives?" the patrol sergeant asked.

"Two detectives," Ben corrected him. "I'm Lieutenant Ben Morgan, and this is Sergeant Devon Evans."

Ben extended his hand and the sergeant took it. "Sergeant Rick Percy, Lieutenant."

"These four men are feds," Ben said. "Just observing. They have a private security firm across the road, a few doors down from the store where the suspects are located."

"Still six of us," the sergeant said. "What kind of des-perado are we after here?"

"A fellow deputy," Ben said. "Sergeant Steven Brady out of the Ramrod substation. He may have been involved in the shooting of another deputy earlier today."

"Marty Phillips?" one of the other uniformed deputies asked.

"Yeah," Ben said. "Outline the situation, Evans."

"We have three suspects inside the store across the highway. The one in the middle with the inside lights on. They went into the back room about twenty-five minutes ago and haven't reappeared. When they entered, I didn't see anyone lock the door, so we'll enter through the front door."

"Brady is in uniform and armed," Ben said. "The other two men are to be considered armed, as well. Sergeant, you take two men to the right. Evans and I, along with one of your deputies will go to the left. We can converge on the store from opposite sides."

"You sure we can't help?" Deuce asked.

"I checked on you," Ben said. "You're not officially a civilian for a couple more weeks, right?"

"Tom here is," Deuce replied. "But the rest of us won't be officially retired from government service until January first."

"Then Tom stays in the car," Ben said. "You three take positions in the bushes ahead of the cars and keep watch until we're in position. Strictly as backup."

"Understood," Deuce said, leading Tony and Andrew to the dense foliage lining the entrance.

Devon fell in with Ben and one of the deputies. They moved north along the residential entrance until they were out of the illuminated area cast by the orange lights of the parking lot. They crossed the street quickly and silently, sidearms drawn. When they reached the corner of the strip mall, they stopped and waited for the other three deputies to get into position.

Ben led the way, as they moved toward the lighted storefront, staying close to the wall, but not too close. Looking across the street, Devon could see Deuce, kneeling in the shadows. He signaled a thumbs-up that it was still clear. The other team approached from the opposite end. They reached the door without incident, and waited a moment, listening intently. There weren't any sounds coming from inside.

Ben held up three fingers. The sergeant on the other side of the door nodded, pulling a heavy flashlight from his utility belt. The other deputies did the same, keeping the lights off until they made entry.

Ben held up one finger. Then two. When he showed the sergeant three fingers again, they all moved in unison. The door was unlocked, and the six of them swarmed inside.

Ben shouted, "Sheriff's department! We have a warrant!"

CHAPTER TWENTY-SIX

A text from Deuce told me that Brady and the other two men had gotten away. When Morgan and Devon entered the store at the strip mall in Islamorada, there wasn't anyone there. Apparently, there was a back entrance and another vehicle was parked out back.

Billy and I took turns at the helm, while the other caught a nap. We both knew that we'd need to be sharp when we arrived. While I'd been napping, Billy had learned that the younger man in the picture, the man who'd shot Marty, was Cedric Harper. He was some sort of small-time criminal from Detroit with a long record. The word Billy got from his contacts in the area was that Harper worked for Ballinger and had helped the man meet the right people and set things up to manufacture the meth.

Billy assured me that his contacts were very reliable. One man he talked to was actually part of the refit on one of the shrimp boats. When he relayed this information after my nap, I didn't ask how he'd learned this stuff in the middle of the night.

I already knew that Ballinger had bought the three trawlers to repurpose as floating labs. I also knew that he used money Charlotte Richmond had stolen from her father to finance the refits. From what Billy's people said, Ballinger was quickly on his way to becoming a serious distributor.

Billy's boat guy told him that each boat had a regular crew of three, plus two *cooks*, as he called them. They sent the trawlers out to anchor during the day with other shrimp boats, to be inconspicuous, but always downwind. The holds on the boats had been partitioned off with a water-tight bulkhead and door. When they were in the lab, the aft part of the hold was filled with seawater and shrimp, trapping the people inside the lab until they were finished making the drugs. Their thinking was that if the boat was searched while the men were in the lab, all the Coast Guard would find was a hold filled with seawater and shrimp. I had to admit, it was a clever idea.

When Billy took his turn for a nap, halfway to Fort Myers, I made my decision, and turned off the sat-phone. Ballinger was facing at least twenty years, I'd bet. Harper would go away for a long time for shooting a cop, and Brady would be dead meat in prison.

Ballinger didn't have much in the way of liquid assets, other than his real estate holdings and yachts, but he did have some powerful friends, one a sitting Florida senator who was once a public defender. One word from him, and Ballinger could be released on his own recognizance. With boats at his disposal, he could disappear.

It was Ballinger I wanted. He was responsible for the deaths of Charlotte and the others on the shrimp boat. He'd sent Harper to kill Marty. He supplied drugs to addicts who died from using them. In my mind, he was as dirty as they come. Cut off the head, you kill the snake.

I could see the lights of the causeway about five miles ahead and was about to flip the switch for the intercom when I heard the salon hatch open and close.

"Still no plan?" Billy asked, when he'd climbed up.

I didn't answer for a moment. Then I turned in my seat and looked at my old friend. "I think you should stay on the boat, Billy. Or catch a cab home to Labelle. I turned off the sat-phone and removed the battery."

Billy's look was grave. He fully understood what that meant. "I'm going with you, brother."

There was no changing his mind. When we were twelve years old, Billy made me his blood brother after helping him out of a bad situation with some other kids that were picking on him. He'd been smallish as a boy, and I'd always been big for my age. There were four of them, and two were teenagers. Billy and I had taken them on, our backs to one another, and beat them. He'd never consider his debt repaid.

"I want to get aboard one of those boats and see for myself."

"And if the shrimpers don't want to let you?" Billy asked.

"At most, there might be five people on each boat," I said. "Odds are we won't find anyone; maybe a single crewman. I want to see the inside of the holds, and if we encounter resistance, we'll meet it with overpowering force."

"You're dead set on this?"

I looked over at him. "These guys make drugs, man. The one called Harper shot a deputy in his own house. The deputy may well be my son-in-law one day, and at any rate, I consider the young man my friend. Ballinger is responsible for the death of a woman I know, plus a few others who were on the boat with her. Running drugs through my backyard is one thing, but now it's personal."

"We go in hard then," Billy said. "Weapons?"

"Mind the helm," I said.

Going quickly down the ladder, I made my way forward to my stateroom and knelt by the bunk. I punched in the code and raised the bunk on hydraulically assisted arms. Beneath it was an assortment of reel and rod cases, along with other boxes labeled as boating supplies. At least that's what they looked like.

Taking two Fin-Nor rod cases out, I placed them on the deck. I also grabbed a large box that said it contained a Shimano reel. Closing the bunk, I picked up the rod and reel cases and returned to the cockpit, handing them up to Billy.

Billy smiled as I climbed up the ladder. "These feel a might heavier than the rods and reels I'm used to fishing with."

Sitting on the port bench, I opened the larger of the reel boxes. Inside were a pair of Sig-Sauer nine-millimeter handguns, along with four magazines. I slid a mag into one of them and handed it to Billy.

"Just the kind of tackle every fisherman needs," he said, taking the Sig and one extra magazine. "What's in the rod cases?"

"A pair of Heckler and Koch rods," I said, opening one of the cases and handing the MP5 it contained to Billy.

He racked the slide on the ugly machine pistol, locking the bolt to the rear with a practiced hand to inspect the chamber. I'd bought both guns from him, along with quite a few more. He slapped the cocking handle, releasing the bolt, then reached over and took one of the thirty-round magazines, slipping it into the receiver. Then he took the other two mags from the case and put them in his pocket.

I did the same with the other handgun and machine pistol, stuffing the extra magazines into my pockets.

"We don't fire unless fired upon," I told him.

Nearing the familiar causeway, I slowed the *Revenge*. Billy had given me a rough idea of where the two shrimp boats were docked. There weren't any other boats on the water as we passed under the bridge and turned up the Caloosahatchee River, barely on plane.

Billy guided me to the marina and we were soon tied up at the diesel dock, behind a shiny, well-kept but older Sea Ray Sundancer.

Before stepping off the boat, I pulled a pair of worn windbreakers out of the bench seat and we put them on to conceal the machine pistols. A sleepy looking dockmaster came out of the little shack, as Billy and I climbed down.

"Two hundred gallons of diesel," I said, as he approached.

The old man looked my boat over. "That's six hundred. Cash in advance."

It wasn't the first time *Gaspar's Revenge* had been mistaken for a smuggler's boat. Who else would fuel up at an out of the way marina in the middle of the night? I peeled off the bills and handed them to the man. Odds were, some of them would end up in his pocket.

"And you never saw us," I said.

"Saw who?" the man asked, exposing several missing teeth, in what I assumed was a conspiratorial grin.

"We're gonna take a walk," I said. "Stretch our legs a little and maybe get some breakfast. My boat be okay here until sunrise?"

"Sure," the old man said, pulling the hose from the pump. "Ain't none of the boats here going out until tomorrow."

"How come?" Billy asked.

"Got me," the dockmaster said. "Only diesel boats here are three shrimpers. One of 'em must still be out. They usually go out for one night, on Monday and again on Wednesday and Friday. They don't catch more than a couple hundred pounds and spend the next day at the dock."

"Never make any money that way," Billy said.

"I don't know," he said with a sigh, his voice carrying the message that he'd seen it all and then some. "Maybe it's just a hobby to 'em. Ain't none of 'em looks like a shrimper. I'd say they was up to no good, ya ask me."

"We'll be back shortly," I said, turning away.

Billy fell in beside me, as we followed the pier toward shore. We'd seen the two shrimp boats as we entered the little marina. They were docked side by side, at the far end of the compound, near the parking lot.

"Last chance," I said, stopping at the foot of the pier.

One corner of Billy's mouth turned up slightly. "Saturday night, brother. Rock and roll."

With that, we each racked the bolts on the MP5s as quietly as possible, chambering a nine-millimeter round. The same round as our handguns, but the machine pistols were full-auto.

The pier connected to a concrete wharf, where a decrepit boatyard stood, machinery rusting in the elements. We walked along the wharf, keeping to the shadows as much as possible. When we reached the far side, I led Billy into a maze of lobster traps to a spot where we could see both boats. Neither had a light on and we didn't see any sign that there was anyone aboard.

"Let's check the nearest one first," I whispered.

Billy nodded, and we moved out of the maze and onto the northern pier. It extended a hundred yards out into a small, natural harbor, just like the pier on the other side, then turned at a right angle, a mirror image of the fuel dock where the *Revenge* lay, with the ends of the two docks a mere fifty feet apart. The shrimp boats were tied up on the outside of this one and the fuel dock was on the outside of the other one.

The two L-shaped docks surrounded another shorter pier in the middle. This one had a couple dozen slips, most of which were empty. None of the boats in the marina showed signs of life, and I had serious doubts if any had been used in months, except the two trawlers. I couldn't help noticing that there was room at the end of the pier for another trawler.

We reached the turn of the pier and crouched next to a large dock box mounted to the dock, the paint peeling and the wood showing signs of rot from the harsh south Florida environment. The stern of *Eliminator* was right in front of us. This was the boat that Al Fader said had a strange odor the night it anchored among the Key West shrimp fleet.

I moved toward the low gunwale of the shrimp boat, Billy right behind me. Just as I lifted a leg to step over, I heard a very distinctive sound and froze. Billy stood motionless beside me. The double clunking sound came from behind us, where a beat up old Silverton was tied up.

Billy and I knew that sound well and it sent a cold chill down my spine. The sound of a heavy, twelve-gauge shotgun shell being racked into the chamber will do that to anyone.

CHAPTER TWENTY-SEVEN

Devon sat at a table idly picking at a half-day-old muffin. Both she and Ben were disappointed that Brady wasn't in the warehouse. She felt guilty that she hadn't figured on another vehicle or another exit. She wondered if she'd been seen, or if one of the men had seen Tom Broderick crossing the street to join her. She doubted that; he was a Marine combat infantry officer.

But more than anything, she felt guilty about her decision concerning Jesse.

"Don't beat yourself up," Ben said, taking a sip of his coffee.

They'd stopped on their way back to Key West to get a bite to eat. It was still a few hours until sunrise, and they both needed coffee for the drive back.

"That obvious?" Devon asked.

"Yeah," he said. "You couldn't watch the front and back at the same time. Uniforms will sit on Brady's car and the APB will turn up one of them, sooner or later."

"I know," she replied, still picking at the muffin. She felt like she should be starved, since she hadn't eaten since lunch. But her stomach was in knots and nothing looked appealing on the menu, so she'd chosen the blueberry muffin.

"It's something else, isn't it?"

"You're not going to like it," she said, her eyes quickly glancing up at her boss and mentor.

Ben stretched his legs and leaned back in his chair. Though only seven years older than her, he always reminded Devon of a concerned uncle, though she never had an uncle.

"The job offer from that City Manager up in Georgia?" he asked. "You should take it."

Devon's eyes came up to meet Ben's steady gaze. "Why would you say that?"

"Don't pretend with me, Devon. You've already decided. You're only thirty-five. Sure, it's a small rural town, but it'll be *your* town. Let me ask you something. How many thirty-five-year-old female police chiefs have you heard about?"

"Not many," she replied.

"Four currently, in the whole State of Georgia," Ben said. "I checked. And the sheriff in the same county you're going to is the first woman sheriff in the state. It's a great opportunity."

"But I have friends here."

"You'll make friends there, too," Ben said, leaning forward, and placing his elbows on the table. "Stop being a dumbass, Devon. There's no such thing as a perfect relationship. Sure, you and McDermitt get along well, and I don't remember you ever mentioning any kind of disagreement, and I'd pick up on that vibe even if you didn't say anything. You two have similar backgrounds, morals, and convictions, but you and I both know it won't work in the long run."

"Jesse will never leave his island," Devon admitted, starting to realize for the first time that her instincts were right. "Not for me, or anyone else."

"And you're a landlocked islander who doesn't like the water."

"It's still not an easy decision to make," Devon said.

Ben grinned. "If it'll make it easier, I can fire you. But you've already made up your mind, haven't you?"

Devon drained her coffee and stood up. "Yes, I have. I've got over a month's vacation time saved up. Can I take it? Starting now?"

"No," Ben replied, standing, and dropping a ten on the table. "You gotta go back down to Key West first, and turn in your vehicle."

Outside, the two detectives stood by their cars. "I'll get started on the paperwork in the morning, but consider your comp time as having started at midnight."

"Thanks, Ben."

"One thing," he said, as she reached for the door handle. "Is your decision based partly on the little girl?"

"How'd you know about her?"

Ben smiled broadly. "I'm a lieutenant. It's my job to know everything."

"Jesse hasn't said anything," Devon said, opening her car door. "But my gut tells me the child is his. Once he knows, he'll want to be a part of her life. I don't know anything about the woman, except that she seems to be a better fit for Jesse than I am, and I would never stand in the way of that."

"Now you're talking like a detective, Chief."

She laughed, though she liked the sound of the title, then turned and hugged him. "Thanks for everything, Ben. I won't forget this."

He hugged her back, though she knew he felt awkward about personal contact. "I'm going home to get some sleep and probably won't be in until noon. By then, you'd better be on the Florida Turnpike, halfway to Georgia."

Devon got in her car and waited a moment until Ben backed out. She waited a few minutes longer, letting him get far down the road. She didn't want him to look in the mirror and see her crying.

CHAPTER TWENTY-EIGHT

The sounds from over at the bar had quieted shortly after midnight. Savannah had put Flo to bed right after Rusty had delivered them back to his little marina.

Sitting on *Sea Biscuit's* fly bridge, Savannah saw Rusty turning off the lights in the bar. A moment later, he stepped outside, locking the door behind him. Her bridge was covered, and she was in the shadows, so he didn't see her when he turned and surveyed his property. Savannah watched as Rusty walked toward his little house adjacent to the bar and then went inside. She waited another twenty minutes, until she saw the lights in the back room of the house turn off. Then she waited a half hour longer, to allow the man to get to sleep.

Right after Jesse and his Indian friend had left the hospital, the ME arrived and told her that his investigation was complete, and she could arrange transport. He'd even had all the necessary documents for her to sign. Sharlee's body would be picked up in just a few more hours and transported back home to Beaufort. It was time to move on, though she didn't have a destination in mind.

Starting the boat's engine, she went quickly down to the aft sun deck to untie the lines, leaving Woden asleep on the bridge deck. As she began to step down from the sun deck, she saw Rusty standing on the dock, next to her boat. He was dressed as he had been when he went into the house. His presence startled her. She thought she was pretty good at reading people and never guessed that a man his size could be very stealthy.

"Dangerous setting out in the middle of the night," he said.

Woden rose and emitted a low, rumbling growl. She silenced him with a raised hand, and turned to face the man. "You knew I was going to leave?"

"Suspected as much," he replied. "Once Doc Fredrick released your sis's body, there just ain't much holding you here, is there?"

Seeing Jesse again had made her want to stay—but there just wasn't any way she could put that burden on him.

"No," she said. "Nothing at all."

Rusty glanced to the front of the boat, where Flo slept in the forward vee-berth. "She's his, ain't she?"

"I told you, Rusty, I just don't know."

"That's why you're runnin' in the middle of the night."

Savannah stepped down to the small cockpit behind her little stateroom and stood with her hands on her hips. "I'm not running."

"Where ya headed?"

"I don't know yet," she replied.

"You're runnin' then."

Savannah sat on the roof of the cabin, a single tear streaming down her cheek. "Don't you get it? I can't saddle him with the knowledge and I just don't want to know."

"You're a coward," Rusty said. "If Jesse is the dad, there ain't no way in hell he'd shirk his responsibility. Being a dad's about all the man's really got going for him."

"And both his daughters are grown women," Savannah said, looking up at the bar owner. "He's nearing fifty years old, Rusty. A man shouldn't be the father to a small child at that age."

"Hah!" Rusty exclaimed. "I've known Jesse for damned near thirty of those years. He's my own daughter's godfather. I seen him around his girls when they were little. You ever seen a warrior in camouflage sipping make-believe tea with a little girl? I have. He looked comical sitting there in boots and utes, but he didn't give a damn what anyone thought, 'cept that little girl. It ain't about the years in a man's life, it's about the life in a man's years. Jesse would make a great daddy for your little girl."

Savannah dropped her head in her hands, sobbing a little. "Don't you see, Rusty? I can't ask him to take that on. Besides, he has a woman in his life."

"He don't love her."

For an instant her resolve melted. If she could only be sure of that, it might make a difference. "Did he tell you that?"

"No," Rusty replied. "But like I said, I know the man as well as I'd know my own brother. She's young and pretty, but she's all wrong for Jesse, and deep inside, he knows that."

Savannah brushed her cheeks with the back of her hand, as she stood. "Makes no difference."

Rusty stood there a moment, looking deep into her eyes. In his, she saw the wisdom of a very old soul. This was a man to be trusted.

"Go on up to the bridge, Captain," he said. "I'll get your dock lines for you."

She started to step up onto the cabin roof, then stopped. "Don't tell him about our conversations."

"I can't promise ya that, Savannah. All I can promise is that I won't bring it up. But if he asks me did I talk to you before you left, I'm gonna tell him the truth. He was really tore up the last time you up and disappeared in the middle of the night."

That stung, but at the same time, it gave her a feeling of warmth. She'd only been here a little more than a week, all those years ago. But it had been an emotional roller coaster of a week. She had to cut it short because she'd known that she was falling in love with a man she barely knew. And she'd still been married.

"I can't stay," she said flatly, and turned to go up the steps to the fly bridge, tears streaming down her face.

CHAPTER TWENTY-NINE

"Turn around real slow," a voice behind us drawled. I knew that voice. As I slowly turned, I saw the old sports fisherman the man was on and recognized the dingy look of it, the faded brightwork and green stains running down from the scuppers. It was the dive boat I'd seen on the wreck and I suddenly realized why it had looked familiar then.

The man pointing the shotgun menacingly at me and Billy was the same Texan who had held a knife at my throat when he delivered me to Tena Horvac almost two years ago.

The rage that had been building inside me and had nearly tipped when Brady walked into the ER now pegged the meter at full tilt. I turned off my mind. I allowed muscle memory to take over. I'd trained many long days, for many years, to move and fight by instinct.

Time slowed. The man's mouth began to open to say something else, but I was already in motion. Some sixth sense told me that Billy was also moving, though my focus was on Tex's midsection.

I dove to my left, my right hand already brushing back the open windbreaker, and falling onto the grip of the MP5, which hung from my shoulder.

I hit the ground in a roll, coming up onto one knee, my cheek molded to the weapon and my sights right on Tex's belly. I pulled the trigger, firing a two-round burst just as he fired at the spot where Billy and I had been standing.

As Tex spun around from the impact of the two bullets, I heard Billy firing. Most civilians are never in a firefight. Many have never even heard a gunshot. But if you're a twenty-year infantry Marine, trained daily in every possible condition and weapon, your situational awareness and your mind and muscle memory will recall things without your mind even knowing. Billy was shooting at something above me.

Suddenly, more men appeared on the other trawler, all firing at us. Handguns and shotguns roared from where they stood on the deck eighty feet away.

A man's body fell onto the dock next to me, two red dots expanding from the center of his chest. Some part of my mind recognized him. It was the kid that'd been on the dive boat, the one who'd tried to kill Marty.

I moved behind a storage box and quickly extended the butt of the HK to its fullest. The MP5 is a great weapon in tight spots. It combines the small size of a pistol and a forward grip like an assault rifle, with a telescoping butt. Though not as accurate as a rifle, in the hands of someone who knows how to use it, it's far more accurate than handguns and shotguns.

I rose, leading with the weapon, my cheek melded to the stock. I heard Billy fire a two-round burst behind me. Again, years of training told me which direction he was firing, which my eyes confirmed when my head came up and I saw one of the men on the trawler drop. I chose a target at random and pulled the trigger again. Another man spun and went overboard, the splash sounding unusually loud and out of place amid the gunfire. My mind registered a man on the roof of the pilothouse, rising and starting for the ladder, just as I dropped back down behind the box.

Billy ran up and took cover behind a post, checking the dock to our rear. He looked over and nodded. I rose and shot the man climbing down from the pilothouse. He fell backward onto the dock with a thud.

Like a cat, Billy rose and moved across the dock ahead of me, dropping behind another dock box. I instantly rolled to my left, taking advantage of the distraction, and came up kneeling by the post Billy'd just vacated. I saw him rise and fire again.

I didn't see, but I knew he'd dropped another man. Though Billy had only spent four years in the Corps, he was one of those guys who was always prepping for a possible government overthrow or some sort of apocalypse. He had a tactical infiltration course on his property, back behind the off-road track he'd built.

Now there were only two. I stood up fully, shouldering the MP5, and advancing toward our assailants. A man on the boat stood, pointing a revolver at me, of all things. I shot him in the chest.

Billy stood, and together we marched deliberately toward the shrimp boat, weapons at the ready. I knew there was one more man on board, but the deck was cluttered with nets, buckets, and bodies.

Suddenly, the back door to the pilothouse opened, and I heard an engine start beyond the trawler. Brady stepped out of the wheelhouse, a shotgun in his hands. Billy's weapon fired before Brady could even raise the barrel.

The engine I'd heard suddenly roared, churning white water directly ahead of us. At first, I thought it was the *Revenge* and someone was trying to steal her. But it was the Sea Ray that had been docked in front of us.

The bridge deck was awash with light and there was only one person at the helm that I could see. He turned and looked back at us. It was Ballinger.

"Back to the boat!" I shouted.

Billy was right behind me as we raced down the dock toward the wharf. We were both breathing hard when we got to the *Revenge*. I tossed off the stern line and jumped aboard. Billy raced past me to cast off the bow line.

In seconds, Billy was aboard, and we were underway. I hadn't seen the old dockmaster. His little shack was empty. He'd probably run off as soon as the shooting started.

The other boat had disappeared in the darkness but the disturbed water from his wake left a trail of bioluminescent plankton that at least gave me an idea which direction he'd gone.

Billy got the radar up and running and pointed to the only moving echo on the screen. "Downriver," he said calmly. "Headed toward the causeway. How fast can his boat go?"

"I don't know," I replied, turning the wheel to go after Ballinger. "Probably forty knots."

"That's how fast we went coming up here."

"But we weren't going full speed," I said, pushing the throttles to the stops. The *Revenge* surged forward, as the superchargers spooled up, creating a high-pitched scream. "Take the wheel. Force him to run for open water."

Descending quickly down the ladder to the cockpit, I dreaded opening the hatch to the engine room. My ears were still ringing, both from the underwater blast and the firefight. When I opened the hatch, the sound of each engine's twin turbos and the superchargers wound up as high as they'd go, made me dizzy. I quickly stepped down into the engine room and grabbed a pair of earmuffs from a hanger on the bulkhead. They helped a little.

In seconds, I had the two hidden compartments open and placed the tripod and mini-gun up on the cockpit deck. Another purchase from Billy. I removed the lower half of the tripod, leaving only the gun mount and pedestal with its two-inch titanium connecting rod. Removing the strap that holds the ammo box and the twelve-volt motorcycle battery below the pedestal, I slung it over my head and shoulder, then picked up the mount and gun.

Holding the gun by its handle with my left hand, I stuck the lightweight mount under my arm and stepped up onto the narrow side deck. Grabbing the handrail of the cabin roof with my right hand, I reminded myself for the millionth time that an access from the galley to the foredeck just made good sense.

A year ago, Tony had mentioned the need for a forward mount. I nixed the idea for obvious reasons. The handrails around the foredeck are barely knee-high, except at the pulpit, and standing up to use the tripod would just be too dangerous. So we'd stripped the tripod from its mount and had a small insert fabricated into the deck next to the anchor chain in lieu of the tripod.

Fortunately, seas were still dead calm as I carefully moved out onto the open foredeck. The *Revenge* rocketed ahead at nearly fifty knots. I had to stay low, with my feet far apart, but I made it to the relative safety of the bow rail. Kneeling and leaning against the rail, I removed the cap from the receiver in the deck and inserted the connecting rod. Fitting the mini-gun into the swivel mount, I latched it in place, then secured the ammo can and battery pack to the opposite rail.

Looking ahead, I was shocked to see how fast we were approaching the causeway. I could see Ballinger's boat; he was just passing under the high arch. Billy was steering toward the opening to the left of where Ballinger was, forcing him to turn around the tip of Sanibel Island.

We flashed under the bridge, and Billy yelled out, "Hang on!"

I gripped the starboard rail, knowing he was going to turn sharp to force his way between Ballinger and the beach. The *Revenge* rolled over onto her side, the starboard chine digging deep into water.

When Billy recovered from the turn, I went back to work. In seconds, I had the belt fed into the mini-gun and the battery cable attached. I flipped on the electric belt feed and waited for the green light.

When it came on, I sat down on the deck, bracing my feet against the raised pulpit and the rail stanchion. Ballinger's boat was less than a mile off the port bow and heading west-southwest, directly toward the setting moon.

A minute later, Billy turned and we crashed through the yacht's starboard wake, just a hundred yards away and coming alongside. I aimed well ahead of the yacht and depressed the firing switch. The motor whirred, spinning the six barrels up to speed. Then the belt feed engaged, and the gun spat a stream of flame, as more than a hundred rounds flew across Ballinger's bow in two seconds. Only every fifth round was a tracer, but the steady stream from the barrel looked like a whip of fire.

Ballinger turned sharply away from us to the southeast, paralleling Fort Myers Beach. Billy turned and crossed his wake again, far too wide, putting Ballinger behind me. The set-up for the pedestal mount had to be off-center so as not to interfere with the anchor chain. The gun could only be fired forward or to port.

Ballinger turned southwest again and I realized Billy had gone wide to give the man a false sense of security and turn him back toward open water. Billy slowed slightly, then turned and crossed the other boat's wake again, bringing it into my field of fire.

Ballinger had gained nearly a quarter of a mile, but we were slowly chewing up the distance. I realized what Billy was doing. There was no turning back once this started. Ballinger wasn't going to stop just because I sent some lead across his bow. Billy was forcing the man farther and farther from shore, into deeper water. Water that a boat could disappear under and not be found.

Ballinger began a series of swerves, trying to avoid being hit. Billy countered like a sheep dog, constantly forcing Ballinger away from shore. I was certain that his boat didn't have the range to cross the Gulf; it was a luxury yacht, not an expeditionary vessel. Maybe he thought he had enough range to just out-distance the *Revenge*. But our tanks were full. We could chase him to Havana or Pensacola, or any part of the Gulf in between. Like the deep waters I was sure we were entering.

Looking behind us, I saw no other boats, and Sanibel Lighthouse was a good five or six miles away and fading fast. We were in forty or fifty feet of water now.

I pointed, pumping my arm, urging Billy to get us alongside. I felt the *Revenge* surge forward, as the superchargers spooled up again, forcing more cool, clean air into the turbocharged engines.

Ballinger attempted to turn away from us. Billy turned with him, slowly overtaking the yacht on the outside. I aimed and pressed the button, holding it down. The flame and loud buzz of the mini-gun split the night air. I moved the wicked line of tracers onto the target and watched as they chewed the aft cockpit and sundeck to pieces. I moved the line of fire like a whip along the waterline.

The yacht exploded in a bright yellow fireball. It broke up, parts and pieces skimming across the surface. The water quickly extinguished most of the flames, as what was left of the yacht rolled and went under, taking Ballinger with it.

Billy slowed. It was over. Pieces of flotsam scattered the surface of the water, some still burning. But the yacht was gone. Ballinger was dead. Brady was dead. Harper was dead. And the Texan was dead.

CHAPTER THIRTY

I kept looking behind us as we cruised south past the Ten Thousand Islands for the second time. We didn't want to risk going back to Fort Myers, or on up the river to Labelle, where Billy lived. It would mean going right past the marina. So we'd set a course for my island. Billy would hang out until we were sure nobody was looking for us.

Taking another person's life isn't something done lightly, at least not for a person of good conscience. But I knew those men were bad, and I was glad they were dead. I just hoped that I hadn't gotten Billy into something we couldn't get out of. Vigilantism isn't what I do. Nor him.

The only one who knew we were going to Fort Myers was Deuce. I'm sure Morgan or even Devon could put things together. And the old man at the dock had seen us.

Billy had spent the first half hour of our return trip on his satellite phone, texting people, trying to get a read on what the police in Fort Myers knew.

An hour into our trip, he finally put the phone in his pocket and looked over at me. "You owe me ten thousand dollars."

"You're a merc, now?"

He chuckled softly. "Taking out the garbage is on the house. I just had one of my people visit Zac Lunsford."

"Who's he?"

"The dockmaster," Billy said. "He said he knew something was going down and as soon as he filled our tanks, he left the marina. My friend gave Lunsford ten grand to say that he never saw us, and only went to get a bottle of rum. He readily agreed."

When we got back to my island, the sun was already up. Pulling into my channel, I half-expected people in FBI jackets to come streaming down the pier. The only greeting we had was from Finn.

Carl and Charlie's boat was gone. We tied up and I took my cell phone up to the deck. I was tired and felt old. Billy went inside to shower and change clothes. I turned on the phone and called Deuce.

"Where the hell are you?" he whispered urgently.

"At home. How's Marty?"

"He's gonna be fine, already complaining to go home."

"That's good," I said. "What's up?"

"What's *up*?" he said more urgently, but still in a whisper. "You go and shoot the hell out of half of Fort Myers and want to know what's up? You need to get to Marathon riki tik."

"Who knows?"

"That you went on a vengeance streak?" Deuce asked. "Only me, and maybe Chyrel. But there have been some developments. You need to get here right away."

I took the time to shower first, after Billy was finished. Dressed in clean clothes, we boarded *El Cazador* and headed to the hospital. When we arrived, there wasn't anyone I knew in the ER lobby. I asked at the desk and a nurse told me there was a waiting area in the wing where Marty had been moved to, and gave me the room number.

When I got there, Kim, Deuce, and Julie were still there. Eve and Nick had gone back up to Miami, but his father, Alfredo was still there.

"Where've you been?" Kim asked, as we entered the waiting room.

I glanced at Deuce and he shook his head slightly, telling me that Kim didn't know.

"I'm sorry," I said, hugging my daughter. "There were things that needed tending to. I was in constant touch with Deuce, though. He told me Marty's gonna be fine."

"They'll probably let him go home tomorrow," she said, eyeing me suspiciously. "I was just about to go visit him. Why don't you come with me? He's been asking to see you."

We started to leave, but Maggio pulled me aside and asked for just a minute of my time.

"What is it?" I asked.

"Last year, I took a case pro bono for a man who was trying to avoid a foreclosure."

"How is this important?" I asked, briskly.

"His name is Zachary Lunsford."

He knew already? I knew he had connections all over south Florida, on both sides of the law. Was he trying to hold some perceived information over me, to get out of our deal?

"I just want you to know," Maggio said, with a half-grin, handing me a business card, "if you should need representation, call me. That's got my private cell number on it."

Sticking the card in my pocket, I thanked him and went with Kim to Marty's room. Billy sat down with Deuce and Chyrel, who had her computer open on the table in such a way that only the three of them could see it. They were speaking in low whispers.

Marty was awake and alert when we entered the room. He smiled nervously. Kim stopped at the foot of his bed and said she was going to go get Marty something to drink.

"I'd like to ask you something," Marty said, after she left. I had a feeling I was being set up.

"And what's that, Marty?" I asked, taking a seat in the chair next to his bed and pushing my hair back over my ears with both hands.

"I saw the guy. He was in my house. Everything happened in slow motion. He shot me, and I thought I was going to die."

"You're a tough man," I said, trying to avoid calling him a kid.

"The thing is," he said, "the only thing I could think of while I lay on the floor bleeding was that I might not see Kim again. I want to marry her, Mister McDermitt. But I want your approval before I ask her."

"Have you heard what happened to Brady?"

"Yes, sir, I did. Fort Myers police think he was trying to stop a drug shipment or something."

"And what do you think, Marty?"

He looked me straight in the eye. "I think the engines on your boat show about eight hours more run time than they did yesterday."

I gazed back at the young man. He knew. "And you want to do the morally right thing, by asking *me* for my daughter's hand?"

The ball was in his court. What Billy and I had done was wrong, and I knew it. Marty also knew it.

"Sometimes," he said, "doing what's morally right might not always be the ethical thing to do."

"Pretty wise statement, considering your age."

He chuckled softly, then winced and put a hand to his chest, where it was bandaged tightly. "I heard it from you."

"From me?"

"A long time ago. You were drinking at the *Anchor* with some of your friends, discussing the difference between ethics and morals."

"I'll have to take your word," I said, not remembering anything about what he was saying. "I'm not responsible if I'm drinking rum."

"Brady's fingerprints were found on my boat, where he put the head. Sergeant Evans saw him with the guy who shot me and the guy who was making the meth. Fort Myers PD found the meth labs on Ballinger's boats. Did you know my dad's from Texas?"

"I seem to remember that, yeah. What's that got to do with it?"

"He says that in Texas, *they needed killin'* is a valid defense."

I stood up and extended my hand. "I'd be honored to have you for my son-in-law, Marty."

He took it, and we shook—I expect in much the same way that men have been doing with prospective fathers-in-law for generations.

Though probably without the specter of the betrothed possibly arresting the father of the bride.

Ben Morgan entered the room. "Ah, Mister McDermitt, I've finally tracked you down."

I went to full alert. Morgan was a good cop, as good as they come. I wasn't going to resist. "You've been looking for me?"

"Yes," he said. "I'm afraid I have some bad news."

He went on to tell me that several weeks ago, Devon had been approached by the City Manager of Apple Valley, Georgia, just north of Athens, about taking on the job of police chief.

I was confused. "What are you saying, Lieutenant?"

"Devon decided to take the job. She left last night."

I was having trouble comprehending. He and Devon had been at Ballinger's store when I left for Fort Myers. Morgan led me out of Marty's room, to a small chapel where we could talk privately. He told me that Devon had been agonizing over it for weeks, more so in the last couple of days. He explained to me what she suspected about Savannah and her daughter.

"Not that it's any of my business," he said finally. "But you're a smart guy, you had to have known it wouldn't work."

He was right. I'd known it right from the start. She wanted the house with the picket fence, and two cars in the driveway. And being eleven years younger than me, she could still have that. But not with the likes of me. I couldn't stomach living in a subdivided neighborhood, even Key West. The logical part of my brain understood and even agreed with that, but the emotional side took a hit. It was fun being with Devon. She made me feel more alive than I had in years.

In nine years, I thought. My mind suddenly reeled with the knowledge that I was no longer attached. A voice in my head chastised me for thinking of Savannah, but I couldn't deny it. Even Devon had thought that Florence was my child. I suddenly needed to know.

Excusing myself, I left the chapel in a hurry. Kim was probably in the waiting room with Deuce and the others. I needed to get to the *Anchor*. The overwhelming urge was more powerful than anything I'd ever experienced.

By boat, I'd have to go all the way around the island. By car, it was just a few minutes. But my car was at the *Anchor*. I could get a ride from Deuce, or even Julie, but I didn't want to waste time explaining, nor could I explain the irrationality of it.

What could I say? Devon just left me, and I need to see Savannah right now? I turned the other way and went to the stairs. If it was minutes by car, it wasn't any longer than running. I went down the steps in near leaps, swinging around the landings by the rail.

Outside, I ran through the parking lot, angling toward the corner and the sidewalk. I ran across the intersection at Sombrero Beach Road, against the light, a car honking at me as I did so. I ran past the Kmart. I turned down the crushed shell driveway covered in foliage. I ran into the small parking area on the other side of the jungle barrier.

I stopped at the edge of the dock, where the sidewalk goes up to the bar. Savannah's boat was gone.

EPILOGUE

Later that morning, Billy flew back with his pilot buddy, but not until Deuce and Chyrel found no mention in the Fort Myers police reports that linked me and Billy to what happened at the marina.

Later that day, Fort Myers discovered that Brady had a BOLO out on him, and his status changed instantly in their eyes, from dead hero to dead criminal. The investigation stalled after just a few days. Everyone dead had a long record and nobody seemed real enthused about solving the mystery of who shot up the drug gang.

Ballinger was listed as missing and presumed to be on the run, since his yacht was gone from its slip. Over the ensuing weeks, his assets were frozen, what little there was, and his passport was revoked. Fort Myers figured that when he surfaced again, wherever it was, he could be extradited. But Davey Jones doesn't have an extradition treaty with Florida.

Marty was released from the hospital the following Thursday. Kim had to race back to Gainesville for two exams, then she was off until after the first of the year. Her grades in the class she missed and the fact that her professor was a former police officer allowed her to retake that exam and she passed them all with high marks. She immediately returned to take care of her fiancé.

Kim told me that she and Marty had set a date for after Kim's graduation. Then she surprised me saying she wanted to graduate in the spring with just an associate degree. They both wanted to go to the Fish and Wildlife academy in the summer, and Marty was finishing his associate degree online.

Marty was given a month of convalescent time and they came out to the island every day to check on me. I was lost. The woman I thought I'd loved was hundreds of miles away. I didn't begrudge Devon for doing it. We both knew it wasn't going to last. The woman I could love was anywhere but here. The idea that I might have another daughter out there consumed me.

Friday was moving day. I arranged a truck to meet the Trents at Old Wooden Bridge Marina and with the help of a dozen friends, we unloaded Rusty's big barge into the truck. Though they were leaving the furniture, just their personal belongings brought out to the island over the last three years amounted to quite a bit. We loaded Carl's little pickup onto a trailer and hitched it to the truck and they were ready to go. Carl Junior wanted to ride in the truck with his dad and Patty rode in Charlie's car, towing Russ's old Grady-White. Their departure was emotional.

As I hugged Charlie, I slipped her an envelope. "Just a little something to help you guys get set up in your new home."

She reached up and threw an arm around my neck, hugging me tightly. "You didn't have to do that."

"It's the least I could do," I said. "I know how difficult starting over can be."

The following week, I flew the *Hopper* to Beaufort for Charlotte's funeral. Savannah wasn't there. Her mother somehow knew who I was and approached me. Though grief-stricken over the loss of her daughter, she was more concerned about Savannah and Florence. She told me that Savannah had called to tell her that she wouldn't be at the funeral, thinking that I might show up there.

"I don't know where they are," Madison Richmond told me. "Her home has always been the sea, since she was a little girl. If I hear from her, I'll tell her you were here to pay your respects."

I flew back to Marathon in a funk. I couldn't just come right out and ask the mother if her granddaughter was the legitimate child of Savannah's marriage. In some places, that might be acceptable, but not in an old southern town dripping with Spanish moss.

When I got back to Rusty's place, I went straight to the bar. It was close enough to five o'clock, but it was getting close to Christmas and there wasn't anyone around. Rusty guessed at my mood and poured me a double from the top shelf. The real top shelf, hidden under the bar. I drained half of the fifteen-year-old Pusser's.

"Find out anything?" he asked, opening a beer for himself.

I started to answer, but the question suddenly struck me as odd. It was a question a person would ask if they knew you hadn't found what you went looking for.

"You know something," I said, flatly.

"I know a lot of things, bro."

"Where'd Savannah go?"

"She left the night you and Billy went up to Fort Myers and killed Brady and Ballinger."

It was still early, and we were alone in the bar. Still that's something you don't just openly talk about.

"You saw her leave?" I asked, avoiding the confrontation on the killings.

"Helped her cast off," he replied picking up a highball glass and polishing it. "It was zero dark thirty, after I closed up."

"You talked to her?"

"Yeah, I did. She asked me to not say anything."

"Dammit, Rusty! What'd she say?"

"Well, since you ask, I can tell you." He put the rag down and set the glass aside. "She don't know who Flo's daddy is and, right or wrong, she don't wanna know. Her ex has no claim to the child and she don't want him in her life in any way, shape, or form. So she just don't wanna know."

"Did she *say* I was the father?"

"Ain't you been listening, ya dumb ground-pounder? She don't wanna know who the daddy is."

Sometimes, talking to Rusty is like dancing across hot coals. You know you're gonna burn your feet, so all you can do is step where the coals might not be as hot. He'd promised Savannah that he wouldn't tell me what they discussed, that was obvious.

But, being an honest man, he wouldn't lie.

"Why doesn't she want to know if I'm Florence's father?"

Rusty leaned on the bar. "She don't want to saddle you with the responsibility of being a daddy at your age."

"At my age?" I asked, a bit too indignantly.

"Well, you ain't no spring chicken, bro. Look at you. Hair's all stringy and you got quite a growth of man-hair on your face, both of 'em about half gray. We're both old farts."

Rufus came through the back door, carrying a platter with a fish sandwich and a rather healthy-looking salad. He slid the plate in front of me. The bread wasn't something from the store. I could smell the coconut. Jamaican coco bread.

"Eat up, Cap'n," he said. "Yuh be needin' to get ready."

The old man was always talking in riddles.

"Get ready for what?" I asked, having had about enough games.

Rufus looked just above my head and spoke, as if talking to someone above me. "Yuh be goin on a long voyage, Cap'n. A voyage to merge yuh pink and purple aura with di rest."

THE END

THE
RUSTY ANCHOR
BAR & GRILL

Lyrics

On a barstool in the corner I strummed on my guitar
for some half-sober locals just trying to unwind
I kept my set list simple just like this rundown bar
just a few windows and old Dade County pine

Julie wiped the bar down while Rusty drank a beer
and the smell of blackened fish and mangos filled the air
It's at the end of a no name shell road and one thing that is clear
it's no accident if you wind up in there

It feels like home and always will at
The Rusty Anchor Bar and Grill
It ain't no Margaritaville, *yeah it's real,*
it's The Rusty Anchor Bar and Grill

Well it ain't no gun and knife club but it ain't too far from it
so if your looking for trouble then you've come to the right place
So just pull up a barstool and if you don't start no shit
then Jesse won't have to mess up your pretty face

It feels like home and always will at
The Rusty Anchor Bar and Grill
It ain't no Margaritaville, *yeah it's real*,
it's The Rusty Anchor Bar and Grill

Come as you are and you will see
you'll be treated just like family
It ain't much to talk about but it ain't hype
yeah they have the best blackened fish and cold Redstripe

It feels like home and always will at
The Rusty Anchor Bar and Grill
It ain't no Margaritaville, *yeah it's real*,
it's The Rusty Anchor Bar and Grill
The Rusty Anchor Bar and Grill

Eric Stone © 2017
Boatsongs Music
(used with permission)

If you'd like to receive my newsletter, please sign up on my website:

WWW.WAYNESTINNETT.COM

Every two weeks, I'll bring you insights into my private life and writing habits, with updates on what I'm working on, special deals I hear about, and new books by other authors that I'm reading.

THE CHARITY STYLES
CARIBBEAN THRILLER SERIES
Merciless Charity
Ruthless Charity
Reckless Charity
Enduring Charity (Spring, 2018)

THE JESSE MCDERMITT
CARIBBEAN ADVENTURE SERIES

Fallen Out
Fallen Palm
Fallen Hunter
Fallen Pride
Fallen Mangrove
Fallen King
Fallen Honor
Fallen Tide
Fallen Angel
Fallen Hero
Rising Storm
Rising Fury
Rising Force (Fall, 2018)

The Gaspar's Revenge Ship's Store is now open. There you can purchase all kinds of swag related to my books.
WWW.GASPARS-REVENGE.COM

Made in the USA
Las Vegas, NV
22 December 2022

63919151R00177